THE CHESHIRE CAT MURDERS

An enthralling crime mystery full of twists

ROGER SILVERWOOD

Yorkshire Murder Mysteries Book 18

JOFFE BOOKS

Revised edition 2020
Joffe Books, London
www.joffebooks.com

First published in Great Britain 2012

ISBN: 978-1-78931-524-0

1

The River Lizard, Little Bottom, Cheshire.
2.45 p.m. Saturday, 25 September 2010

'This is the 999 emergency service, police, fire and ambulance. Which service do you require?'

'Police, please,' the man said.

'Police. Hold the line. Putting you through.'

'Little Bottom Police Station. Sergeant Gurney speaking. Please give me your name and the number of the telephone you are speaking from.'

'Oh, dear. Yes. I'm Sir Giles Brownlee . . . I'm on my mobile. I don't know the damned number. I have a terrible thing to report . . . Oh it's too awful. Dreadful. I don't know where to start.'

'Is somebody hurt, sir?'

'A man — I think it's a man — has been torn to pieces. I saw the rear end of it. It had a long black tail. I saw it eating . . . actually eating the poor man's leg. It was that big black wild cat that's on the loose. It ran off when I turned up. If only I had had my shotgun. If it had come towards me, I would have given it both barrels, I can tell you. Anyway, it ran off into the long grass.'

'The man attacked, sir, do you think he's dead, Sir Giles?'

'Of course he's dead, man. The cat's eaten huge lumps of his leg, his arm up to his shoulder, a big piece out of his face and . . . it's dreadful, dreadful, a bloody, bloody mess and unbelievable.'

'And have you or anybody else there suffered any injuries at all?'

'There's only me. No, I'm all right. I shall never forget it, though, man. I can't stop my hand shaking.'

'We'll get a doctor to you as soon as we can, Sir Giles. Where are you?'

'Oh I'm all right. On the south bank of the river . . . about two miles up. I think the poor man must have been fishing.'

'Can an ambulance get there, sir?'

'Ambulance? Don't need a bloody ambulance for him, man. Just send the mortuary van.'

30 Park Street, Forest Hill Estate, Bromersley,
South Yorkshire, 7.30 a.m. Monday, 25 October 2010

Michael Angel was upstairs in the bathroom drying his face after a shave when he heard the clap of the flap of the letter-box followed three seconds later by the clink of the catch on the front gate. He leaned out onto the landing and called out to his wife. 'It's the post, love!'

Mary Angel pulled the grill pan out from under the heat, ran into the hall and looked down at the mat.

Angel hovered at the top of the stairs awaiting her reply. He was hoping there weren't any bills. Bills were not welcome in the Angel household at that time. Food and heating costs were rising insidiously and he was not expecting an incremental rise in his copper's salary until next year.

'There's only one,' she said, looking towards the stairs. 'It's addressed to you,' she added, turning it over.

'Who is it from?'

'Don't know. It says, 'Gilson, Wimpey and Hetty'.'

'Don't mess about,' he called.

'I'm not messing about,' she said.

'I thought you said, 'Wilson, Keppel and Betty'.'

She frowned. 'Looks like a firm of solicitors.'

Angel's eyebrows shot up. He didn't like the sound of the word 'solicitors'. He dashed downstairs.

She handed him the letter. He glanced at it, rushed into the kitchen, pulled open the cutlery drawer, took out a knife and slit the envelope open. He read the letter quickly and then re-read it. He pulled an unhappy face.

Mary mashed the tea. 'What is it then?'

'Uncle Willy's died,' he said.

She looked up from the gas stove. 'I'm sorry,' she said. 'Which was Uncle Willy now? Wasn't that your Uncle Reg's brother, the antiques dealer?'

'Yes,' he said. 'He must have been ninety-five. He had a daughter, Doreen. I remember her.'

'Yes, lovely woman,' Mary said. 'But I hardly knew *them*. Only seen your Uncle Willy once, at your dad's funeral.'

'I wonder how she's taken it,' he said, rubbing his chin. 'I don't suppose — strictly speaking — they are relations of ours.'

He passed her the letter.

She read it aloud.

Dear Mr Angel

We regret to advise that William Edwin Gardiner of Brentwood, Gildersome Road, Wakefield, died on 21 September last.

In his last will and testament he bequeathed you a safe and contents therein. It is located at the address above. In order to facilitate the sale of the house, and the winding up of the estate, would you kindly remove the item as soon as possible? Access to the house can be made by contacting the late Mr Gardiner's daughter, Mrs Doreen Goodman.

With thanks.

Yours sincerely

Gilson, Wimpey and Hetty

Angel dropped the letter on the worktop and said, 'Well, he'll be in a better place now.'

'Poor Doreen. I wonder how she'll manage?'

'She'll be all right. She won't be short of anything, that's for sure.'

'Didn't you say he was very well off? I wonder what's in the safe?'

'He was loaded. He owed my dad some money from way back. A hundred pounds. When money was money. When you only bought one kettle in a lifetime. The 1940s I think. Uncle Willy needed to pay somebody off who was on his back and my dad told me he helped him out, that's all. He had an IOU for £100. I bet that this is a sort of repayment of it. He could have paid out sooner. He took up antique dealing . . . made a lot of money. Never paid any tax. Dealt a lot in old silver and jewellery.'

Mary's eyes shone. 'Would there be enough to have the sitting room decorated and some new curtains?'

'Hang on, love,' Angel said. 'We've still got the mortgage and the gas to pay.'

She didn't seem to hear him. 'And I'd like a really nice coat for Christmas.'

Angel rubbed his chin. 'We've got to get the key for the safe from Doreen. I must phone her. We could go over tonight . . . maybe.'

'Yes, we must,' she said. 'Red shoes. I've always wanted a really good pair of red shoes . . . with three-inch heels.'

Detective Inspector Michael Angel's office,
Bromersley Police Station, South Yorkshire,
8.28 a.m., Monday, 25 October 2010.

Angel parked the BMW in the police vehicle park at the rear of the station. He dashed up to the rear door, swiped his card down the door jamb and pushed open the door into the station. He passed the cells and made his way up the green-painted corridor. He was breathily whistling to himself, 'Oh what a beautiful morning, Oh what a beautiful day.' He had something to be happy about. He was a beneficiary. When he reached the CID office, he stopped the whistling and looked through the open door.

PC Ahmed Ahaz was seated at a desk near the door. He was gazing at his computer screen, waiting for it to load up. He recognized Angel's breathy whistling, he turned, saw him and quickly got to his feet.

'Good morning, sir. You wanted me?'

Angel took a break from the melody. 'Yes, lad,' he said. 'In my office.'

Ahmed followed him across the corridor.

Angel opened his office door, took off his raincoat, put it on the hook at the side of the stationery cupboard and turned back to face him.

'Get a cardboard box, Ahmed,' he said. Then he pointed to the table behind his desk. 'And pack up all that stuff . . . those files, papers, witness tapes, exhibits and stuff. It's all to do with that ticket clerk and vicar's murders. Take it across to the CPS and leave it with Mr Twelvetrees. He's expecting it.'

Ahmed's eyebrows shot up. He nodded and said, 'Is that case all wrapped up then, sir?'

'It is, lad,' Angel said. 'And it's as tight as the chief constable at the Christmas booze-up.'

Ahmed grinned.

The phone rang.

Angel looked at it, frowned and reached out for it.

It was the woman civilian on the switchboard. 'I have a call from somebody called Sister Mary Clare from St Magdalene's Hospital,' she said. 'That's that private hospital on Rustle Spring Lane. She asked for the chief constable, but his secretary said he wasn't in. He is around somewhere because his car is in its car space. Anyway, I tried Superintendent Harker and he said he was too busy and that I was to push her onto you. Will you speak to her? She won't tell me what it's about . . . except that it is very important.'

Angel let out a long sigh. 'Put her through.'

There was a click and he said, 'Sister Mary Clare, sorry to have kept you waiting. Detective Inspector Angel. What seems to be the trouble?'

'Ah yes, Inspector,' she began, in an accent as thick as a garda's shillelagh, 'It is a bit delicate. I wouldn't want it to get out to the newspapers or become general knowledge, don't you know.'

Angel's face muscles tightened. He rubbed his chin roughly and said, 'Has a crime been committed, Sister?'

'Oh yes, Inspector.'

'Well, you *are* obliged to report it, Sister. What exactly has happened?'

'You see, our chairman was out of the country and I have been unable to reach him. He would probably deal with this robbery his own way.'

'What exactly has been taken, Sister?'

'A bottle of ethanol and a quantity of saltpetre,' she said. 'The pharmacy was broken into last night, Inspector. A pane of glass was smashed and a window opened, would you believe?'

Angel blinked at the word saltpetre. It could be used to make gunpowder. It worried him.

'The pharmacist is still taking stock,' she said. 'There might be other items.'

Angel wrinkled his nose. 'Get everybody out of the pharmacy, Sister,' he said, 'and lock the door. Your pharmacist might unwittingly be destroying evidence.'

'Oh but he's a very intelligent, professional man, Inspector.'

'I don't care if he's the winner of Mastermind, Sister. To give us the best chance of catching the thief, the crime scene has to be preserved. Please have the area cleared immediately and lock up all points of access.'

Sister Mary Clare was wondering whether reporting the burglary had been a wise move. 'Very well, Inspector,' she said at length.

'And how much saltpetre, and how much ethanol has been taken, Sister?'

'A five-litre bottle of ethanol, and a twenty-kilo paper sack of saltpetre.'

Angel's eyebrows shot up. There were the constituents of many a crime. 'I'll send the forensic team to you immediately, Sister, and I'll be down there myself as soon as I can.'

He ended the call and promptly tapped in the number of Bromersley's Scene of Crimes Officer, Detective Sergeant Taylor. It was ringing out.

Ahmed had overheard the conversation and was still at the door. 'What's ethanol, sir?'

Angel glared across at him. 'It's a fancy word for alcohol, lad,' he said. 'Now buzz off. Find that box, and be quick about it.'

'Yes. Right, sir,' he said, and he went out quickly and closed the door.

The phone was answered by DS Taylor.

Angel quickly briefed him and instructed him to get his team to St Magdalene's Hospital promptly, then he returned to fingering through the pile of envelopes in front of him. After a few moments, he frowned and his fingers stopped moving. He looked up, reached out for the phone again and tapped in a number. It was the station incident room.

'Duty officer, DS Olivier,' a voice said.

'Have any fires or cases of arson, or explosions large or small been reported during the night, Callum?'

'No, sir. It's been pretty quiet for a Sunday night.'

'A burglary has been reported . . . enough saltpetre to blow open a bank vault for example, and more than enough ethanol to organize a booze-up afterwards. If any incidents come up that could be linked to this burglary, let me know.'

Angel replaced the phone and returned to the pile of envelopes.

Shortly afterwards, Ahmed arrived with a cardboard box that had originally contained fingerprint ink he had found among the station rubbish. He cleared the side table, filled the box and went out.

Angel sighed and returned to checking through the pile of post. He was quick to pull out mail shots advertising membership of a local gun club, life insurance at special rates for police officers, and a buy-one-get-one-free offer of motorized scooters for the disabled. He promptly dumped the lot in the wastepaper basket in the kneehole of his desk with a gesture of satisfaction. He had resumed the search through the pile when the phone rang. His face muscles tightened. He ran his hand through his hair and reached out for it.

It was Detective Superintendent Harker.

'Ah, Angel,' he said, then he coughed loudly and persistently for several seconds. Angel held the phone away at arm's length.

Eventually Harker managed to speak. 'Just had a triple nine. A man walking his dog in that field at the back of Ashfield Lodge Farm came across the remains of a body. He said the "mangled remains", so I don't know what you might expect.'

Angel's heart began to thump. 'Mangled remains, sir?'

Harker said, 'It is in a bad way, the witness said. He only knew it was human and that it was male.'

The corners of Angel's mouth turned downwards as he visualized the scene. He had seen many horrific sights in his time, and in spite of what people say, for him it never had become any easier.

'The witness is standing by,' Harker said, 'and a patrol car is in attendance. I have instructed DI Asquith to send a squad of uniformed to the scene ASAP.'

'Right, sir,' Angel said, and he replaced the phone.

His chest was buzzing like a queen bee's boudoir on a hot sunny day.

He phoned Ahmed, summoning him to his office, then tapped out Don Taylor's mobile number. He instructed him to leave a fingerprint man and a photographer at St Magdalene's Hospital until they had completed that job, then to direct the remainder of his team to the field at the back of Ashfield Lodge Farm.

He replaced the phone as Ahmed knocked on the door and came in.

Angel stood up, reached out for his coat as he told Ahmed about the finding of a body and its location, and instructed him to phone the mortuary at Bromersley General Hospital to inform Dr Mac, then to find DS Trevor Crisp and DS Flora Carter, inform them and ask them to join him there promptly.

'Got all that, lad?' Angel said, as he brushed past him through the office door.

'Yes, sir.'

2

A field at the rear of Ashfield Lodge Farm, Bromersley.
9.00 a.m. Monday, 25 October 2010.

The narrow lane along the side of Ashfield Lodge Farm, at the end of Ashfield Road was crammed with police vehicles. Radios chattered in distorted monotones. Blue lights buzzed round incessantly.

Angel parked his BMW on Ashfield Road and walked between the vehicles and the perimeter wall of the farmyard to the rear of it to a large open field bordered at the far side by bushes over-hanging a small stream.

About a tenth of the field including part of the stream was taped off, and six men in white overalls were erecting a small marquee over an area by the stream. Twenty officers in high visibility orange coats were positioned strategically round the outside of the perimeter of the taped area. A small group of onlookers fingered the tape and gawped across it expectantly.

As Angel approached the tape, several officers saw him and saluted. He acknowledged them. Then he heard a voice call from behind.

'The witness is up the road, sir. I took him home.'

He turned to see Patrolman Donohue waving his hand in the air to draw his attention. Angel acknowledged the wave and waited for the constable to catch him up.

'Right, Sean,' Angel said. 'Where does he live?'

'Number 46, sir. His name is Bullimore.'

Together they walked back past the police vehicles and round the corner.

'Mr Bullimore is sixty-nine and was shaken up,' Donohue said, '. . . well, the remains are . . . very messy. He was upset. He wanted to come home. He's had a drop of brandy, sir.'

Angel nodded.

They walked up the street a little way.

Donohue stopped and turned to face the house door.

'Is this it?'

'Yes, sir.'

'Right,' he said. 'Introduce us, then get hold of three other officers and do the house to house . . . every house that has windows overlooking the field.'

'Right, sir,' Donohue said and knocked on Bullimore's door.

It was answered by an elderly man with a stick.

Angel heard a dog barking.

'This is Detective Inspector Angel, Mr Bullimore.'

'Come in. Come in,' Bullimore said. 'Sit down here. Wherever you like.'

The barking became louder and more passionate. It was accompanied by banging and scratching noises from the internal door.

'Don't worry about Caesar, he's locked in the kitchen.'

Angel nodded to Donohue, and the officer rushed off.

'Quiet, Caesar.' Bullimore called. 'Quiet.'

The dog whined, barked a couple of times then all was quiet.

Angel waited for Bullimore to select a seat. He sat in an easy chair by the fireplace then Angel chose the chair facing him.

'What sort of a dog is he, Mr Bullimore?'

'He's a German Shepherd. He's three years old, and as keen as mustard. I'm not afraid of anybody or anything when he's with me.'

Angel understood that only too well. German Shepherd was the force's first choice of breed for guard duties, and Ashfield estate was home to a few unsavoury residents, especially among teenagers.

'You live here on your own?' Angel said.

'Yes. That's why I have him. He's good for company as well as protection.'

'Yes, indeed,' Angel said.

'The policeman said your name was Inspector Angel. Are you that Inspector Angel who the papers say always gets his man . . . like the Mounties?'

Angel avoided his eyes and said, 'Yes, I suppose I am.'

'And is it true?'

He shuffled uncomfortably. He didn't want to tempt providence. 'I've been very lucky. I have a great team.' He wanted to move on quickly and said, 'Tell me about this morning, Mr Bullimore,' he said. 'What time did you get up?'

Bullimore blinked. 'Seven o'clock. I always get up at seven o'clock. Caesar needs to go out. I opened the door into the backyard. He can't get out of there. And he comes back in when he's ready. I gave him his breakfast and I had my own. I got ready and we came out for a walk at about half past eight. We go into the field as a general rule. I let him off the lead and he darted straight away down towards the stream. He sniffed round something, then barked and looked round for me. He often does that. I walked towards him. Then he bounded back up to me and led me towards the stream. Then I saw it.'

The elderly man swallowed, rubbed his jaw and said, 'It looked as if a load of meat had just dropped off a butcher's van. I couldn't understand it. Then I saw a pair of leather shoes, socks and the bottom of a pair of trousers and realized what I was looking at. I felt sick. I thought I was going to throw up.'

The hair at the back of Bullimore's hands stood up and he gave a little shiver. 'It couldn't have been done by a human being, Inspector,' he said. 'It would have to have been the result of a wild animal of some sort . . . or several of them . . . maybe starving, desperately hungry, fighting over the dead body . . . I can't say any more. I slipped the chain over Caesar's neck and we came back here. I immediately dialled 999 and reported it in. And that's all I know.'

Angel frowned, made a note with a ballpoint on an old envelope, and then said, 'Did you see anybody around the field before or at the same time you were there?'

'No. It was deserted. Spooky even. I didn't hang about. If I could have run, I would have.'

'Did you see anything at all suspicious that morning or last night. By the look of it, this house overlooks the field. You could probably have seen the incident from a back window.'

'Mmm. Possibly, but I sleep in the front. I didn't see anything anyway, and Caesar would have kicked up hell if he had heard anything in the night. I think this house is too far away from the stream for us to have heard anything.'

Angel nodded.

Bullimore said, 'He sometimes hears things from Ashfield Lodge Farm. The woman there keeps cats in the house and she feeds a fair number of feral cats, and if Caesar hears them courting . . . making their peculiar noises . . . that always makes him bark, in fact, he goes mad. I always have to keep him on the chain as we go past her place.'

Angel raised his eyebrows, paused and said, 'Do you happen to know the lady's name?'

Bullimore wrinkled his nose. 'It's Sharpe, and she's no lady.'

Angel pretended not to hear his last four words, and said, 'Mrs Sharpe,' as he wrote the name on the back of the brown envelope.

‘It’s *Miss* Sharpe,’ Bullimore said. ‘Miss Ephemore Sharpe.’

‘Ephemore Sharpe,’ Angel said while still writing. ‘You know her well?’

‘I’ve met her, Inspector. She’s not nice to have as a neighbour, I can tell you. She’s a retired schoolmistress, never married, has no friends . . . well, nobody ever goes there except on business . . . Has cats in the house, cats in the barns and outbuildings. People go to her from all over the place sometimes, if they have a sick cat and they’re desperate. She sets herself up to know more about cats than anybody.’

‘But you don’t like her. Why?’

‘Well, Inspector, I’ll tell you. I came to live here about thirty-six years ago. She was already living there in the farmhouse with her father and mother. Her father ran the farm, worked like a dog, and was as miserable as sin. Mother kept house, helped with the milking sometimes, never smiled, and grumbled all the time about everything and everybody. Ephemore went out to teach at the grammar school and put the fear of God into all the kids. She taught history. My, what a family. And they were all ugly. Uglier than the devil’s totem pole. But I suppose, out of the three of them, Ephemore was the ugliest. She is like the wicked witch of the west from the Wizard of Oz. Anyway, me and my wife had a nodding relationship with all three. If we passed any of them in the street, we’d say, ‘Good morning’, or ‘Good afternoon’, and walk on as quickly as we could. And they were only tolerably civil back. Anyway, her father and mother died about ten years ago. Ephemore sold the herd — got a very good price for it, I heard. Anyway, she retired from school teaching straightaway. She took to keeping cats. About eighteen months ago, I was passing her place with Caesar, and her yard gate was open. It was a bit unusual. I had Caesar on a lead, but unfortunately he saw a cat, somewhere in her yard, and charged off after it, pulling the lead out of my hand. It dodged through a small hole under one of her outbuildings. Caesar made a mighty effort to follow it, but, fortunately, couldn’t get through the hole. However he scratched around it, but made no progress, so he stood barking at the hole, kicking up hell. I eventually got hold of the lead and was pulling him away when Ephemore appeared at her front door. She glared at me, demanded that I left her yard and said that if my dog ever entered her property again, she would have it shot. Of course, I protested and tried to apologize, but she wouldn't have any. She's a nasty old cow. All the pupils at the school hated her, and there's no wonder.'

Mr Bullimore was interrupted by a knocking on the door. It was immediately followed by renewed wild and angry barking from the dog.

Angel looked round.

'Quiet, Caesar! Quiet! It's all right!' Bullimore called, then he turned to Angel and said, 'It's the door,' and he reached down to the floor for his stick to assist him to stand up to answer it.

'I'll get it,' Angel said, and he jumped up, crossed the room and turned the copper doorknob.

It was Flora Carter, one of the two sergeants in Angel's team and quite the prettiest female police officer in Yorkshire.

'Ah, Flora,' Angel said, and he stepped out of the house and closed the door to speak to her in private. He briefed her about the phone call from Sister Mary Clare and the burglary at St Magdalene's Hospital, and instructed her to go down there immediately and see what she could make of it.

Carter nodded and rushed off.

Angel then went back in to Bullimore's front room.

'It was one of my sergeants,' Angel said.

Bullimore nodded.

Angel resumed his seat, frowned, rubbed his chin and said, 'When you saw what was left of the body, did you immediately turn away?'

'If you mean did I touch anything, Inspector? No, I didn't. I put the chain round Caesar and came straight back here.'

'Good. It might be necessary to have your footprints to eliminate *you* from the scene.'

Bullimore blinked. He looked down at his feet and said, 'I was wearing these shoes.'

'You'd better take them off and give 'em to me. You'll get them back tomorrow.'

Bullimore grunted, pulled the bow on a shoelace and began to kick the shoes off.

Angel stood up. 'I think we've finished here for now, Mr Bullimore. Thank you very much indeed. You've been most helpful. If anything further occurs to you, give me a ring at the station, will you?'

Angel came out of the house with the man's shoes swinging by the insides of heels from his fingertips.

Trevor Crisp, Angel's other sergeant, was strolling up the street towards him. Their eyes met.

Angel glared at him.

Crisp increased his speed. He noticed the shoes Angel was carrying. His lips began to develop a smile.

Angel's eyes missed nothing. 'It's taken you long enough to catch up with me, lad,' he said. Then as he came level with the sergeant, he lifted up his arm and swung the shoes at him. 'Catch!' he said. 'Witness's shoes. For SOCO. And I said that *you'd* see that he got them back tomorrow. All right?'

Crisp caught the shoes. Mud from one of them smeared the sleeve of his light-coloured raincoat. He looked at the brown smear, and rubbed it making it worse. He glanced angrily at his boss, who was walking on briskly nonchalantly unaware of any mishap.

The sergeant ran after him. 'Don Taylor ran out of Denstone KD plaster, sir,' he said. 'He knew I'd be coming here. He asked me to get some from the stores on the way in. There are a quite a few clear prints around the body in the clay at the edge of the stream.'

Angel's eyebrows went up. Clear prints were practically unheard of in today's criminal investigations. He was pleased. 'Clear footprints? Good.'

'Not exactly footprints, sir,' Crisp said. 'Don said that they are paw prints probably from a cat.'

Angel glared at him. 'A cat?'

Crisp shrugged. 'That's what he said.'

The sergeant found himself conveniently passing his car, so he took the opportunity of dumping the witness's shoes in the boot.

Angel stopped, wrinkled his nose, turned back to him and said, 'Come on, Trevor. Let's see this woman Ephemore Sharpe.'

They walked together to the end of the street, then went through the farm gate into a big yard. There was a smart stone-built farmhouse with a large immaculately maintained garden behind it, and three stone-built barns at the other side facing it. Several cats rushed in different directions from one outbuilding to another as the policemen made their way over uneven cobbles to the farmhouse door.

Angel banged the big knocker hard and waited. Nothing happened for a while so he looked at Crisp and pulled a face. Crisp was about to reach up to it to knock again when the door opened and a woman appeared.

Angel gasped. From Bullimore's description, it was certainly Miss Ephemore Sharpe and he hadn't exaggerated at all.

She looked them up and down suspiciously, using sharp jerky movements like a vulture.

'Miss Sharpe?' Angel said.

'Yes,' she said. 'Are you policemen?'

She had a hard, nasal voice, a big nose with nostrils so wide that you could see that the insides were bright pink with thread-like violet veins. Very unusually, her septum was Z shaped.

'Good morning,' Angel said. 'Yes. We need to speak to you about a very important matter.'

'It's not convenient just now,' she said, and began to close the door.

'I'm afraid that I have to insist,' Angel said. 'These are police inquiries about the death of a man.'

'Don't you dare speak to me like that, young man,' she said. 'The police are *our* servants and not the other way round. These are enlightened days. I know my rights.'

Angel blinked. He was not usually stuck for words. In this case, the woman had surprised him. He took a deep breath and said, 'As an inspector of police, madam, I know mine. You *are* obliged to assist us in our inquiries. If you will not do it voluntarily, I can get a warrant. That would be very time consuming and unnecessary.'

She considered the matter a few moments then, opening the door wider, she said, 'I can give you a couple of minutes. You may come in. Wipe your feet. But you must make it quick. I have a lot to attend to.'

Inside, she ushered them into a drawing-sitting room, comprising a settee, four upholstered chairs, a grand piano and a television. Framed paintings and photographs, predominantly of cats of all sizes, almost entirely obscured the wallpaper. The largest photograph was of a man with a big moustache and wearing a leotard. He was in a big cage wielding a whip and a chair surrounded by six huge, clawing tigers.

Angel looked at them and then at Crisp who nodded to indicate that he had seen the photograph and would remember it.

On the piano, there were in addition a dozen or so family photographs in polished silver frames. They were of people of all ages, in groups or single portraits. Each person in each photograph had a huge nose, big ears, sunken cheeks, staring eyes, a thin, pointed chin and sparse grey hair. Angel felt confident that they all must be relatives of Miss Sharpe, and that each one must have scowled deliberately as the photographer clicked the button.

The old woman indicated seats where they should sit, while Angel introduced himself and Crisp to her.

She said, 'I would like to know why there are all these police vehicles cluttering up the only access to the field.'

'They are there to assist in the investigation of a dead body found by the stream,' Angel said.

'You do realize, Inspector whatever your name is, that the presence of those vehicles there will disturb the cats — both feral and tame — who regularly come here to feed. Your big, noisy vehicles with flashing lights, and your men banging about in heavy boots are ruining all that and frightening the cats away. It's disgraceful and as a taxpayer — a very big taxpayer, as it happens — it is not right that I should have to put up with this nuisance.'

'I'm sorry, Miss Sharpe, that you are being inconvenienced,' Angel said, 'but a man *is* dead and we *do* need to find out the cause of his death . . . for the sake of the community. I am here just now specifically to ask you if you saw or heard anything suspicious anywhere in the field, but in particular near the stream, yesterday, last evening or during the night.'

'I haven't seen or heard anything unusual at all,' she said.

Angel said, 'All the windows at the south side of the house look onto the field and from your upstairs rooms, I expect you have uninterrupted views down to the stream . . . are you sure?'

'Positive. What is the dead man's name? And how did he die?'

'We don't know that yet.'

She sniffed. 'You don't know much, do you?'

'That's why we're here,' Angel said. 'I was hoping you could help us. Anyway, that's all I need for now. I may be back with additional questions when we have more information,' he added, then he looked at Crisp and the two men stood up to leave.

She opened the door and said, 'Well, I can't say it has been a pleasure because it hasn't.'

The two men made for the hall. She followed them to the front door.

'If you recall hearing or seeing anything at all in the field, please let me know,' Angel said, 'it is vitally important.'

'I know nothing at all about it, young man,' she said.

Before he could reply, the door slammed.

As Angel and Crisp picked their way over the cobblestones on their way up to the farm gate, Angel turned to Crisp and said, 'Get onto the PNC asap, Trevor, and see if there's anything known about her.'

‘Right, sir,’ Crisp said. ‘I don’t suppose there will be.’

They reached the gate and Crisp said, ‘She was a schoolteacher, wasn’t she?’

Angel nodded.

‘I thought so. What was her main subject?’

‘History, I believe,’ Angel said.

‘Modern history, sir?’

‘Aye. Gestapo techniques to the under fourteens.’

3

*The field behind Ashfield Lodge Farm,
Bromersley. 2 p.m. Monday, 25 October 2010.*

Ds Taylor phoned Angel to advise that his team and Dr Mac, the pathologist, had completed their inspection of the scene, and that they were ready to remove the remains of the body to the mortuary.

Angel, in a white one-piece overall with hood, boots and gloves, picked his way across the field towards the stream. The first person he came across at the site perimeter was Dr Mac who silently led him to the body.

Angel stared at the blood-soaked victim, with no chest, leg gouged and one arm almost severed. He sighed. The horror of the scene caused his pulse to beat so hard that his eardrums pounded like a tambourine at a Salvation Army meeting.

He tried to wave away a score or more flies hovering over and landing on the open flesh and on the trail of dried brown blood that led to the stream, but it was a waste of time. They were insistent.

Angel shook his head. He exchanged glances with Dr Mac in silence. Eventually, through the mask, he said, 'I've never seen anything like this.'

Mac nodded and said, 'I remember my father telling me about attending to an animal trainer after he had been savagely killed by a Canadian bear that was part of an animal act. It happened in the wings of the Hippodrome in Glasgow a hundred years ago. The trainer had had his ear and one cheek actually bitten off. The bear had taken several bites. It was ghastly.'

Angel wrinkled his nose under the mask and turned away. He looked around and in the muddy ground at the edge of the stream he saw sixteen numbered moulds the size of saucers. They had been filled with quick drying Denstone KD plaster. This plaster is both strong and fine enough to record small detail in the impression, and can be lifted with care after thirty minutes, although it may take up to forty-eight hours for them to set completely hard. He was optimistic that the moulds would produce both useful and adequate forensic information to conclude the case.

Taylor came up to the two men and saluted.

'Now, Don,' Angel said. 'What you got?'

He shook his head and lowered his eyes. 'It's pretty horrific, sir.'

'Aye.'

'Worst I've seen,' Taylor said. Then he brought up a clipboard, looked at it and said, 'We've got what seems to be the remains of a male, white, aged sixteen to fifty. There are animal paw prints around the edge of the stream.'

Angel said, 'Are there any human footprints?'

'No, sir.'

Angel frowned. He went to rub his chin, but the mask prevented him. 'Are you sure?' he said. 'Smudged or partial?'

Taylor didn't like Angel doubting him. 'There are no fresh human footprints at all, sir,' Taylor said. 'I have checked all round.'

Angel frowned again. 'Right,' he said. The unavoidable conclusion was that the death of the victim must have been caused by an animal of some sort.

Eventually Taylor said, 'The prints are undoubtedly from a very large cat, sir. The sort that was seen in Cheshire a month ago.'

'I read about that.'

'It was thought to be a black panther.'

'Yes. It couldn't be the same one, could it?'

'I don't know, sir. I suppose they roam around the country at night.'

'Or there might be more than one? I'll look into it. Any means of the victim's ID?'

'There is a small bulge in his inside pocket, sir. It could well be a wallet. I haven't yet looked there. Didn't want to risk contaminating the scene.'

'Pass it to me.'

Taylor leaned over the remains, gently turned back the suit coat, put his gloved fingers inside the pocket, lifted out a brown leather wallet and passed it up to him.

Angel opened it carefully. It wasn't easy to handle wearing rubber gloves. There was a pocket for business cards which had four or five of them sticking up. He took one out by its edges and read it out, 'Julius Hobbs, property developer, The Old Manse, Ripon Road, Bromersley.'

He blinked. 'I've heard of him,' he said. 'I've seen his ads for posh, expensive houses in the *Bromersley Chronicle*.' He wrinkled his nose. 'Somebody will have to go there . . . tell his wife.'

* * *

'I'm sorry to have been the bearer of such tragic news, Mrs Hobbs,' Angel said. 'I came as soon as I discovered that the body was that of your son, and I regret that it will be necessary for you to identify the body formally in the next day or so.'

The elderly lady nodded and wiped away a tear.

Angel said, 'Are you up to answering a few questions now? I am afraid they are necessary, but I can come back another day if it is too much for you.'

‘No. No, Inspector,’ she said. ‘I would rather deal with matters now.’

‘Well,’ he said, ‘if you’re up to it, I need to confirm that you are Julius’s next of kin.’

‘Of course. He’s not married, if that’s what you are getting at. He *was* married for four years but, well, he wasn’t the marrying kind, Inspector. He was not a man for settling down and living the quiet life, if you see what I mean. He married a very nice girl, Dorothea Webber . . . but she was not his type. It didn’t last long. She wouldn’t put up with his travelling around the place and never at home. You see, my Julius was very intelligent. He was always top of the form in school. Did well. Went to university. Got a first in architecture. Opened an office on York Street opposite the Town Hall. Never looked back. He was interested in property in different parts of the country, and Dorothea simply didn’t want to travel around. She wanted to stay at home and start a family. He didn’t want that. They had a clean, straight divorce, two years ago. No children. In a way I was sorry for her, but I loved my son.’

‘Have you got her address?’

‘Oh yes. In my address book, Inspector. I’ll give it to you, before you go.’

‘Thank you.’

Then suddenly she lowered the damp tissue and raised her head. ‘These days he was seeing that actress Celia Hamilton,’ she said proudly, then she lowered her eyelids, rolled each shoulder round alternately several times and slowly turned her head from left to right and back.

It was a routine she employed to emphasize a point.

Angel knew of Celia Hamilton. She was the present darling of every television and film producer. She was very beautiful, played romantic roles and was hardly ever off the screen.

‘I take it they didn’t marry?’ he said.

‘No. She has a flat in London. He stayed there sometimes. Occasionally she stayed here, especially when she was filming or appearing in a theatre nearby. I don't know what will happen now. You see this is *his* house. He persuaded me to come and live here after my husband died a few years ago. But I can't stay here on my own. Look at the size of it.'

Angel nodded and smiled. 'I am sorry to have to ask you, Mrs Hobbs, but do you know the whereabouts of your son's will?'

'It's at the solicitors, Bloomfields, but I know the contents, Inspector.'

'Would you be good enough to tell me?'

'Yes, of course. It's very simple. After his divorce from Dorothea, he left everything to me. I am sure that he would have told me if he had altered it.'

Angel nodded and then said, 'Did your son have any enemies . . . in his personal life or his business life?'

She frowned. 'What sort of a question is that, Inspector?'

'We have to look at all possibilities, Mrs Hobbs.'

'But if my son was killed by a . . . an animal, isn't the question irrelevant?'

'We have to be very thorough, Mrs Hobbs. Because your son's death is so unusual, the cause of his death will have to be heard in a coroner's court and these questions may very well arise.'

She shook her head in disbelief, wiped away a tear and said, 'Well, his ex-wife is not kindly disposed to him. I did tell you about her. And there's a young lady he was with after that, Imelda Cartwright. They were together a year or more. That was a rather vindictive split . . . then there's a man he was always in competition with, buying property — Sir Raphael Quigley. Julius used to bid higher prices for property making Sir Raphael offer more. Then Julius would withdraw. The result was that Sir Raphael invariably paid out more than he had originally intended. I never did approve of that, and I told him so. Sir Raphael Quigley came here once. He was furious. Julius just laughed.'

Angel eagerly wrote these names down on the back of an envelope. He would get the addresses afterwards. He stayed quiet, pen poised ready in case there were any more names to come.

'I don't believe there were any others,' she said. 'Anyway, if there were, he never mentioned them to me.'

'What do you know of Julius's movements yesterday, Mrs Hobbs?'

'He was in his office yesterday morning as usual. He works from an office here. A girl from an agency comes in to do his letters. We had a quick light lunch together in the sitting room. And he said he would be out for dinner and that I wasn't to wait up. He left at about two o'clock . . . and that was the last I saw of him.'

'Did he seem all right? Was there anything troubling him?'

'He seemed absolutely normal, Inspector.'

'And you've no idea where he went, or what he did yesterday afternoon and evening?'

'No.'

'I will need to look at his diary and through his recent correspondence and so on, see if that assists us.' He stood up.

'Of course, Inspector,' she said. 'His office is facing the front door. His diary with any appointments is on his desk. Please help yourself.'

'Thank you very much, Mrs Hobbs.'

'Oh dear,' she said. 'While you are doing that, there are some phone calls I must make.'

* * *

Angel had a look at Hobbs's diary, address book and the post on his desk. Then he headed back to the station. It was almost five o'clock when he hurried down the corridor and saw Ahmed coming out of the CID office.

'There you are, lad,' Angel said. 'Come in my office and close the door. Sit down there a minute. There are some jobs I want you to see to.'

Ahmed took out his notebook and held his pen at the ready.

‘First thing in the morning,’ Angel said, ‘I want you to find out the name of the local newspaper that covers the village of Little Drop Bottom in Cheshire. It’s near Evensfield Prison. It’ll likely be a weekly. Ask for the editor or chief reporter, and pour on the charm, lad. Ask him if he would be kind enough to let us have copies of any photographs, also any description he might have, of the animal that attacked and killed one of their local men a few weeks back, and if he would kindly send whatever he has to us by email. Tell them that we would be most grateful. All right?’

‘Yes, sir,’ Ahmed said.

‘Now, there were three women in Julius Hobbs’s life,’ Angel said. ‘They were Dorothea Webber, Imelda Cartwright and Celia Hamilton. I want you to find out if anything is known on the PNC. The first two are local and the third has a London address.’

Ahmed’s eyebrows shot up. ‘Is that Celia Hamilton the actress, sir?’

‘It is, lad,’ Angel said.

Ahmed’s eyes glowed. ‘Wow,’ he said. ‘Saw her on television last night, sir.’

Angel gave a little shrug. ‘She’s on *every* night,’ he said drily, ‘like *Vick* on the super’s chest.’

Ahmed smiled. ‘She’s very good, sir.’

Angel blinked. ‘She’s only a woman, lad. A competent actress and just about old enough to be your mother. And if you stop fantasizing, I’ll move on.’

‘Sorry, sir.’

‘Then I want you to phone the NCOF at Wakefield and ask them to put us in touch with a wild animal expert. They might have different specialists, Ahmed. We need one on big, wild cats.’

As Ahmed scribbled away, he said, ‘Do you really think the man Hobbs was killed by a big cat, sir?’

‘Unless the murderer could fly, Ahmed, I am left with no other alternative. There were only big cat prints near the body. Now you push off home. See to all that in the morning. And *stop* thinking about Celia Hamilton. It'll put you off your curry, and your mother will worry about you.'

Ahmed grinned. 'Right, sir,' he said. 'Good night.'

* * *

Mary wound the car window down and said, 'It'll have a 'For Sale' board up won't it, darling?'

The cold night air swirled into the car and round their ears.

Angel slowed the BMW right down. 'I would have thought so,' he said. 'I seem to remember it was somewhere around here. The house is called Brentwood. It was the only house with tall trees at the front.'

Suddenly Mary said, 'It's this *next* one. *There's* the 'For Sale' sign. *There* are the trees. Brentwood. This is it, darling.'

'Right,' Angel said, as he tugged on the steering wheel.

The house was in total darkness.

The BMW went through the open black wrought-iron gates, veered round to the right. Three floodlights suddenly illuminated the front of the house, the drive, the cluster of bushes and trees and the double garage at the side.

He drove up to the front steps and then stopped. As he turned off the car engine, a light went on in the hall, the front door opened and an elderly lady in a long overcoat came out to greet them. It was Doreen Goodman. They exchanged warm courtesies, with pecks on the cheeks and hugs. Angel said how sorry he was that her father had died. She seemed to have come to terms with it easily, in view of his long years. She said that he was still dealing until a year ago, attending auctions and a few local antiques fairs.

She then led them into a small ground-floor room which was empty except for a large old safe in the corner standing on bare floorboards.

'This had been Dad's office cum study,' Doreen Goodman said. 'There was a desk, bookcase and a filing cabinet over there . . . and a television and easy chair over there.

They've all been sold. In fact, I've also put all his stock into a London auction, while silver prices are high. There's only the house and this safe, and Dad was most insistent that you should have the safe.'

Angel stood back and looked at it. It was obviously old, very heavy and much bigger than he had expected. He rubbed his chin.

Mary stepped forward and looked closely at the big door handle, keyhole and manufacturer's moulded brass plaque bearing the words, 'J. P. Phillips, Birmingham — Mark II'.

Angel turned back to Doreen and said, 'What exactly did Uncle Willy keep in here, love?'

She shrugged. 'Anything and everything valuable. But I don't believe that I have seen it wide open for ten years or more. Dad was always very secretive, you know. It was his way.'

Angel nodded. 'Do you have the key?'

Doreen Goodman shook her head. 'I haven't, Michael. Now I hope that's not going to be a big problem. My father became a little forgetful during the last couple of years. He always used to carry it with him. It was a big key by today's standards and it made holes in his coat pocket lining so I persuaded him not to keep it there and to find a different place for it, but after he died I couldn't find it anywhere. It wasn't among his clothes, his papers or anywhere in here. I am afraid it seems to be lost.'

Angel pulled a face.

Mary looked at him and said, 'You can easily deal with that, darling, can't you?'

Angel wasn't so sure it could be dealt with *easily*, but he smiled weakly. He didn't want to seem to be tiresome. After all, he was getting a safe for nothing with who knows what inside it.

'You've solved bigger mysteries than that, haven't you, Michael?' Doreen Goodman said.

He turned to her with eyebrows raised.

'I keep reading complimentary things about you in the papers,' she added.

Mary looked at him and smiled. He gave a slight shrug and looked away.

* * *

'Good morning, sir,' Crisp said.

'Come in, lad. Sit down.'

Crisp sat down in the chair nearest Angel's desk.

'There's nothing known about Ephemore Sharpe, sir.'

Angel was disappointed. And confused. He pulled a face. 'And it looks like Julius Hobbs *was* killed by a wild cat,' he said.

Crisp looked at him closely. 'But you don't really believe that, do you, sir?'

'If this was certain parts of Africa or we were in the South American jungle I might be persuaded to believe it, but on the outskirts of Bromersley, it stretches the imagination.'

'It happened in Cheshire a month ago, sir, and there was a witness.'

Angel shrugged and began to look through the morning's post.

Crisp said, 'I understand that there are only paw prints near the body.'

Angel looked up. His face creased. He dropped the letters. 'That's right,' he said. 'That's the problem. The animal presumably devoured part of the poor man by the stream, having killed him somewhere else and dragged him there.'

'Have you any idea where that was, sir?'

Angel wrinkled his nose. 'Not an inkling. Nobody has reported seeing a wild cat anywhere round here.'

'Do you think the one that was in Cheshire has somehow worked its way across the Pennines and finished up here, sir?'

Angel shook his head. 'I really don't know. I don't think so. Not unless someone physically transported it in a cage or something. It is well known that there are a few animals that have been let go free or have escaped from private zoos, or have been smuggled in the country somehow and that the keeper can't afford to keep them, or gets bored . . . or for whatever reason, they are set free.'

'They want shooting,' Crisp said. 'The keepers I mean. The least they could do for the poor animal is to return it to its country of origin and give it a chance to survive and reproduce among its own kind.'

Angel grunted in agreement. He rubbed his chin for a moment then impatiently ran his hand through his hair.

'You crack on with your reports, lad. And don't go far away. I'll want you to do a job for me, when I get sorted.'

'Right, sir,' Crisp said. He went out and closed the door.

Angel thought about the possibility of the Cheshire cat making its way across the Pennines probably by night, killing a sheep for its sustenance on the way. It was possible, he supposed. He resumed sorting through the post.

The phone rang. Angel reached out for it. It was the civilian switchboard operator. 'I've got a call for you from that Selwyn Plumm, the reporter from the *Chronicle*,' she said. 'Do you want me to tell him you are out?'

There's many a time Angel had wanted to say that, but from experience it resulted in the man being more persistent and phoning every hour. Besides, there was many a time he needed the help of the local newspaper.

'No, put him through, please.'

There was a click and then a cheery voice said, 'Hi there, Michael, you old fox. You have a juicy killing by a big, wild cat and you don't tell me about it. What's the dead man's name?'

'I don't know how you found out about it, Selwyn, but there's no proof yet that the victim *was* killed by a wild cat.'

'Makes a great headline, Michael. You're always so guarded. You know I can always say that a *police source* said that the victim was killed by a wild cat, then if fresh evidence shows that things are different, nobody loses face. Have you got any pictures?'

'Pictures of what?'

'Anything! Well, anything interesting, the wild cat, the dead body . . . you *know* . . . anything that will get the people of Bromersley animated.'

'No. Nothing I can release yet, Selwyn.'

'Pity. Never mind. I know we've got a library shot of the mortuary van. I suppose we can use that, with a caption that the remains of the body were taken to the mortuary. What was the name of the victim, Michael?'

'We think it is a thirty-year-old local man. He has not been formally identified, so I can't reveal his name.'

Plumm's voice changed from friendly to wheedling. 'Come on, Michael, you can let an old friend know. I can hold it back a day or two if you like.'

'No. No,' Angel said. 'I really can't say any more about him.'

'Can you tell me his trade or profession?'

'No,' Angel said, rubbing his chin thoughtfully. 'But I tell you what, Selwyn. You could possibly help me.'

'In what way, Michael? What do you want?'

'I want to know if anybody has seen a large, wild cat around these parts in the past month or so. You could make an appeal, Selwyn.'

'An appeal to our readers?' he said slowly, then he brightened and his voice took on a lighter tone. 'Yeah. That might be good. What colour and how big?'

Angel shook his head. He didn't want to prompt any of the *Chronicle's* readers and encourage any publicity-seeking reader to fabricate a sighting. 'Just say what they saw, where and when, and what it looked like . . . and a photo would be helpful.'

Plumm blinked. He thought how much his editor would like a picture of such an animal on the front page of the *Chronicle. 'A photo would be great.* All right, Michael, I'll write it up and we'll publish it on Friday. Ta for now.'

Angel replaced the phone. He rubbed his chin and wondered what he must deal with next. He picked up the post and began sorting through it again. It should be done every day, and it usually was, but this was yesterday's. There was no time to worry about it. There was simply too much to do.

There was a knock at the door.

'Come in,' he called.

It was Flora Carter. 'About that break-in at the hospital, sir.'

'Yes. What you got?' he said, putting the letters back on the pile then pointing to the chair by his desk.

She sat down.

'Entry was made through a ground-floor outside window, sir,' she said. 'A simple brown paper and treacle job. No sign of the treacle tin, though. Looks like the thief came with a shopping list: ethanol and saltpetre. Nothing else was disturbed. No footprints. And no fingerprints. The fingerprint officer said the thief wore gloves, and from the size of the dabs, he thought it was probably male.'

'How did the thief transport the stuff?'

'Don't know, sir. It would be awkward because both items were bulky. The thief may have brought bags and carried them to a car.'

Angel frowned and rubbed his chin. He suddenly stood up. 'I'm going down there. Who did you see?'

'Sister Mary Clare.'

'What's she like?'

'Nervous. Scared of her boss, I think.'

Angel looked at her and frowned.

There was a knock at the door.

'Come in,' he said.

It was Ahmed smiling and waving a sheet of A4. He stopped when he saw Flora Carter.

She smiled and made a gesture to him to indicate that he should carry on. He still hesitated.

Angel wrinkled his nose. 'Come on, lad,' he said. 'What is it?'

'Right, sir,' Ahmed said. 'I had an email from the *Cheshire Courier* with the print of a photograph of the cat that killed that man who was fishing, sir. And a report on the case.'

Angel took the sheet of paper from him and sat down. He looked at the photograph. It showed the rear half of a large muscular black cat with a long black tail, about fifteen to twenty centimetres taller than a German Shepherd. Its head and most of the body was obscured by long grass. Then he skimmed through the report and handed it to Carter.

She read the report and shuddered slightly when she saw the photograph.

'I wouldn't like to come across an animal like that, sir,' she said, as she handed the email back to him.

Angel nodded.

She said, 'You don't think that *that* cat actually made its way across here, do you, sir?'

'That's nearly thirty or forty miles away, Flora. I don't know.' He looked up at Ahmed. 'Don't they have a wild animal expert at Wakefield then?'

'They say they'll come back to us on that one, sir, later on today.'

Angel shrugged. 'Must be having difficulty in digging one up.'

'They were surprised when I put it to them, sir,' Ahmed said. 'I told them you were looking for someone who knew about large, wild cats . . . that we had somebody who had been killed by one.'

Angel frowned then eventually nodded. 'Right, lad,' he said. 'Carry on.'

Ahmed went out.

Angel stood up. He turned to Flora. 'I'm going down to that hospital now, before anything else crops up.'

4

Angel steered the BMW off Rustle Spring Lane and through the black iron gates into the grounds of St Magdalene's Hospital. He drove past the manicured lawns and symmetrical floral borders. He noticed a man in overalls behind a noisy mower in the middle of a big lawn, cutting grass in lines as straight and parallel as iron bars in a prison. He looked up at the grimy, grey Georgian stone construction with its black stone window surrounds. The main building had smoke-stained red-brick extensions built on at one side and to the rear. There were white on black signs all over the place. Several of them read, 'All visitors must report to reception'. However he carried on past the main door and drove round the back of the building through extensive areas of trees, bushes, plants and grass on both sides with cars parked higgledy-piggledy on the service road up to the delivery door. On the short journey, he spotted a boarded-up ground-floor window and stopped the BMW twenty metres away from it. He got out of the car, crouched down and peered at the ground around him. Then he stood up and made his way slowly towards a window that was partly boarded-up. He looked through the glass next to it. There were rows and rows of bottles, jars and boxes. On the bench underneath he could see several small bags and packets which appeared to be prescriptions awaiting delivery or collection.

As he was taking all this in, he heard footsteps behind him. He turned round to see a man in overalls advancing towards him at speed. The man was carrying a garden hoe. It was the man he had seen minutes before mowing the lawn at the front. He didn't look friendly. He stopped two metres away and said, 'Here. What you doing?'

Angel reached into his pocket and pulled out his ID. 'Detective Inspector Angel, Bromersley Police,' he said. 'I am investigating a robbery. Who are you?'

The man's shoulders dropped and he sighed. 'Sorry about that,' he said. He seemed relieved. 'I am the gardener here, Pryce is my name. I know about the robbery. The boss, Dr Rubenstein said I should keep a lookout for strangers behaving in an unusual manner. I was only doing as I was told.'

'That's all right, Mr Pryce. Did you see anything unusual?'

'No. I would have reported it if I had.'

'Have you seen anything of a bottle of ethanol and a bag of saltpetre?'

He shook his head. 'No,' he said.

Angel reached into his pocket and took out a business card and gave it to him. 'If you see or hear of anything give me a ring.'

Pryce glanced at it and put it in his pocket. Then he produced a card of his own and waved it in front of him before handing it over. 'And if ever you need any gardening doing, Inspector Angel, I'll do it for you at a special rate.'

Angel smiled. He took the card, looked at it and said, 'You never know. If my back gives out, I might have to call on you.'

Pryce waved, turned and walked quickly away.

Angel then returned to the car and started the engine. He engaged gear and let in the clutch. It was then that he noticed an unusual sickly sweet smell. He sniffed carefully. It was strong and sweet but not unpleasant. He looked round to be sure that nobody had entered the car without him knowing. There was nobody there. The smell reminded him of his mother. As a boy, he remembered being out shopping with her and a smart, overdressed woman, hair piled up, wearing a fur coat, lots of make-up, and strong perfume had sailed past them. The sickly sweet smell had lingered after she had passed out of sight, and Angel's mother had said, 'You want to beware of women smelling of cheap scent, like that, Michael.'

Since then the situation had happened more than once. He smiled at the memory.

Mystified, he drove round to the front of the building to the car park. It was a large marked out area but at that time, only a few cars were there. He parked the BMW next to a grey Bentley just as his mobile phone began to ring. It was Ahmed.

'What is it, lad?' Angel said.

'I've had a wild animal expert from NCOF, Wakefield on the phone, sir. He can see you in your office this afternoon at one o'clock. Will that be convenient?'

Angel had a surge of encouragement just when he needed it.

'That would be great, Ahmed,' he said. 'Is he their best man on wild cats?'

'He's their *only* man on wild cats, sir. A professor. He said he had recently been in Africa on conservation work.'

'Good,' Angel replied. He was enthusiastic about meeting the man. There were so many questions he wanted to put to an expert. 'Tell Don Taylor I want to see him at twelve forty-five,' he added, 'and I want the plaster casts of the animal's paws and all the info from the scene of crime he's got. All right?'

He closed the phone, dropped it in his pocket, got out of the car and made his way smartly up to the hospital entrance. The sickly sweet smell was still hovering in his nostrils. He wondered if it was something in the air, released by the hospital, or a factory close by. But, as he thought about it, there weren't any factories at that side of town.

The reception desk faced the revolving door. The area was very clean and well lit.

Behind the polished pine counter was a strikingly beautiful young woman in a neat black suit. Her body had more curves than Silverstone and she was gifted enough to suckle for Yorkshire.

She fluttered her eyelashes, raised her eyebrows, smiled and said, 'Can I help you?'

Angel took note of her name. He had an excellent memory, and remembering beautiful women was not difficult.

'I'm Detective Inspector Angel from Bromersley Police. Could I see Sister Mary Clare, please?'

'Thank you,' Candy Costello said, picking up a phone. 'There's a Detective Inspector Angel to see Sister Mary Clare.'

She replaced the phone, turned to Angel and said, 'Won't keep you a minute.' She pointed to the right of the desk to a block of chairs against the wall. 'Please take a seat.'

Angel looked across at the line of eight upholstered chairs and beyond them down a long seemingly endless corridor with a highly polished parquet flooring. He turned back to her. 'Thank you,' he said.

However, before he had chance to move, a door behind him opened and an American or Canadian voice said, 'Inspector Angel? Are you Inspector Angel?'

Angel turned to see a man with a bushy beard holding out his hands.

The man grabbed Angel's hand and shook it firmly. 'So very pleased to meet you, Inspector. My name is Doctor Edward G. Rubenstein. Come on through,' he said. 'I'm the President of St Magdalene's. Sister Mary Clare is on her way, but I didn't want to keep our Chief of Police waiting. Please, come into my office.'

Angel followed the man into the office. He felt the plush carpet beneath his feet and took in the polished oak-panelled walls.

He grinned. 'I'm not the Chief of Police, Dr Rubenstein,' he said.

'No matter. I expect you soon will be. You *are* that famous policeman, aren't you? Sit down,' he said, pointing to a red leather chair. 'The homicide detective with the unbroken record, who always gets his man, aren't you? I have read about you.'

Angel's eyes narrowed and he looked away. It was a tag given to him years ago by a crime reporter after digging into the history of his career. Reference to it always embarrassed him. It also made him conscious that someone might be observing him carefully . . . hoping he wouldn't be able to maintain the record.

Angel sat down and ran his hands down the chair arms. Rubenstein sat in a leather swivel chair behind the desk and looked across at him.

Angel said, 'I suppose it would be me, Doctor.' Then he added quickly, 'I understand that you've had a robbery of some ethanol and saltpetre from your pharmacy?'

'Yes indeed, and as president of this hospital, Inspector Angel, I want to assure you that we want to do everything possible to stay at the right side of the law in every particular. And I intend to take a personal interest in this business . . . though I must say, Inspector, we are not overly-concerned about it. It is the only robbery we have had in years, and the value of the stolen items is less than a hundred pounds.'

'It is not the value of the robbery solely that concerns me, Doctor. It is that both commodities could be used for dangerous activities, such as the making of explosives or as a means of starting a serious fire. The ethanol is, of course, alcohol and you can do all sorts of weird and wonderful things with the stuff apart from drinking it. And in that regard, I hope you will do all that you can from now on to make your pharmacy safe.'

'Oh yes, indeed. I have that already in hand, Inspector. We are having iron bars fitted across the three outside windows.'

Angel nodded. 'Good. Good. I am very glad to hear it. Now perhaps you would be kind enough to take me there?'

'Of course,' Rubenstein said. He pulled open a drawer, took out a bunch of keys, closed the drawer and stood up. He crossed to the door. 'Your fingerprint men and photographers have been over it . . . and one of your detectives has had a good look round and taken a statement from Sister Mary Clare.'

'Nevertheless, I'd like to have a look for myself,' Angel said.

'Of course. Why not?' Rubenstein said, getting to his feet. 'That's all right. Please follow me, Inspector. I don't know where Sister has got to.'

They trudged along corridors, passing or being passed by the occasional uniformed nurse or hospital worker. Angel noticed how clean and quiet and well decorated the corridors and everywhere seemed to be.

As they were passing a room with the number 21 on the door, it was suddenly opened and a woman in a nightdress looked out. She had long grey hair.

Rubenstein stopped, looked at her and smiled. 'Hello there, Maisie,' he said.

She smiled back at him, touched him on his crisp navy-blue suit jacket and said, 'Philip. Are you all right, dear?'

'Shouldn't you be resting, Maisie? Isn't there a nurse with you?'

From behind the old lady a much younger woman's voice called out, 'I'm here, Dr Rubenstein. It's Nurse MacNeil. Sorry about that. I was in her bathroom, cleaning the shower. Come along, Maisie. Let's get you ready.'

'Goodbye, Maisie,' Rubenstein said, as he closed the door. He looked at Angel and shook his head. 'That dear lady suffers from amnesia. It went suddenly when her husband died two or three years ago.'

Angel nodded. 'Very sad,' he said. 'But memory goes with age.'

'So they say, but Maisie isn't very old. She is still in her fifties.'

Angel's eyes narrowed, his mouth tightened and he shook his head. After a few moments he said, 'Is this a mental hospital, Doctor?'

'No. Not at all. We nurse anybody who is sick or has undergone a procedure or a major operation. In fact we provide nursing for anyone who needs it.'

'For which they pay?'

'Why yes indeed, Inspector. We are not subsidized by the state or anybody else.'

Angel wondered with dismay what it would cost to spend a week in the place.

They continued down the corridor until they were outside a brown door with six small panels of patterned glass framed in it. The words 'Pharmacy — No Admittance' were painted on it in cream.

Rubenstein produced the bunch of keys, selected one and opened the door. He went inside and switched on the light.

Angel followed him into the tiny room. 'Don't you have a pharmacist to dispense prescriptions?' he said.

'We do, but he spends most of his time with the doctors and on the wards. We page him if we need something urgently.'

Angel suddenly heard the bustle of starched skirts and rapid breathing behind him. He turned to see a woman in a blue uniform and white hat.

Rubenstein said, 'Ah. Sister Mary Clare.'

'Sorry to have kept you waiting, Doctor,' she said. 'A small problem in the kitchen. It's all right, now.'

'This is Detective Inspector Angel, Sister.'

Angel smiled at her. He recognized the unmistakable accent. 'We've already spoken on the phone, haven't we, Sister?'

She nodded back at him. 'Indeed we have, Inspector. You'll be wanting to know about the stolen items?' she said.

'Yes, please.'

She passed in front of him and pointed up to the shelf. 'Well, the ethanol was in a tall brown bottle on that shelf up there. It contained five litres full, but it wasn't quite full. And the paper sack of saltpetre was in the cupboard under the workbench. Our stock records show that there were four and a half litres of ethanol and twenty kilos of saltpetre taken.'

'Thank you, Sister. Have you any idea who might have stolen the items?'

Rubenstein said, 'You mean it was an inside job?'

Sister Mary Clare's eyes opened wide. 'To be sure, Inspector, I have not,' she said.

'The window *was* smashed from the outside, wasn't it, Inspector?' Rubenstein said.

'It was,' Angel said. 'But it doesn't mean to say that access was made through the window. If it was an inside job, it would be a good ploy to have the window smashed from the outside *after* the robbery, by the thief or an accomplice, wouldn't it?'

Rubenstein blinked, smiled, and said, 'You've a devious mind, Inspector. No wonder you've such a reputation!'

Angel ignored the compliment. It was standard police practice to take nothing for granted. Rubenstein should have known that.

'How many keys are there to this room?' he said.

'Two,' Rubenstein said. 'I have one and the other is currently in the hands of the pharmacist. It is passed from duty pharmacist to duty pharmacist, and signed for as it is handed over. Some nights and weekends, when we might not have a qualified pharmacist on duty, a doctor or a senior member of the nursing staff may have the key. That's only in case a patient needs some medication urgently.'

Angel rubbed his chin. 'That means quite a few people have had possession of the key at some time or another.'

'Yes, but . . . but they are all professional people, Inspector,' Rubenstein said.

Angel wanted to point out that Crippen and Shipman were also professional people, but he didn't.

'You are certain that nothing else was taken, Sister?'

'We have checked off the rest of the stock with the book and it matches precisely, Inspector,' she said.

Angel nodded, had another quick glance round the shelves, the workbench and the floor. He went over to the door, opened it, examined the keyhole, then locked and unlocked the door. He seemed satisfied. He turned back to them and said, 'Well thank you. That's about all I can do here.'

Sister Mary Clare said, 'Well, if you will excuse me, Inspector, I have a lot on this morning. I will return to it.'

'That's fine, Sister, thank you,' Angel said.

She looked across at Rubenstein, who said, 'Yeah. That's fine, Sister. Thank you.'

She rushed out.

On the way back to reception, Rubenstein turned to Angel and said, 'Perhaps you and your good lady — I assume you are married, or have a partner as they say these days — would care to come to dinner one evening at my house? My housekeeper is an excellent cook.'

Angel frowned. The suggestion didn't appeal him, and he knew Mary definitely wouldn't want to. She didn't know him and she'd be worrying all the time about asking him back to their small, unpretentious house.

'Sounds very . . . nice,' he said vaguely. But he hoped that Rubenstein would quickly forget about it.

* * *

'Excuse me eating my sandwiches, as we talk, Inspector,' the veterinarian said from behind his desk. 'As I said on the phone, the first free time slot I had today was my lunch break. And I only take twenty minutes for *that*, and I usually do some office work while I'm chewing.'

Angel sat down at the other side of the desk facing a colourful poster illustrating the innards of a dog. He wrinkled his nose and turned away from it.

'My receptionist can make you a coffee if you would like one?' the man said, biting into another sandwich.

'No thanks,' Angel said, involuntarily licking his lips.

'What can I do for you?' Fairclough said.

'I'll try to be brief. Thank you for seeing me promptly, but the matter is urgent and you being probably the oldest and most experienced vet in the town, I naturally came to you first.'

Fairclough nodded.

Angel rubbed his hand across his chin. 'The fact is, a local man has died having been savagely half eaten by a large catlike animal,' he said.

Fairclough stopped chewing. His eyes locked onto Angel's face. His mouth dropped open momentarily showing bread and the red of tomato. 'Goodness me,' he said. 'Did this happen in Bromersley?'

Angel nodded then said, 'Yes. The cat must have originated in Africa or South America or somewhere like that. Can you tell me if you have treated such an animal recently?'

'This is absolutely dreadful. No. Not recently. No. Let me see. It's twenty or more years since I had any contact with a large cat and that was a leopard with a skin rash. It was at the Scholes travelling circus in Jubilee Park. It seems a lifetime away now. But the cat you are looking for must have escaped from some private owner . . . or been deliberately set free?'

Angel looked down and frowned. 'I really don't know that yet. Have you any knowledge of anyone who keeps or has kept such an animal?'

'No. It would need to be somebody eccentric. And rich.'

'And stupid,' Angel said.

Fairclough smiled and nodded in agreement. 'He or she would need space to exercise it . . . a place in the country or a farm. There was a recent case the other side of the Pennines —'

'In Cheshire,' Angel said. 'Yes, the animal killed a man. I wondered if we had a similar animal round here?'

'Do you know, Inspector, my father spoke about the proliferation of small circuses in the late Victorian and Edwardian period, all the way up to the 1930s. Apparently it was possible then to make a handsome living from them.'

'That was *then*,' Angel said. 'There are stringent laws prohibiting the caging and exhibition of animals for the purposes of entertainment now.'

'I know. I know,' Fairclough said. 'Was the poor man who was killed anyone I would know?'

'I can't say. He hasn't been formally identified yet.'

Fairclough had finished eating. He looked at Angel wistfully, put the lid back on the sandwich box and said, 'No, Inspector. I know of no one. It is absolutely tragic. What breed of cat was it?'

'We don't know that yet either,' Angel said, getting to his feet. 'Well, thank you very much, Mr Fairclough.'

The man's face suddenly brightened and his eyes opened wide. 'Just a minute,' he said. 'Don't go, Inspector. I don't know if this has any relevance, but many years ago, Haydn Sharpe had a small circus . . . back in the early 1900s.'

'Haydn Sharpe?' Angel said. He frowned and added, 'Who was Haydn Sharpe?'

'Ephemore Sharpe's grandfather, it would have been. In fact, I believe *he* was the actual animal handler. There were six tigers. I've seen a poster of him somewhere. He was in a leotard standing in the middle of them. You know Ephemore Sharpe, Inspector, don't you? She lives at Ashfield Lodge Farm, Bromersley, end of Ashfield Road. Cat mad. Wants locking up.'

Angel blinked. He didn't say that the dead body of Julius Hobbs was found less than 200 yards from her farm. 'I've met her. She must be a client of yours.'

Fairclough's face changed to granite. 'I found her to be personally the most obnoxious and charmless woman I have ever met,' he said. 'I had need to call on her a few years back now, to try to sort something out, but it was to no avail. She has never been in these premises, nor does she call on the services of any of the other vets in town. We compare notes at veterinary association branch meetings, you know. Ephemore Sharpe reckons she is an authority on anything and everything feline. In fact she has almost set herself up in competition with the veterinary profession and I know she has actually taken some business away from me. Oh that doesn't matter, I don't mind *that*. I can afford it. But she was only a history teacher at the grammar school before they changed its name. I don't know what it is called now. She thinks she is an expert in the feline world because of a long-term family interest and devotion to photogenic domestic cats and cute kittens. But, you know, Inspector, she doesn't stand a chance against modern drugs and prevailing scientific diagnostic techniques. There must be fifty cats roaming about her house and in those barns and outbuildings in her yard. Could even be a hundred. If she really cared for her pets, she would seek professional help, modern drugs and the latest advice. But she won't. Some people call her 'The Cat Woman'; they admire her, but they don't know the truth of the matter.'

Angel frowned. "The Cat Woman," he said. 'Indeed?' he added, and gently rubbed his chin.

Fairclough reached out for a beaker of coffee and took a sip.

Angel slowly stood up. 'Well, must get back to the office. I have an appointment. But thank you very much, Mr Fairclough. Thank you.'

5

It was 12.45 a.m. exactly when Angel arrived back at the office. There was no sign of DS Taylor. Angel frowned. He looked up at the wall clock to check that his watch was correct, then wrinkled his nose. He picked up the phone and tapped in a number.

There was a knock at the door.

He replaced the phone and called, 'Come in.'

It was Ahmed.

'I thought you were Don Taylor,' Angel said. 'Where is he?'

'On his way, sir.'

'He'll have to get a move on, lad. See if you can chase him up.'

'Right, sir.'

'And when that professor arrives bring him straight in.'

'Right, sir.'

'And organize some tea for us? Where has that nice blue and white teapot and four-cup set disappeared to?'

'Last time I saw it, it was on a tray outside the chief constable's office, sir. It must have been nicked by the chief constable's secretary.'

Angel's eyes flashed. 'It was antique,' he said. 'It belongs here. It was given to *us* by Phoebe Wilkinson as a thank you for finding the murderer of her friend, Father Gulli. Go and fetch it back.'

'Supposing she sees me.'

'Supposing she *does*? She won't bite. Tell her I sent you. It belongs in this office by rights. Ask her for it. If she's not there, *take* it.'

Ahmed's mouth opened. He was about to protest when there was a knock at the door.

'See who that is,' Angel said.

Ahmed turned and opened it. It was DS Taylor.

'There you are,' Angel said. 'Come in, Don. You're late. We haven't much time.' He turned back to Ahmed and said, 'Off you go, lad. And get on with that little job, smartly.'

Ahmed looked like a patient waiting to have a colonoscopy. He went out and closed the door.

Taylor was carrying a big wooden tray with four-inch high sides like a deliveryman's bread tray. On it were thirty-eight pink wax moulds resting on their corresponding plaster casts. Also pressed under his arm was a clipboard holding several sheets of A4.

'Can I put this tray on your desk, sir?'

Angel moved the day's post which he had not yet seen and put it on the table behind him.

Taylor carefully placed the tray in the middle of the desk. Angel peered down at the contents.

Each pink cast had a number 1 to 38 in blue felt pen on white paper stuck to it. Underneath each cast was the matching white plaster mould of an animal paw mark taken from the muddy ground around the remains of the body of Julius Hobbs.

'Are they set hard enough to handle?' Angel said.

'Yes, sir,' Taylor said.

Angel tentatively picked up one of the casts and its pink mould. He pressed the cast several times. Then he looked under the mould at the paw mark. Then replaced it on the mould and put it back on the tray.

'The numbers refer to the location of each paw mark? You have the chart?'

'And photographs, sir.'

'Good. Did you make any of the paw prints on paper?' Angel said.

'Yes, sir,' Taylor said. He handed him the first sheet off the clipboard. On the next sheet were labelled illustrations in black ink of the front pawmarks and the back pawmarks of three breeds of cats. They were puma, lynx and leopard.

Angel looked at them attempting to make a comparison.

'There's very little difference between them,' he said.

Taylor pointed to the top one and said, 'I think it's this one, sir. The puma.'

Angel nodded. 'Could be. What colour is a puma?'

'Don't know, sir.'

Angel rubbed his chin. 'The prof will know,' he said tidying up the papers. 'Anything else?'

'Yes, sir. The body was moved. There were hypostasis marks all down the body. It had been face down for at least six hours before being turned over onto its back.'

Angel's face creased. 'The body was moved?' he said.

'Yes, sir. It was discovered at the side of the stream on its back.'

As Angel was digesting that important piece of information, the door suddenly opened. They both turned towards it. It was Ahmed.

'Professor Stevenson is here, sir,' he said.

Angel stood up. 'Ah, good,' he said. He had been looking forward to meeting the man. 'Show him straight in, lad.' Then he whispered, 'And bring in that tea ASAP.'

Ahmed nodded, stood to the side and said, 'Professor Vincent Stevenson.'

A thin young man with spectacles came in. He didn't look happy and hardly looked up.

Angel held out his hand to shake it. The young man looked at it, seemed uncertain at first what to do, but eventually responded to what was expected, taking only the tips of Angel's fingers, lifting them up and down twice then releasing them.

'I'm Detective Inspector Angel and this is Detective Sergeant Taylor,' he said.

'Hello,' he said. 'Very nice. Yes. I'm Vincent Stevenson. Please call me Vince.'

Angel pursed his lips. 'Please sit down, Professor Vince,' he said, rubbing his chin.

'No,' the professor said. 'Just Vince.'

The young man sat down on the edge of the chair.

Angel continued to rub his chin. 'You *are* on the Wakefield-based panel of experts of the National Crime Operations Faculty, aren't you, Vince?' Angel said. He wanted to be certain that he was the right man.

'Yes,' he said.

'And are you conversant with big wild cats . . . cats that could kill a fully grown man?'

'Yes, sir.'

'Good,' Angel said. 'By the way, you had better call me Michael.'

'Right, Michael,' the professor said. That seemed to please the young man. He smiled and shuffled backwards to occupy the full seat of the chair.

Taylor leaned forward and said, 'And I'm Don Taylor. Please, call me Don.'

The young professor looked up, smiled and said, 'Yeah. Right, Don.'

Angel smiled and said, 'We're in need of your help, Vince.'

The young man leaned forward and looked at them.

Angel quickly told him about the finding of the body near the stream on the wasteland behind Ashfield Lodge Farm, and showed him an aerial photograph of the area. He then showed him the more intimate photographs of the crime scene, the wax casts of the animal paw marks, the prints and said, 'There are no human footprints anywhere near the victim, but these paw prints are all over the place, distributed as the chart shows. We are obviously led to the conclusion that the killer therefore is a big cat. We have no sighting of any animal but inquiries from the general public are being canvassed. To begin with, can you tell us what animal made those paw marks?'

The professor looked carefully at the sheet of A4 with the prints produced by Don Taylor and said, 'There are only minuscule differences between the prints of the puma, lynx and leopard,' the professor said. 'But looking at these, I am inclined towards the puma, or the cougar as it is more correctly known.'

Taylor smiled. 'The cougar, Vince?' he said.

'We don't have an example of the paw prints of a cougar,' Angel said.

The professor said, 'The cougar, mountain lion, mountain cat, panther and puma are all the same animal.'

Angel raised his eyebrows. 'Really? And these are the paw prints of a cougar?'

'Yes, Michael. I believe so. An adult cougar.'

'And how big is an adult cougar?'

'Pretty big. It stands two feet to two feet six at the shoulders.'

Angel frowned as he visualized the animal standing next to him, the height of the desk top. He didn't like it. He was thinking of the people of Bromersley: they wouldn't like it either, if they knew.

'It is big, Vince,' he said.

The professor smiled. 'Yes. And it's a beautiful animal, Michael.'

'From North America, aren't they?' he said.

'Mainly,' the professor said. Then his voice hardened. 'In the UK, of course, cougars in the wild are out of their own environment. It should shame those who, on a whim, smuggle an animal into an environment unfamiliar to it, and then later, when they become bored with it, release the poor animal into a world it doesn't understand. It's cruel and disgraceful. And then, whatever goes wrong . . . if anyone gets hurt, the animal gets all the blame!'

Angel rubbed his chin and shook his head at the same time. This was obviously a subject close to the professor's heart. He exchanged looks with Taylor then said, 'And is the cougar black, Vince?'

'No. Despite anecdotal evidence to the contrary, an all-black pigment has never been documented in cougars.'

Angel hesitated. 'But I have heard the term 'black panther' many times,' he said.

'Yes, Michael. The term 'black panther' is used colloquially, particularly in fiction, to refer to occasional freak instances of *other* species that have a pigmentation that causes the darkening of their coats, but that applies specifically to jaguars and leopards.'

'So what is the colour of the cougar, Vince?'

'Well, typically, it is tawny, but it could range to silvery-grey and even to a reddish brown.'

Angel's eyes narrowed. 'I think for our purpose, we'd better say light brown.'

The professor smiled and said, 'Michael, the cougar's great majesty, beauty and range of coat colour is far too fascinating to be described merely as light brown.'

Angel sighed. 'That cat might be attractive to you, Vince, I simply need to know what it looks like so that I can tell people. You see . . . to most Bromersley people, coming across a cat like that — particularly at night — could mean a death sentence.'

The professor nodded and said, 'Yes Michael, I understand that, but the cougar does not generally regard the human animal as prey and, interestingly, prey recognition is a learned behaviour. It's true that if the cougar was cornered by a human, of course, it would fight, but then, usually only to escape. Only because of great starvation, or because the human looked a very easy target, being small, or a child, would it attack. There are instances in the US of a cougar attacking and killing children, but few indeed of attacking and killing adult humans.'

'I wouldn't have described our victim as small, Vince. He was average build and aged thirty.'

'What was he doing?'

'We don't know,' Angel said.

'You see, if the victim looked small, and therefore appeared to be an easy target, the cougar might attack, particularly if it was a male cat.'

'You mean if the victim was kneeling down or something like that?'

The professor nodded. 'Or, perhaps seated.'

Angel rubbed his chin. That was a possibility, he thought. He turned to Taylor. 'Was there a fishing rod or any of that sort of thing anywhere around, Don?'

Taylor thought a moment, 'No, sir. Were you thinking that he could have been crouched on a fisherman's stool?'

'Could have been.'

'No, sir. There was no kit of any sort around the body.'

The professor said, 'Well, I'm sorry. I can't explain it. We are all made differently. Maybe this cougar has an unusual and therefore dangerous temperament.'

'Something else unusual, Vince.' Taylor said. 'There are marks of hypostasis on the victim.'

The professor said, 'He could have been killed in one place, but eaten later by the stream where the body was found.'

Angel's eyebrows shot up. 'That would mean someone else, a human had been involved, to move it,' he said.

'Not necessarily,' the professor said. 'It is quite usual. The cougar is typically an ambush predator. It stalks through brush and trees, across ledges, or other uncovered spots, before making a powerful leap onto the back of its prey and delivering a lethal neck bite. It might then drag the kill to a preferred spot, cover it with brush and return to feed over a period of days.'

Angel looked at Taylor. 'That could have happened in this case, Don.'

'I suppose it could, sir. But if it did, we have no idea where the actual killing took place.'

'Were there any signs that the body had been dragged to the stream?' Angel said.

'No, sir,' Taylor said.

Angel turned back to the professor, and said, 'Would the cat be able to drag a twelve-stone man, Vince?'

'Oh yes. They have been known to bring down both wild and domestic horses and even large moose.'

There was a knock at the door.

It was Ahmed carrying a tin tray with a teapot in blue and white, with matching sugar, milk, cups and saucers.

Angel gave him a knowing grin. Ahmed smiled back.

'Thank you, Ahmed,' Angel said, then he turned to the other two men and said, 'Tea break. Come and get it.'

Ahmed did the honours, then turned to go. Angel reached up, grabbed his jacket sleeve and pulled the young man towards him. 'I want DS Crisp, DS Carter and DC Scrivens here at two o'clock,' he said.

Ahmed nodded. 'Right, sir.'

Then, in full throttle, waving the cup around, Angel said, 'The tea's great, Ahmed . . . tastes much better out of this teapot.'

Taylor and the professor looked across and nodded.

Ahmed smiled and went out.

The three men finished their tea. Then Angel thanked the professor for his useful knowledge about wild cats, delivered in words, he said, he understood, and the professor thanked Angel for his friendly reception. The professor took a business card out of his top pocket, wrote a number on it, handed to him and said, 'Don't stand on any ceremony, Michael, if I can help you anytime, ring that number.'

Angel took it, looked at it, put it in his pocket and said, 'Thank you, Vince. I might have to take you up on it.'

The professor nodded, smiled and went out.

As the door closed, Angel and Taylor sat down, and looked across at each other. Angel sighed.

Taylor said, 'What do we do now, sir?'

Angel ran his hand through his hair and said, 'Well, I can't send you and Scrivens out to bring in a male, brown cougar, 2'6 inches at the shoulders, for questioning, can I?'

Taylor nodded.

Then Angel said, 'It's the old, old story, Don. We simply haven't enough info. We don't even know *where* Hobbs actually died. I want to see the place where the cougar actually killed the poor man. I would expect to see bloodstains and signs of a struggle. It might also be where the cougar is hiding in the daylight hours. So you had better get a team together. Search a quarter of a mile radius from the spot where the body was found. It isn't a large area, so I want it searched thoroughly, including the stream, and all the outbuildings, huts, sheds, garages and so on. I want every square yard scratched and sifted through. I don't think a cougar would have ventured *inside* a house to kill anybody, so at the moment I am not including searching living accommodation. However every house — except one! — in that area must be visited and the residents asked if they saw the dead man at all yesterday, and if they have seen a wild cat roaming the neighbourhood over the past few days. Now you are going to need a lot of help, so take everybody available from the CID office, the canteen and the general office. I'll phone Inspector Asquith and get him to let you have whatever uniformed he can spare. All right?'

'You didn't say which house it was you didn't want anybody to call on,' Taylor said, getting to his feet.

'Ah yes,' Angel said. 'That's Ephemore Sharpe's place, Ashfield Lodge Farm. I'll call on her myself. I don't want any of your team being scared by her — could put some of your probationers off women for life.'

Taylor grinned.

But Angel's face was as straight as the crease in the chief constable's trousers. 'Don't stand there grinning, Don,' he said, 'buzz off and get on with it, before that big cat finds another victim.'

6

It was just after two o'clock when Crisp, Carter and Scrivens filed into Angel's little office and settled down on the tubular steel framed chairs.

'Find somewhere to sit and listen up,' Angel said, then he brought them up to date with the latest facts gleaned from the professor and Don Taylor minutes earlier and then said, 'There were three women in the victim's life: Dorothea Webber, Imelda Cartwright and Celia Hamilton. Ahmed has their addresses.'

Then he turned to Crisp and said, 'Now, Trevor, I want you look up Dorothea Webber. She was married to Julius Hobbs briefly. Not happily, according to his mother, and that was not entirely her fault. A bit odd for the mother not to blame the daughter-in-law, but that's what she told me. Anyway, see what you can find out about Dorothea, the relationship she had' with Julius and the reason for the break up and subsequent divorce. Also where she was on Sunday evening. All right?'

Crisp's forehead creased producing a dozen parallel lines. 'If a wild cat killed Julius Hobbs, sir, why do we need to make these inquiries?'

'It's called thoroughness, lad.'

Crisp wasn't satisfied, but he didn't want to say so. He involuntarily shook his head and said grudgingly, 'Right, sir.'

Angel said, 'You see, there's one thing that cougar will never tell us, Trevor, and that is, its motive.'

'Hunger, sir,' Crisp said.

'Yes, sir,' Carter agreed.

'He wanted something to eat, sir,' Scrivens put in.

'Maybe,' Angel said. 'But satisfying its hunger is what happened *after* the killing. What made the cougar select Julius Hobbs?'

'Because he was the first accessible human being, sir,' Crisp said.

'*Where* was he accessible? We don't know. It was a cool evening, very cool. It is not likely that the wild cat was inside a house, and it is not known why Hobbs would be out of doors in October without a topcoat. He was not noted to be particularly interested in hobbies or sports that might have required him to be out of doors that autumn evening. Now there might be very satisfactory explanations to these questions but I don't know what they are yet. So we must keep on with our inquiries until we have answers that will satisfy a coroner. All right?'

'Right, sir,' Crisp said.

Flora Carter shuddered and said, 'I am not sure I would want to be out at night in Bromersley if a cougar is on the prowl.'

Angel tried to think of something to say to lessen her fear. 'Flora,' he said, 'the odds of you bumping into it are millions to one. You've a better chance of winning the lottery. And while I have you in my sights, Flora, I want you to inquire into the activities of that actress Celia Hamilton and her relationship with Hobbs. His mother said that they had been seeing each other a few months now. Contact her and see what you can find out. Obviously, it may require you to break the tragic news to her. Also find out what she was doing on Sunday evening.'

Crisp and Scrivens exchanged glances.

'Right, sir,' she said.

Angel then turned to Scrivens and said, 'And you, Ted, I want you to inquire into Hobbs's relationship with a Miss Imelda Cartwright. Hobbs's mother said that they were together for about a year and the split was rather vindictive. Ask the same questions I have told the others. All right?'

'Yes, sir.'

Angel then glanced round to check that he had the attention of the three of them and said, 'I want you to see if you can find a motive for the killing. Hobbs seems to have been a regular sort of chap. There must be *something* bad about him. Also see if you can find out where he was and what he was doing on Sunday evening. All right? Any questions?'

There was none. 'Right,' Angel said. 'Off you go then.'

They went out and, as the door closed, Angel pulled open a drawer in his desk and took out a telephone directory. He opened it, found the page he wanted, scanned down the column, and then reached out for the phone. He was soon speaking to Sir Raphael Quigley, the property developer. And forty-five minutes later he was seated in his modern office with glass walls on two sides, in a new, multi-storey building in Leeds city centre.

'Now then, young man,' Quigley said, peering over his half lens spectacles, 'as I told you on the phone, I fail to see how I can be of any help to you in connection with this Julius Hobbs person?'

'I think you may be able to help me quite a lot, Sir Raphael,' Angel said. 'Firstly, you can tell me what kind of a relationship you had with him.'

Quigley blinked. His nostrils quivered as though he had been hovering too close over the gravy vat in the cookhouse in Strangeways. 'I didn't have any kind of a relationship with *that* young man,' he said.

Angel sensed prevarication. 'Come along, Sir Raphael. Don't mess me about. Hobbs was a competitor of yours, wasn't he? He used regularly to outsmart you at auctions and when submitting tenders, didn't he?'

Quigley's small black eyes suddenly glowed like the flame of a safe-breaker's acetylene cutter.

'Nothing of the kind,' he said. 'He certainly did not.'

'That's what Hobbs's mother said.'

'What do mothers know about their sons? She doesn't know what she's talking about.'

'You knew his mother then?'

'No. Well, yes. I've *met* her.'

'So you've met her son then?'

'Well, yes. Hobbs was a small-time, impertinent young opportunist who drifted in and out of the property business . . . buying and selling in an entirely irresponsible manner to make a quick buck.'

Angel thought that that was what every property developer did.

'So we've established that you knew Julius Hobbs, Sir Raphael,' he said.

Quigley raised his eyebrows, lowered the corners of his mouth and looked across at the big modern clock on the wall facing him.

'Yes of course,' he said. 'You'd better get a move on, Angel. The time is three fifty-two. I have an appointment in London in an hour. And my helicopter leaves in eight minutes.'

'If you answer my questions in a helpful and complete manner, Sir Raphael, it *is* possible that you *might* be able to keep your appointment,' Angel said.

Quigley's face went scarlet.

Angel continued, 'Did you and Hobbs have any financial proposition pending?'

'Certainly not. I didn't . . . I couldn't have dealt with him. He wasn't . . . he wasn't ethical.'

'Really? In what way?'

'In every way.'

'For instance?'

'Well, for instance, at some property auctions, where we might have had competing interests, he would often run my estates manager up to some outrageous figure and then drop out at the last moment leaving him having to agree to pay a greater sum than would have been necessary. When I subsequently spoke to Hobbs about it afterwards, he just laughed . . . laughed in my face.'

'He probably thought it was fair competition, Sir Raphael, after all, anybody can bid in an auction, and he could have misjudged how high your company would bid and have finished up having to buy the property at the price he bid at. What would he have done then?'

'He would probably have attempted to sell it to me, the impertinent rascal. However, it never happened. He seemed to know when to stop bidding.'

'Wouldn't that be because he knew the property's true value?' Angel said.

Quigley growled and looked away through the glass wall. The office was on the eighth floor so all he saw was cloudy, grey sky.

Angel rubbed his chin and said, 'Have you any notion of any transaction in which he was currently involved?'

'How would I know that?'

Angel shrugged. 'I don't know. I thought it might be possible.'

Quigley lowered his eyebrows, with very long manicured fingers tapped his chin several times and said, 'No. I don't know much about his business, but there is one project I heard of that had very probably been of interest to him. It was, perhaps, too small for my company . . . and it is in Bromersley, right on his doorstep, so it certainly would not have missed his eagle eye. There is a plot of building land, around six hectares that is ripe for development into a small estate of semis. There is an old farm in front of it that needs to be purchased and demolished to allow adequate sewerage and road access. It is the sort and size of project that might just have suited young Hobbs.'

Angel blinked as he experienced a small tingle of pleasure. He might just know the plot of land to which Quigley had referred.

'Who owns it?' Angel said.

'I don't know, but it is in the hands of an agent,' Quigley said. 'Adrian Hastelow Estate Agents. He's in the book.'

'Thank you,' Angel said and he scribbled the name down on the back of an envelope taken from his inside pocket. 'Just one more thing, Sir Raphael, for the record. Where were you on Sunday evening last?'

Quigley's eyebrows shot up again. 'Sunday evening?' he said. 'Am I obliged to answer such an intrusive question? Am I under suspicion of having committed a crime of some sort?'

'No, sir. Not at all, and you are not obliged to answer the question. I will perfectly well understand if you find the question . . . embarrassing.'

Quigley's lips tightened. 'The question is not in the least embarrassing,' he said.

'Oh good,' Angel said brightly and he looked expectantly across the desk into the man's face.

Quigley instantly looked away, his jaw set harder than Dartmoor granite. He breathed in and then out slowly, three times, then he looked back at Angel and said, 'If you must know, I was at my home in Harrogate.'

'With your family?'

'I have no family. I live alone. I was relaxing . . . listening to music and re-cataloguing my butterfly collection.'

'You were alone all day?'

'No. My housekeeper left at four o'clock. I was alone after that.'

'Did you receive any phone calls at all after four o'clock?'

'I don't think so, why?'

'A phone call to you might have helped confirm that you were there.'

'I *know* I was there!' he said banging the top of the desk with a clenched fist.

The phone rang. He snatched it up. 'Yes? . . . I'm coming.' He slammed it down, turned to Angel, raised his eyebrows and said, 'Well, Inspector, have you any more questions for me?'

Angel rubbed his chin. 'No, Sir Raphael, thank you,' he said, standing up. Then he added slowly, 'That's all *for now*.'

Quigley glared at him across the desk.

A door flew open and a woman dashed in carrying a laptop case and a black overcoat with black silk-faced lapels. She had the laptop under her arm and was holding the overcoat shoulder-high by the collar.

As Quigley slid his arms into the coat sleeves, he said, 'Miss Prendergast, immediately after I have gone, show this . . . this person out.'

'Yes, Sir Raphael,' she said.

Then Quigley snatched the case from her and dashed out of the office buttoning the coat.

Angel watched the door close and wrinkled his nose.

* * *

Angel returned immediately to the station and, as he made his way down the corridor to his office, he heard his phone ringing. He dashed through the door and snatched up the receiver.

'Angel,' he said.

Nobody replied, but there was the sound of a loud wheezy cough and a splutter. Angel pulled the phone away from his ear. He knew the caller was his superior, Superintendent Horace Harker. There was nobody who could cough and splutter like he did. There was another cough and a splutter, and that was again repeated.

Eventually Harker spoke. 'Angel, are you there?' he said, breathily.

'Yes, I'm here, sir,' he said.

'Aye, well, come up here, smartish,' he said, then he banged the receiver hard down into its cradle. It clicked noisily in Angel's ear. Angel's jaw muscles tightened. He replaced his receiver, then blew out a yard of breath. He went up the corridor to the last door, where there was a sign screwed to it that read: DETECTIVE SUPERINTENDENT HORACE HARKER.

He knocked on the door and went in.

Harker was at his desk. There were two piles of papers and files standing up to eye level, and the rest of the desk was littered with letters, reports, a bottle of lemonade, a coffee cup, jar of Vick, bottle of paracetamol tablets, box of tissues and a transistor radio.

The superintendent was holding a white plastic inhaler up a nostril and taking a long hard sniff while blocking off the other nostril with the forefinger of his other hand. His eyes followed Angel as he came into the office. He looked and nodded at the chair opposite.

Angel sat down, looked across at the superintendent and wondered what was coming next.

Eventually, Harker withdrew the inhaler, put the cap on it, placed it on the desk, and sniffed.

'You wanted me, sir?' Angel said.

'Aye,' Harker began. 'You're spending too much time on this Hobbs case, lad. I know his death is unusual, but don't you realize that your time, supported by the specialist services, forensic, research, security and legal, costs the force a hundred and sixty-six pounds an hour? Not a *day*, lad, an *hour*. And that's only for you. It doesn't include the other members in your team. They are separately costed at figures proportionate to their rank and qualifications.'

Angel ran the end of his tongue along his bottom lip. 'I don't think I get your point, sir.'

Harker's red, shiny eyes looked as if they might burst out of their sockets.

'Your reports clearly show that Hobbs was killed by an animal. We can't arrest it, can we? We can't charge it with murder, even if you could find it and prove that it was that particular creature. This case needs to be handed to the coroner's office without delay. In turn, I expect the court would pass a verdict of 'accidental death'. End of story, until someone with a rifle — hopefully somebody from this force — sees the blasted animal and kills it. In the meantime, you should move onto something else. There is a case you have in hand . . . the stealing of dangerous substances from that hospital. Now *that* is urgent.'

Angel pursed his lips. 'The thing is, sir, I haven't had the post-mortem report from Dr Mac yet. Hobbs has only been dead about forty hours, I felt that it was too early to —'

Harker said, 'But in this case, the cause of the man's death is obvious. He has bite marks in places, and pawmarks all round the body. What more evidence do you think a coroner will need? You can't simply hang onto a case, Angel, for whatever purist reasons you may have. Our budget simply won't stretch to it. I know that you get very possessive about your cases, and that you are a bloody perfectionist. But this case is different. Although there *is* obviously a victim, there *isn't* a criminal as such. The party responsible is an animal who is only seeking food, or maybe the victim alarmed it, or it felt threatened by him, but whatever the motive, it doesn't matter as far as the law is concerned. We don't try animals in a court of law. Now I know you're a bit of a celebrity and some people think you are something special, but you don't have to play the part all the time. There's no justification in trying to make this slightly unusual case seem more important than it really is. It certainly attracts the newspapers, but the verdict will still be accidental death, and you will look such a fool. So give the facts to the coroner's office now . . . oh, look at the time . . . it's ten to five . . . I have to go.' He stood up.

'But, sir —' Angel said.

'I know. You obviously can't do it *today*,' Harker said, as he reached into the green steel wardrobe behind his chair and took out his overcoat and hat. 'But do it in the morning, then get on with that theft from the hospital. All right?'

But it was not all right. Angel stood up. His lips pulled tight back against his teeth. There was a lot he wanted to say.

'I knew you'd see reason if I explained it to you carefully,' Harker said as he passed behind him on his way to the door. 'Now, I really *do* have to go,' he added as he put on the hat, aimed an arm into a sleeve of the overcoat and grabbed hold of the door handle. 'I've an appointment at five for drinks with the chief constable, the mayor and aldermen at the Town Hall,' he added as he rushed out of the office.

Angel followed him to the door and glared down the corridor after him.

* * *

He looked across the kitchen table at Mary and said, 'And then, would you believe it, the super dashed off saying that he was having drinks at the Town Hall.'

'Never mind, darling,' Mary said. 'Have another piece of chocolate cake?'

'No thank you,' Angel said. 'But it is delicious.'

She smiled.

'Just coffee,' he said pushing away from the table.

'Go in there,' she said, with a nod towards the sitting-room door. 'I'll bring the coffee through in a minute.'

Angel went into the sitting room, switched on the table lamp, slumped into his favourite easy chair, leaned back onto the cushion and closed his eyes.

A few minutes later Mary came in with the two cups of coffee and put them on the library table.

'Thank you, love,' he said as he reached out for the cup. He stirred the coffee a few moments and then said, 'I definitely think that there is a human involved in the death of young Hobbs. I haven't much to go on, but, if I am right, the investigation becomes a murder inquiry. But you see if I hand the case over to the coroner's office tomorrow morning, the crime might never be uncovered and the murderer might get away with it. And all the blame for his death would be attributed to a wild cat.'

'You worry too much.'

'Listen to this, Mary. If only an animal is the killer, it killed the man in a place we have not yet found and devoured some of the poor man's body there. Then, some time later, we don't know how much later, the animal supposedly dragged the body to the place where it was discovered by the stream, where more of it was eaten. But the strange thing is that there were no drag marks anywhere near the place, nor were the body's clothes muddied or wet, which they certainly would have been.'

'So how was the body moved?'

'That is the question precisely. Also, the body was found outside *not* wearing a topcoat. This is late October. It is almost certain that he would have been wearing an overcoat and we have not found it. And I haven't met a cat yet that could, or would bother to, take the coat off a man.'

'The victim could have taken the coat off . . . beforehand, voluntarily.'

'Of course he could, but why would he do want to do that when he was out of doors, on a cold night?'

'Well, Michael, what's your explanation then?'

'Simple,' Angel said, 'I believe that he was murdered *in*doors.'

Mary frowned. She picked up her coffee, took a sip then said, 'It's not much to go on, love.'

'It's enough,' Angel said. Then he added, 'Now you can see that I must find the human partner in the murder, and why I can't pass the case on to the coroner's office.'

'Never mind, sweetheart,' Mary said. 'You'll solve it. You always do.'

Angel looked down at the carpet, shook his head and rubbed his chin. 'I dunno, love,' he said. 'I've got to solve it before I get into the office tomorrow morning.'

Mary suddenly sat upright in the chair. She breathed in and then out loudly. 'Now look here, Michael,' she said. 'I've had enough of work, and enough of Superintendent Harker. If he orders you to pass the inquiry to the coroner's office, that's what you'll have to do, isn't it?'

He shrugged.

Mary looked straight at him. '*Isn't it?*' she repeated.

Eventually he said, 'Yes, of course.'

'Well, let's leave it until tomorrow morning then.'

He considered the matter for a moment then he nodded. He had to agree, it was the most sensible thing to do.

They both sipped coffee for a moment then she assumed a brightness she didn't feel and said, 'Now what have you done about the safe?'

Angel's mind didn't change direction as quickly as his wife's. His jaw dropped. 'What safe?' he said, then he raised his head quickly and added, 'Oh Uncle Willy's safe.' He returned the coffee cup to the table. 'I phoned Williams, the house removals firm, and they said they would need specialist lifting tackle for a safe that big, so they declined to quote. Then I phoned Smith's the safe furniture retailers in Leeds, for a quote. They wanted two hundred and twenty-five pounds. I thought that was a bit steep. I didn't have the time to make any other inquiries.'

Mary's face dropped. She couldn't hide her disappointment. And she did want to know what was in that safe. 'Doreen Goodman wants it out of the house so that she can sell it you know.'

'A safe stuck in the corner of a room won't stop her from selling the house,' he said. 'And look at the cost it's going to be to move it.'

'I think as Uncle Willy has left you the safe, the least you can do is get a move on and take delivery of it. It will look to Doreen as if you don't want it.'

'Well, I don't. We've nothing to put in it, have we? And it makes us potential targets for villains who might think it's stuffed full of money or diamonds and pearls or whatever.'

Mary's eyes shone as she considered what he had said. 'But, Michael, we don't know what's in it. Doreen said she hadn't seen it open for more than ten years. It might really be full of all sorts of fabulous antiques.'

Angel blinked several times then rubbed his chin. He thought about the gas bill and the mortgage. 'Shall we get Smith's to transport it here, then?'

'As soon as they can,' she said. 'Then we will have to find a way of opening it.'

'Yes,' he said. 'I must give that some thought.'

Mary nodded quickly several times.

7

'Good morning, sir.'

'Yes, Ahmed. Come in. There's something I need you to do.'

'Yes, sir?'

'I want you to ring round Sergeants Carter and Crisp, and DC Scrivens, and tell them that the Hobbs case is to be handed over to the coroner, and therefore I do not require them to pursue their inquiries into the women with whom the victim had had a relationship. All right?'

Ahmed blinked. 'Does that mean that poor Mr Hobbs *was* killed by a wild cat after all, sir?' he said.

'No, lad, it doesn't,' Angel said, 'It means that the super *thinks* that the man was killed by that wild cat. *He's* wrong, but *he's* the super and *I'm* only the inspector. Got it?'

Ahmed nodded knowingly. 'Oh *yes*, sir,' he said, then he went out.

Angel watched the door close. He shook his head and sighed. It was a deep sigh. It seemed as though he had drawn breath all the way from his toes. He looked round the little office and wondered what he was doing there. He rubbed his chin as he reminded himself that he was just one of millions, earning money to afford to keep himself and Mary warm and fed in a comfortable house. He used to believe he had the best job in the world, being a police inspector, solving crimes, bringing murderers to court and seeing them put away. It had all seemed very satisfying, and he had felt that he had a certain aptitude for it, but now, the job was becoming more difficult and he wasn't enjoying it like he used to. It was more like an obstacle race. The foremost problem was Harker, who made illogical decisions in the face of evidence to the contrary, as in this instance. Angel could only think that it was to show his superiority. It had happened time after time. The superintendent was always putting in his oar in a most unhelpful way. There were also other reasons. Since he had been made an inspector, there had been changes to judges' rules in favour of the criminal, always making it more difficult for Angel, his team and the CPS. In addition, the chief constable was frequently demanding statistics on the most obtuse aspects of crimes and criminals, and new restrictions were often made on current methods of evidence gathering to meet the ever-changing pernickety requirements of Health and Safety. And so it went on.

Was the job losing its magic? Was it time to get out of the police service? A few years ago, he had had a dream of opening an office in Bromersley as a private detective. He thought he might have made a good living at it. But as murder was his primary business, he didn't see that he would have had many private clients with a murder they wanted him to solve. He reckoned that most of any prospective clients would be husbands wanting their wives followed, and wives wanting their husbands followed. He had talked this over with Mary at length and she had said she'd support him in whatever he wanted to do, but that she didn't think that he would be fulfilled with a business mostly involving tailing errant spouses, so the idea was abandoned. Maybe now was the time to resurrect it.

The phone rang and brought him back to reality. He snatched it up.

'Angel,' he said.

It was Harker, who coughed several times and then said, 'There's a triple nine. An anonymous caller reported a body found on Fish Lane, wherever that is.'

Angel's heart began to race. A body. All thoughts of leaving the force vanished. He knew exactly where Fish Lane was. It was a footpath between Salmon Cottages and Ashfield Lodge Farm.

'Constable Weightman was on early shift and near the place,' Harker said. 'Control room sent him to investigate. He's just confirmed it's a body. Looks like another attack by that animal. See to it, lad.'

'Right, sir,' Angel said. He cancelled the call then tapped in a number. As it connected, he waited, gripping the phone tightly. The back of his hand suddenly felt unusually ice-cold. He glanced down and saw that the hairs were as stiff as a judge's collar.

Ahmed knocked on the door and came in.

Angel replaced the phone. 'I was just ringing you, lad. There's a triple nine . . . a body found on Salmon Lane.'

Ahmed's jaw dropped.

'Ring DS Taylor and Dr Mac immediately on your phone and ask them to attend.'

'Right, sir,' Ahmed said.

'And have you contacted Crisp, Carter and Scrivens yet about the Hobbs case being handed over to the coroner?'

Ahmed looked embarrassed. 'I'm sorry, sir. I haven't had a chance. The phone's never stopped and you —'

'That's OK. Cancel *that* order. Say nothing about it to them or anybody.'

'Can I ask why, sir?'

'I have the feeling that we'll find that this body has been murdered in the same way as Julius Hobbs, which means that, in my opinion, a human is involved and therefore the inquiries would be justified.'

Ahmed looked troubled. 'But what about the super, sir?' he said.

Angel hesitated then gave him a political reply: 'He'll be delighted if we crack the case, Ahmed.'

'I didn't mean that, sir. I mean, didn't he give you an order?'

Angel looked at him closely and shook his head. 'I *know* exactly what you meant, Ahmed,' he said. Then he added significantly, 'But we're *not going to tell him*, are we?'

The young man's face brightened as realization dawned. 'Oh no, sir,' he said.

'Good.'

Ahmed went out.

Angel reached for his coat.

* * *

Angel drove the BMW down Ashfield Road to the front of Ashfield Lodge Farm, which was as close to Fish Lane as he could get by car. He stopped the BMW, pulled on the handbrake and got out. He had arranged to meet DS Carter there. He looked around for her. His eyes alighted on a black and white cat through the bars of the grey, tubular steel gate across the front of the farmyard. The cat sped silently across the yard from the direction of the house. Angel watched it push its head into a hole in the side of a wooden barn. As it advanced further into the hole, its bottom wobbled rapidly and then disappeared. Angel rubbed his chin. Then he heard running footsteps behind him. He looked round and saw Flora Carter rushing towards him.

'There you are, sir.'

'What you found out, Flora?' Angel said. 'Don Taylor here?'

'Yes, sir. And Doctor Mac.'

He nodded. 'Good. Where's the body?'

'Down here, sir.'

'I'll follow you. Have you set up the door to door?'

'No, sir. Only just got here myself.'

'It should have been done. See to it as soon as we've finished here. But not Miss Ephemore Sharpe's farm. She wouldn't help us anyway. But every house, coal-hole, caravan, dog kennel and rat trap that has a door or a window that overlooks the scene. All right?'

'Right, sir. It's along this path. It veers to the right. Between the farm and Salmon Cottages. I wish I'd worn my boots. It's a bit muddy.'

They went down the side of the farm wall, turned left and then picked their way along the back of a row of houses, passing the usual array of police vehicles with lights flashing and RTs chattering. They reached the taped area where PC Weightman, a big man who had been in the force more than twenty years, was on guard. He threw up a salute.

Angel acknowledged it and said, '*You* found the body, John, I heard?'

'Yes, sir,' Weightman said, as he lifted up the tape. 'After a tip off,' he added.

'Is it male or female?'

'Couldn't tell, sir.'

Angel's eyebrows went up and he wrinkled his nose as he followed Flora Carter down the lane towards a white canopy that was set up across the muddy footpath forty yards ahead.

Carter said, 'I heard it's female, sir. Couldn't say how old. Apparently the straps of a vest or slip . . . and a bra are partly distinguishable. She's been badly chewed up by the animal.'

The corners of his mouth turned down as he realized he would have to view another atrocity.

DS Taylor came out of the canopy. He was in the obligatory sterile, white, one-piece overall with hood, boots and gloves. He saw Angel and Carter and walked towards them.

'What you got, Don?'

'Not a lot, sir. Looks like another attack from a cat,' Taylor said. 'This time on a female. Age indeterminate.'

Angel frowned. 'How bad?'

'Bad, sir. Face and the top half of her body are mutilated. She's been badly mauled and parts of her have been eaten, her face, breasts and most of an arm. And there are claw scratches on her arms and legs. Again there are paw prints, twelve clear enough to take moulds of, but no human footprints.'

'Time of death?'

'Not sure. But like the previous case, the woman wasn't killed here. The body was moved. There are hypostasis marks on her arms and a leg that I could see. It had been face up for at least six hours before being turned on its side.'

'You found it on its side?'

Taylor nodded. 'I know it's a bit unusual, sir. Its shoulders and hips are on their side, but the arms and legs are not. They're all over the place. You'll see for yourself.'

Angel frowned. He was in no hurry to view the body. 'Any ID?' he said.

'No, sir. There's no sign of a bag or a coat with pockets or laundry marks on the bits of clothing as far as we could see. Dr Mac might find something when he has the body on the slab.' Taylor pointed to the canopy behind him and said, 'He's about finished here.'

Angel nodded then turned to Carter and said, 'Have you any gloves, Flora? Did you bring any?'

Her mouth opened and her eyes flashed. She wasn't pleased. 'No, sir,' she said.

Angel frowned. He wasn't pleased either. 'We need gloves,' he said. 'Well, don't touch anything.'

He pushed his hands firmly into the pockets in the sterile suit.

Taylor looked sympathetically at Flora and then said, 'There isn't a lot you would want to touch, sir.'

Angel and Flora Carter followed Taylor into the canopy.

A powerful stark light on a tripod illuminated a mess of pink flesh, a head of dark hair, two open eyes, and torn remnants of clothes. There was dried blood everywhere. The body was located mostly on the grass verge but one leg was stretched out at an extreme angle on the muddy path.

Dr Mac in the white sterile overalls, was crouching over the body, packing his bag. He looked up. His eyes over the mask showed his distaste.

The horror of the scene caused Angel's pulse to bang in his ears as loud as a Salvation Army drum.

Angel methodically looked over the scene and the body. It consisted of dried blood, raw flesh and torn clothes. He noted the long naked shapely leg with claw marks in three places. He counted twelve numbered casts of paw prints in the mud on the path. He looked for signs of human footprints and saw none. He rubbed his chin. He wrinkled his nose. Then he opened the canopy flap and emerged.

Flora Carter followed him out into the field, then quickly rushed past him and darted behind a bush, a handkerchief to her mouth.

Angel's face creased when he heard the throaty noise followed by the sound of vomit landing on the ground.

Doctor Mac came up from behind him. He cast a quick glance in the direction of the bush. 'A stiff brandy cured me, Michael. I used to carry a bottle in here,' he said holding up his bag.

Angel strode out, eager to get away from the place.

PC Weightman held up the boundary tape for them. As they dodged under it, Angel said, 'I think you must be slipping in your old age, Mac.'

The little Scot raised his bushy eyebrows and said, 'What's that supposed to mean?'

'I'm waiting for an update on Julius Hobbs.'

'I've only had him two days.'

'It's not like you to dally about.'

'I've not been dallying about. I've all the hospital PMs to do as well as police work, you know. Anyway, I *have* almost finished.'

Angel didn't reply. They walked on a few more steps in silence.

'I think I know what's getting at you, Michael,' the doctor said.

'Well, you old fox, if you know, why do you keep me in suspense?'

'You don't think the death of Hobbs and therefore probably the death of this woman has been brought about by an animal, do you?'

Angel sighed impatiently. 'Don't dance around it, Mac. If you've something to say, say it!' he said.

'I can't say it, Michael, because I have nothing conclusive to say.'

'But you have an opinion. A professional opinion, I mean.'

'My professional opinion is that we have to wait and see, but I promise to phone you if I find anything remotely suspicious about that young man's death or about this woman's death.'

* * *

'Now, Vince, this might seem a very strange question,' Angel said into the phone. He spoke slowly and deliberately. 'But is it possible, by use of some sort of bait, or signal, or smell, or some other way, to train a cougar to attack and kill a specific person?'

Professor Stevenson didn't reply immediately.

'You mean by sticking bait in his pocket or spraying him with a specific smell?' he said.

'Well . . . yes . . . any way at all, like that. And . . . so that the target doesn't realize he, or she, has been marked?'

The professor took a deep breath before he replied. 'I am not sure, Michael. Unusual relationships *do* exist between animals and humans, but I really can't see how a person could develop a sophisticated rapport with a cougar that would enable him to train it to that sort of degree. Almost all big cats I have had dealings with are simple creatures, interested in survival, copulation with their own kind, the protection and nurturing of their cubs, food . . . and little else. They are not looking for trouble. If they attack a beast or a human, it would be because they are hungry, or because they believe they are trapped, or because the beast or human is a threat or thought to be a threat to their cubs. In situations where they might find themselves cornered they would only be interested in escaping and would attack only to facilitate their escape. And when they are hungry, they would only attack a human if there is nothing else to eat. Believe me, Michael, the young flesh of a gazelle or a sheep would always be preferred to that of a wiry human.'

Angel rubbed his chin. The professor's reply seemed pretty comprehensive.

'Right, Vince. Thank you,' he said. Then he added, 'There's something else. It might seem to you to be a bit far-fetched, but this is a very difficult case, and it came to me . . . and I thought . . . I wondered . . . erm . . .' His voice faded to silence.

The professor said, 'Yes, Michael?'

Angel began slowly. 'Is it likely, Vince . . . nay, is it possible . . . actually to . . . to hypnotize a cougar? You can possibly see where I am going with this?'

'I think I can see *exactly* where you are going,' the professor said. 'I can't say I have any knowledge of large cats of any kind being hypnotized, Michael. Mmm. But . . . well, a few years ago, I saw a Chinese girl hypnotize alligators.'

'Alligators?' The pupils of Angel's eyes froze. He looked straight ahead. 'So it *is* possible?' he said.

'Well,' the professor began, slowly, 'bear with me. Fifteen years ago, I went to an out-of-the-way village in the Sichuan mountains of China, and there was a big, round, wooden, purpose-built structure about fifteen metres across, and had walls about four metres high, but it didn't have a roof. Inside was a small pool and a few rocks and bushes, and languishing by the pool were eight alligators. There was a high viewing platform built all round the outside of the structure so that visitors on payment of a few yuan could mount the steps and look down at the alligators below. It was quite alarming. Anyway, I paid my money, climbed up the steps, chose a place to stand, leaned over the top of the rail and looked down at them. I must say, I love animals, but *they* took a bit of taking to. They were mostly somnolent until the music — if you can call it that — started. It was Chinese, of course, and very noisy. Then the alligators began excitedly running around in every direction. They can move at great speed, you know. I couldn't identify any pattern or explanation except that the music must have warned them what to expect. Outside the pit, at ground level, a Chinese girl dressed in a big colourful gown and wearing a huge headpiece the shape of a fan appeared. She was carrying a torch. There was a door into the pit and, on cue, the torch was ignited and the girl went through the door into the pit. The animals slowed down and stared at her and the flaming torch.'

'Was it *that* girl who hypnotized them?'

'Yes, but I'm coming to that. The girl paraded confidently among them, waving the torch. They all stared at her and slowly edged towards her . . . they began making a circle round her, which made me feel very uneasy, I can tell you. I knew that if she had been bitten by any of them, that initial smell of blood would have incited the other alligators to attack her, and eight alligators would have made very, very short work of her. Anyway, they walked round her, then as they felt brave enough, one by one they advanced towards her. As she spotted one coming, she waved the flame in front of it, stared into its eyes until it stopped moving. She held the gaze for a couple of seconds then turned away from it with a flourish, and the alligator was transfixed. It had its eyes — and often its jaws — wide open. She looked up at the audience, waved the torch and everybody cheered and applauded. She did the same to each of the other alligators, until all eight were like statues. Then the door into the pit opened and men rushed in with meat and fruit on a trolley, which they left in the centre of the ring. Another man went to the pool and did something to it. They all carefully avoided actually touching the animals. The girl stood on a rock in the centre of the pit, I suppose she was watching the reptiles, making sure that none of them woke up. Anyhow, when the men had finished — it took about a minute . . . they went out, and when the door was safely closed again, the girl went round to each alligator in turn and either touched it, or looked into its eyes, or spoke to it, or all three, I couldn't be sure. The reptile instantly came back to life, looked round, seemed all right and dashed off to the pile of food left in the centre of the room and began eating ravenously. When all eight were concentrating on eating, the girl came safely out of the pit to tumultuous applause.'

Eventually Angel said, 'That's amazing, Vince, truly amazing. But it isn't quite what I meant.'

The professor frowned. 'Oh?' he said.

'Well, I mean the girl didn't instruct them to go anywhere or do anything,' Angel said.

'She didn't command the alligators to fetch a ball, or jump through a hoop, or anything like that, Michael, but she certainly got them to stay stock still until she 'released' them.'

Angel nodded. 'Were they actually hypnotized?'

'I don't know if each alligator was actually hypnotized, but she clearly had great power over them.'

Angel rubbed his chin. 'Mmm. But could that be replicated with a cougar, or a team of cougars? Would it be possible for a human to be able to control and direct cats to attack and kill a particular person?'

'I honestly don't know, Michael. But, thinking about it, I don't rule it out.'

Angel permitted himself a slight smile. The outlook was improving. His heart felt lighter. He smiled and breathed out a long sigh. 'All right, Vince. Let's assume that it *could* be done. Then how would you direct a cat, specifically a cougar, to attack and kill an intended victim?'

The professor rubbed his chin for a few moments then he said, 'Well, I would cage the cat up so that it could not obtain food elsewhere, then feed it its favourite food, say raw, fresh flesh from a sheep, to which I had applied a small amount of a particular scent. I would reduce the amount of meat and increase the strength of the scent each day for about two months, so that the cougar would still be healthy but also ravenous and in no doubt that that scent indicated 'good food'. Then I would apply that same scent to my target and arrange to have the target victim somewhere near where the cougar was being kept. Then I would release the cougar.'

Angel nodded. Things were looking up. It was a dreadful thought but the professor had made the proposition viable. He sighed, smiled and said, 'Thank you very much, Vince.'

8

Angel arrived home in a heavy rainstorm at just after half past five.

He came in by the back door as always which opened directly into the kitchen. He closed the door and locked it. It was warm and there was the comforting smell of cooking. He noted with satisfaction that something was simmering in a pan on a ring and he saw that the oven was on.

There was no sign of Mary.

'Anybody home?' he called.

He was pleased to be inside on such a filthy night. He began to unbutton his wet coat.

Mary came in from the hall. Unusually, she was all dressed up in a blue costume, high-heeled shoes and in full war paint.

Angel's eyebrows shot up. He was tired and in no mood to go out or have visitors. 'What's happening?' he said.

She smiled and said, 'You're late. Everything all right?'

He leaned over to give her a kiss.

She offered her cheek but said, 'Mind my hair, love.'

He kissed her then said, 'What's this? Are you going out?'

She was surprised. She looked at him and said, 'Haven't you asked anybody to come?'

He frowned, looked at her curiously and said, 'What do you mean?'

She straightened up, put her hands on her hips and said, 'Haven't you asked anybody to come and open the safe?'

With furrowed brow, Angel finished removing his coat and went into the hall to the boxed-in space under the stairs to hang it up. That's where he kept his top coat, umbrella, gardening shoes and other miscellaneous bits. As soon as he opened the door, he understood better what Mary was talking about. Inside the little cubby hole, much to his surprise, stood the safe. It looked even bigger than it did at Uncle Willy's. His jaw dropped. He turned back to her.

'Just after you left this morning,' she said, 'I had a phone call from Mr Smith himself. He said that they suddenly found that they had a time slot this morning in which they could move the safe, so I said if it was convenient to Mrs Goodman then it would be all right by us. Smith's men actually delivered it at twelve o'clock. I knew you'd be pleased.'

Angel wasn't pleased. He threw his coat on the chair in the hall and ran his hand through his hair. That's why she was dressed up. She had been expecting him to have found someone to come that evening to open the safe. She always liked to look her best to strangers, particularly on first acquaintance. He sighed.

She produced a crumpled piece of paper, which she passed to him. 'Oh yes, Michael, and here's the bill.'

The corners of his mouth turned down. He slowly unfolded it, saw that the bottom figure was as quoted, then stuffed it into his back pocket.

He crossed in front of her and went into the kitchen. 'What's for tea?'

Mary followed him in. 'Aren't you pleased?' she said.

'What's all the rush about? Why didn't you ring me?'

'Well, we agreed that we were going to get Smiths to move it, didn't we?'

'Yes, but not necessarily *today*.'

'Well, what's wrong with today?'

'Nothing, I suppose. I just wonder what all the rush is about?'

'I thought you'd be pleased. I haven't bothered you with it. It's out of Doreen's hair. It's ours — well, *yours*. You wanted it here. You agreed that Smiths should move it. I don't know why you are so — so difficult?'

'I didn't want it under the stairs, for one thing.'

'Where else was I supposed to put it?'

Angel knew that his only legitimate gripe was that he hadn't been consulted. He also knew he wouldn't have been pleased to have had a phone call from Mary about the safe in addition to everything else that happened at the station that day.

'I don't know,' he said quietly. 'But it can't stay there. If it leaks out that we have a safe like that in the house, we'll be burgled. Now what's for tea?'

'What about getting a key for it?'

'Can't. It's a Phillip's and they were bombed out of business in 1942.'

'Well how *are* we going to get it open then?'

'We'll have to get an expert. There will be somebody at Wakefield who will know what to do about it.'

'You mean one of your police contacts? They'll take for ages. Isn't there anybody nearer who will do it *now*?'

Angel shook his head.

Mary's eyes flashed excitedly. 'There's bound to be one of your old customers who could open it,' she said. 'They'd do it for *you*.'

Angel frowned. He pursed his lips. Since safes, alarm systems and CCTV had become more sophisticated, there were fewer top-class safe breakers around. Many were serving time in prison. It was a highly specialist art often passed down from father to son. 'There's old Geoffrey Rollings, known as 'Gelly Roll Rollings',' he said. 'Lives on Barber Street. One of the best. But I can't approach *him*.'

Mary glared at him and flashed her big eyes. 'Why not?' she said.

His jaw tightened. He ran his hand through his hair, looked at the pan boiling on the oven top, and said, 'Because it's tea time, and I want my tea. We can deal with all that tomorrow, or Friday, or over the weekend. Right now, I want something to eat, *please*! I'm starving.'

* * *

When Angel arrived the following morning, Ahmed, who had been on the lookout for him, followed him through the door into his office.

'What is it, lad?' Angel said as he took off his coat.

'There's an urgent message for you from Sergeant Clifton, sir. He's the duty sergeant on the desk. Will you phone him as soon as possible? He's off in half an hour.'

Angel reached out to his phone, tapped in a number and put it to his ear.

Ahmed turned to go.

'Hang on. There might be something I want you to do.'

Angel heard a voice in the earpiece: 'Night desk, Sergeant Clifton.'

'DI Angel here. You have something for me?'

'Ah yes, sir. It might be of interest. A man came into the station at four twenty-two this morning. He had obviously been drinking. He said his name was Maxwell Green. He was inquiring about his son, Jamie, and his ex-wife, Wendy Green who, he said, were not at home, and he was anxious to know where they were. I said that it was not a police matter and that he should make inquiries elsewhere. But he wouldn't leave it at that. He said that he had been in his car outside the house waiting for them from four o'clock yesterday afternoon until four o'clock this morning. He said the house was obviously deserted but that his ex-wife was unlikely to be far away because her car was still in the garage, the upstairs bathroom window was slightly open and the sink was full of pots. Also he said that his son, Jamie, who is eleven years of age, wasn't there. Now, because the lad is a minor, I thought you might want to get involved, sir.'

Angel's face creased. He already had two mysterious deaths to deal with. He had to make up his mind whether in addition he wanted to be involved in that inquiry or leave it to the uniformed branch. There were several questions needed answers before he could make that decision.

'Yes, Sergeant,' Angel said. 'Did he say why he wanted to get in touch with his ex-wife at that ridiculous time?'

'No, sir. Didn't ask him directly. Didn't want to encourage him. I thought it was a simple domestic'

Angel nodded. 'Did *he* have any thoughts about where his son might be?'

'Not specifically. He *did* say that he spent a lot of time with her parents.'

'What's their address?'

'He didn't say.'

'Didn't you ask?'

'Never thought it was going to lead into an inquiry *we'd* be concerned with, sir. We had a very busy night and were shorthanded. I have three men off with 'flu. I was greatly occupied in processing the work and moving him on.'

Angel knew the feeling. It was honest of Sergeant Clifton to admit it.

'How can I get in touch with this Maxwell Green?' Angel said.

'Well, sir, I know he's staying at The Feathers, but actually he's back . . . been here half an hour. He's in the reception area.'

* * *

Ahmed showed Maxwell Green into Angel's office and then went out and closed the door.

'You must be Inspector Angel?' Green said.

'Come in,' Angel said. 'Please sit down.'

Green was wearing a smart, expensive suit, but no tie and he needed a shave and his hair brushing down. Angel was quick to smell whisky on him, and he saw a gold and red coloured screw-cap bottle top sticking out of his jacket pocket. He recognized it as a half-bottle of MacFarlane's Scotch Whisky. He wrinkled his nose. Whisky. The smell of second-hand whisky was not pleasant.

'The duty sergeant tells me that you are worried about your son, Jamie, Mr Green,' Angel said. 'Also that you cannot find out where your ex-wife, Wendy Green has disappeared to.'

'That's right. Have *you* any news?'

'No, sir,' Angel said. 'I have sent an officer to the address you gave us. He should be reporting to me by phone soon.'

The man made a grunting noise indicating his disappointment.

'You understand, Mr Green,' Angel said, 'that more than five thousand people a year in this country are reported missing. The police service does not, indeed cannot, commit time to trying to find out where these people have gone to, nor investigate the reasons why they have disappeared.'

Green glared across the desk at him. 'All right, all right,' he said. 'I don't need a lecture.'

Angel's jaw muscles tightened. 'It's not a lecture. I am just familiarizing you with the facts, and I haven't finished.'

'Well, hurry up then. I am concerned for my son. I don't need a lecture and excuses why you haven't yet made any efforts to find him.'

'I don't deal in excuses, Mr Green. If there are any shortcomings at this station, I assure you they are dealt with severely. I was going on to say that two-thirds of the people who go missing are people who, for reasons of their own, want to disappear to avoid something or somebody, and they reappear months, or sometimes years, later. We are, however, greatly concerned in cases where a minor goes missing or where it is thought a crime has been committed.'

'Well my son, Jamie, is a minor, isn't he? He's only eleven.'

'Yes. I know. So let's start with trying to find out where he is. All right?'

Green's eyes brightened and he leaned eagerly forward in the chair. 'Yes,' he said.

Angel noticed that the man's eyes were pink round the rims, possibly indicating that the man had been crying. Angel was beginning to develop an uneasy feeling about him.

'Is there anywhere your son might be where you have not already looked?'

'I haven't looked anywhere. I didn't know where to start. I waited outside Wendy's house in my car hoping to see him as he came home from school yesterday afternoon, but he didn't arrive. Wendy sometimes asked her mum and dad to take care of him if she was going to be late or away or whatever. He could be there.'

'What's their name and address?'

'Woods is their name. They live at 120 Hoyland Road.'

'What's their phone number?'

'Don't know. They changed it and went ex-directory to stop me ringing them up.'

'Why did you ring them up?' Angel said, as he tapped in a number on his mobile.

'I *had* to ring them up. They were often the only people who knew where Jamie was . . . he was often with them. Of course, they were on her side. But I had to know he was all right. I had to know whether she was looking after him or not. And, in the early days, to find out *where* she was. You have to understand they were difficult days.'

Angel heard a voice from his mobile. It was Ahmed.

'Excuse me,' Angel said to Green, then into the phone he said, 'Ahmed, find out quickly who lives at 120 Hoyland Road and get me their phone number.'

He closed the phone and turned back to Green, who was holding his head in his hands.

‘That shouldn’t take long,’ Angel said. ‘You were telling me about when you were phoning Mr and Mrs Woods, and that they were difficult days.’

‘It doesn’t matter now,’ he said through his hands, ‘finding Jamie is what matters now.’

Angel nodded then ran the tip of his tongue along his lower lip as he thought how he might progress the questioning.

‘How long had you been married?’

‘Nine years. We divorced two years ago. What’s that got to do with it?’

‘You told the sergeant that Mrs Green’s car was in the garage, there were some pots in the sink and that there was a window open. You must have been up to the house and had a good look round?’

He suddenly looked up. ‘Yes. No harm in that, is there?’

‘Not at all.’

‘I didn’t go into the house, if that’s what you were thinking. I stood like a good boy on the front door mat — the mat I bought, incidentally — and rang the bell, which I also paid for. There was no reply. I rang it three times and then walked round the house and peered through the windows and the garage window. I thought she couldn’t be far away, and that Jamie would be back from school in ten or fifteen minutes.’

‘When he didn’t arrive, you knew the address of your wife’s parents, why didn’t you go there and ask *them*?’

‘You make it sound so simple and so easy. I was expecting Wendy, also Jamie, any second, wasn’t I? *Any second.* If I had pushed off to 120 Hoyland Road, I might have missed him. I didn’t want to risk that.’

Angel rubbed his chin.

‘Besides,’ Green added. ‘I didn’t expect to get a good reception there. They don’t like me. I wasn’t in any hurry to ask them whether my son was with them or not. It might have led — almost certainly would have led — to more argument.’

'Had your relationship with them always been difficult?'

'What has it to do with the case?'

Angel's mobile rang. He fished it out of his pocket, glanced at the LED. 'It's my sergeant,' he said. 'Excuse me.'

'Yes, lad?' he said into the phone. 'What have you got?'

'I'm inside the house now, sir,' Crisp said. 'There's nobody here and it looks like there's been nobody here all night. The central heating is switched on. There's plenty of food in the fridge. Beds made. It seems to be clean and orderly apart from a few dirty pots in the sink. Even the garden is in good order.'

'Do you think it has recently been occupied?'

'Oh yes, sir. Fancy underwear on the bed. Very sexy.'

Angel blinked. 'How did you gain access?'

'The front door was unlocked, sir.'

Angel's eyebrows shot up. His heart began to thump. 'Say that again.'

'I said, the front door was unlocked. I knocked a couple of times and waited, then tried it and walked in.'

Angel pursed his lips. Everybody locks the house door when they are going out, particularly if they expect to be away overnight. The situation was beginning to look strange. He needed to speak to the boy's maternal grandparents, and he needed to speak to them very soon.

'Right, lad,' he said. 'I hope you haven't put your dabs everywhere. I may have to have SOCO to go over it. Anyway, get out of there and wait in your car. I'll send somebody to relieve you. Obviously if anybody turns up, detain them and let me know.'

Green jumped up and said, 'What's happening? Has your man found anything?'

Angel closed the phone and turned back to the man. 'My sergeant's in the house now,' he said. 'And there's nobody there. He found the front door unlocked. Was it unlocked when you were there?'

'I don't know. I did not try it. Never thought of it. It may have been. I am an ex-husband, Inspector Angel. It is no longer *my* house. I have no legal rights there. I *bought* it and I *pay* to maintain it, but I am not even allowed in the bloody place.'

'Did your wife usually lock the door when she left the house?'

'Always. She wouldn't dream of leaving it unlocked.'

The phone rang again. It was Ahmed. 'Yes?'

'The name of the people who live at that address, sir, are Mr and Mrs Ian Woods and their phone number is Bromersley 221337.'

'Thank you, lad,' Angel said. Then he cancelled the call from Ahmed and tapped in the Woods' number.

Green said, 'What's happening? What have you found out? Who are you phoning now?'

Angel said, 'Your ex-in-laws, the Woods.'

'Oh my God!' he said.

It rang out for about a minute but it wasn't answered.

Angel rubbed his chin. He really needed to speak to them.

He cancelled the call and re-entered the number. It rang out a good while and then it was answered by a man with a little voice. 'Hello,' he said. 'Who is that?'

'Is that Mr Ian Woods?'

'Yes. Who is speaking?'

'Detective Inspector Angel of Bromersley Police. I am urgently seeking the whereabouts of your grandson, Jamie Green. Is he with you?'

'No. He left here for school at half past eight. That would be in plenty of time for assembly at nine o'clock. He should be there. Why? He's all right, isn't he? He's not been in an accident?'

'He's fine, as far as we know, Mr Woods,' Angel said, 'just checking. What's the name of the school and what form is he in?'

'St John's on York Street. He's in 2B.'

'Thank you. Did he stay with you last night then?'

'Yes, he did. He does frequently . . . when our daughter goes out for the evening, or whatever. He stayed Wednesday night, as well. What is this all about?'

'Did your daughter go out last night?'

'Well, now . . . there's a funny thing . . . I don't rightly know. What's this all about, Inspector?'

'Have you any idea where your daughter is now?'

'No. I don't. To tell the truth we are a bit worried . . . we haven't been able to reach her on the phone since Tuesday morning.'

That was it, the confirmation Angel had needed. His heart began to pound. In his chest, an angry volcano spewed out white hot lava. It was a reliable indicator. It augured that something dreadful had happened to Wendy Green.

'I'll be with you in fifteen minutes or sooner. Please don't go out.'

'We are not going anywhere, Inspector, but —'

Angel closed the phone and turned to Green. 'Jamie spent the night with Mr and Mrs Woods. He's OK and appears at this moment to be at school. I'll get my officers to see him and check that he is all right in every particular and then call you within the hour to report on what they find. In the meantime, I suggest that you go back to The Feathers, have some breakfast, a shower and get some sleep.'

9

Angel ran down the corridor followed by Flora Carter. They went out of the station by the rear door and got into the BMW. He started up the car and drove it out of the car park.

'There's a lot I want you to do, Flora,' Angel said, as he took the corner towards town, 'and there isn't much time to tell you, so get your notebook out and listen up.'

'Right, sir.'

'We are going to the Woods' house; I am going to interview them. While I'm there, I want you to take my car, go to St John's school and find young Jamie Green in Form 2B. Have a word with him and see if he's OK. Gently ask him if he knows where his mother is. Then take a photograph of him, print it and take it to his father, Maxwell Green. He's staying at The Feathers. Room 22. Make sure you get there by nine fifty-five. I promised him that. Tell him how his son is and check that the pic is that of his son. All right?'

'Yes, sir.'

'Then phone Don Taylor at SOCO and ask him to fingerprint Wendy Green's house at 16 Creesforth Road, ASAP. I want him to take prints from all the vital places, door handles, telephones, taps, ledges, rims and so on. He'll know where. It's a precaution, really, just in case there has been any foul play. I want to look over the house myself sometime today. Also ask Inspector Asquith to have the property guarded twenty-four seven until further notice, also ASAP. And I need an officer immediately to relieve Trevor Crisp who is there outside in his car waiting. See that they understand that I want anybody approaching the house stopped, identified and detained. Then come back here and collect me. Have you got all that?'

'Yes, sir.'

Angel was near his destination. He slowed down the BMW and lowered the window. 'Right. This is Hoyland Road,' he said. 'I want number 120.'

'There's a 111 on your right, sir,' Flora said. 'So the Woods will be on your left.'

'This is it,' he said, and he stopped the car in front of a small terrace house, amid a long row of similar houses.

He jumped out quickly, crossed the pavement, opened the little gate up to the front door as Flora Carter took hold of the steering wheel and drove the BMW away.

The front door was opened before he could ring the bell. A small man in his sixties said, 'Are you from the police?'

'Yes,' he replied. 'Detective Inspector Angel, Bromersley Police.'

'I am Ian Woods. Come in. Come in, Inspector,' he said. 'I'll close the door. Please go through to the back. My wife is in there.'

Angel made his way through a small room with a three-piece suite squeezed around a coffee table, passed the bottom of a stairway that was pitch-black at the top, through another half-open door into the kitchen. A small, neat lady was sitting in a rocking chair at one side of a range. Angel nodded and smiled, but the woman responded with a look as hard as Bromersley water.

'It's the Inspector, Isabel,' Woods said dashing in behind Angel and closing the kitchen door. He glanced at Angel and said, 'Sit down, Inspector. Is our daughter Wendy all right? Where is she exactly?'

'I am still seeking information about her, I'm afraid, Mr Woods. When was the last time you made contact with her?'

Mr and Mrs Woods looked at each other with drawn, pained faces.

Angel experienced some of the concern and fear they were going through.

Woods took a deep breath and said, 'It would have been Tuesday lunchtime. She phoned at about one o'clock to ask us if we would have Jamie to sleep over that night, to give him his tea, see that he did his homework, give him breakfast and send him off to school yesterday morning.'

'And there was nothing at all unusual about that?'

'In itself, no. Not at all. Since her divorce, we have had Jamie for sleepovers many, many times. We like having him. He's got some clothes and pyjamas here. He's a grand lad and we love him to bits. But she *didn't* phone us yesterday at all to see how he was or anything, or arrange to collect him. And I phoned her several times but didn't get a reply, so we told Jamie to come back here yesterday. After school as well. We've still not been able to reach her, and she hasn't contacted us.'

'Why did she ask you to look after him? Was there any particular reason?'

Woods looked at his wife again. The corners of her mouth turned downwards. She lowered her eyes and shrugged. Woods looked down, sighed and then said, 'Well, Inspector, to tell the truth she was going out with other men.'

Angel pursed his lips. 'Well, she is a free woman, isn't she? She is divorced.'

Woods' eyes flashed. 'The wrong sort, Inspector. That has been her trouble all her life. She doesn't want a proper, decent, upright citizen. She always chooses flashy chaps in smart suits, filled to their gills with drugs and booze . . . who have never done an honest day's work in their lives. We thought that when Maxwell Green and she split up and finally got a divorce that she'd learned her lesson and would look for someone decent.'

'What caused the split between them?'

'It was his drinking. He's an alcoholic. He can't leave it alone. He's always half cut.'

Isabel Woods suddenly came to life. She shook her head and said, 'It was *her* fault. My own daughter. She had an affair with that hairdresser with the bleached hair and the ear-ring. *I* thought he was a poof. *Everybody* thought he was a poof, but he wasn't. Maxwell Green found out and they had a flaming row.'

Woods' eyes flashed. His face went scarlet. 'You don't *know* that, Isabel,' he said. 'It's only what we *thought*.'

Her eyes grew big. 'She told me,' she said. 'She admitted it. I shamed her into telling me. I wasn't going to tell *you*. I was too ashamed, but things have gone *too* far.'

'But now Maxwell Green wants her back,' Woods said. 'He's hardly ever away from the place.'

'She's a beautiful girl, with a heart of gold,' she said. 'Of course he wants her back, but in his drunken state, who would want *him*?'

'He's worth hundreds. *Thousands* even!' Woods said, waving his hands in the air.

'Money isn't everything,' she said.

Angel said, 'What does Maxwell Green do?'

'He manages pop stars,' Woods said. 'You'll have heard of Purple Sandwich?'

Angel looked as blank as a stolen prescription pad. 'No.'

'They're all over the pop charts,' Woods said. 'He manages *them*. And lots more.'

'They're disgraceful rubbish,' Mrs Woods said.

Woods turned to Angel, put his hands out in front of him, palms upwards and said, 'She doesn't understand, Inspector. I keep telling her, it isn't important what *we* think. Purple Sandwich *are* rubbish, I agree, but whatever we say won't change things. In young people's eyes they are wonderful, and for a month, a year, or five years they'll continue to be wonderful, until somebody, or something else comes along. And it will. Then it'll be all change. Purple Sandwich will be history. It will be goodbye. No more. Dead as a dodo. And the new thing — whatever it is — will be all the rage. And so it goes on. Every so often, the young have to have change. They make change into a virtue. Now our daughter is like that. She's all over the present for a while and then has to have something different. She has got sucked into that way of living. She has absolutely no common sense. She wants to be in a world of loud drums and guitars, flashing coloured lights, short skirts, low necklines, and a man with a tan, a six pack, a guitar, a white Mercedes, a walletful of money, who is able to bawl to tuneless music. She won't take any notice of us. That's why she behaves as she does.'

Angel's mind had now one thought only and it wasn't pleasant. He wanted to say something cheerful and optimistic to sustain the Woods and keep hope alive, but it didn't come easily.

'Wendy has only been missing about forty-four hours,' he said, 'she might have met someone she likes and is with him. She could be back anytime.'

Mrs Woods pulled a face as long as a stick of rhubarb.

Woods shook his head. 'No. There's something wrong. She wouldn't have left Jamie like that, not without making arrangements.'

Angel thought that he was probably correct, but he kept up the pretence and said, 'When we do find Wendy, she'll have to answer a lot of questions and may be at the station for some time. Would you arrange to look after Jamie until she can return home and assume her responsibilities?'

* * *

DS Carter duly returned the BMW to the front of the Woods' house and changed over from the driver's seat to the front nearside seat.

Angel was expecting her and was waiting on the kerbside. 'Everything all right, Flora?' he said, as he got into the driver's seat.

'Yes, sir,' DS Carter said.

He engaged gear, let in the clutch and pulled away.

'I caught up with Jamie Green,' Carter said, 'who is a delightful boy. Of course, he didn't understand why I wanted to talk to him. I had to explain who I was and why I was there. He had no idea where his mother was and knew nothing at all about the company she might be keeping. He didn't show any signs that he was worried, but he was pleased when I told him the photograph I was taking of him was to show to his dad.'

Angel wrinkled his nose. 'So he knew nothing about where she was going on Tuesday evening?'

'No, sir. She must be making a very good job of keeping all that sort of information away from the boy.'

Angel had to stop at the traffic lights on Park Road.

'You showed the picture of Jamie to Maxwell Green?'

'Yes, sir. His father was delighted with it, and he confirmed that it *was* Jamie all right.'

'Good. And has Don Taylor sent a fingerprint man to Wendy Green's house?'

'He went himself, sir. He will have been there about half an hour.'

'Good.'

The traffic lights changed to green.

Angel turned left onto Creesforth Road which comprised mostly architect-designed houses.

'We'll soon know,' he said. 'That lass lives at number 16. I think that's at the far end.'

As Angel drove along the road, he saw a police car on the drive of one of the houses and a uniformed officer in a bright orange high-profile coat standing by the front door which was wide open. The figure 16 was neatly painted in white on a black stone pillar.

Angel turned right up the drive, pulled up behind the police car and stopped.

Angel and Flora got out of the car and made for the house.

The uniformed officer at the door recognized him and threw up a salute. 'Good morning, sir,' the young man said.

'Good morning,' Angel said and acknowledged the salute. 'How long have you been here?'

'About ten minutes, sir.'

'Who is here beside yourself?'

'DS Taylor, sir. DS Crisp left when I arrived.'

At that moment, Don Taylor came to the doorway of the house holding a canister containing aluminium powder in one hand and a fingerprint brush in the other. 'Oh, it's you, sir. I thought I had heard a car.'

Angel said, 'What you got, Don?'

'Up to now, only two persons' prints, sir. A woman's, I think, or a small man or a youth's, and a child's.'

Angel sniffed. He wasn't pleased. 'Just the two people who live here, probably?'

Taylor realized that he was disappointed. 'If there's a 'warm' print of a third person, sir, I'll find it,' he said.

'I hope so, Don. Have you finished downstairs?'

'Yes, sir,' Taylor said.

'We'll come in then,' Angel said, 'you carry on.'

'If you want me, I'll be upstairs,' Taylor said.

Angel licked his lower lip thoughtfully, then looked at Flora Carter and put out a hand, inviting her to lead the way.

She smiled acknowledging the courtesy and made her way up the step into the house.

The entrance hall had wood-panelled walls, a cantilever staircase and a dazzling white, cut glass chandelier hanging from the ceiling.

Carter took that in then disappeared down the hall to a door at the end.

Angel had not taken a step inside when he suddenly noticed a familiar smell. It was the distinctive smell of the cheap scent he had first experienced briefly by the BMW when it was parked on St Magdalene's Hospital car park. He stood motionless in the doorway. He did not move. His pulse raced. His muscles tightened. He suddenly shivered. It was as if a frozen rat had run down his spine. The cold spread along his arms and legs. The skin on the back of his arms and hands turned to goose flesh. After a few moments, he shook his head in defiance, and began to sniff around the door way.

'Flora,' he called. '*Flora*!'

She appeared through a door, with eyebrows raised. 'What is it, sir?' she said.

'There is an unusual smell here. Can you trace where it is coming from?'

'What sort of a smell, sir?'

'It's sweet, strong and . . . my wife would describe it as cheap and common scent.'

'Where exactly?' she said.

'Here. Where I'm standing,' he said.

Flora sniffed round the doorway, and the hall, twitching her nose like a rabbit.

'Yes, sir. I can smell it, sickly sweet.'

'That's it!' Angel said. 'Can you smell where it is coming from?'

'It seems to be coming from you, sir.'

The muscles of his face tightened. 'No, lass. It *can't* be.'

'It must be round the doorway then. It's outside, I think.'

They both spent some time searching around.

He came into the entrance hall, opened the doors into the three main rooms of the house, looked round and closed them. He went three steps up the stairs and then down again. He even went back outside.

The officer on sentry duty saw him, came up to him, looked at him strangely and said, 'Are you all right, sir? Can I do anything for you?'

'Have you noticed a peculiar smell? A sickly sweet pong, especially round this doorway?'

The PC gave Angel a strange look. 'I had a shower this morning, sir, and clean underwear, I don't think it could be me.'

Angel clenched his fists. His face muscles tightened. 'I'm not suggesting it *is* you, lad. If I had thought *that*, I would have torn a strip off you and sent you home. No. There's a smell, a sickly sweet, tarty perfume. Two minutes ago I noticed it, now I can't place it. I need to know what it is and what it's about. I noticed it in this doorway. Now, you have been here a quarter of an hour or so. Have you noticed it or anything like it?'

The officer looked at him with a blank expression. 'No, sir,' he said, 'I haven't.'

Angel nodded in acknowledgement. 'Right, lad,' he said. 'Carry on.'

Then he stepped back into the house, gave a last sniff round the doorway and then closed the door.

He hoped that Flora Carter might have found the source of the smell, and he looked across at her.

She shook her head.

His lips tightened back against his teeth. 'It's gone,' he said, holding his arms out shoulder-high, hands facing upwards, fingers stretched open and tense. 'It's ridiculous, but it's gone!'

She saw how important he seemed to think the smell was. 'Sorry, sir,' she said. 'Smells do that sort of thing. They're here and then they're gone.'

'True,' he said. Then he shrugged. It was very annoying. He would have to find out where it was coming from or he would go mad. It was the sort of thing that would keep him awake at nights. But he must move on.

'Did you find the kitchen?' he said.

She smiled. 'It's this way, sir,' she said.

Flora Carter went down the hall to the door at the end which led to the back of the house.

Angel followed quickly.

She led him into a big kitchen with all the domestic machinery and utensils you might expect in such a large house. It was tidy and clean except for silver-coloured aluminium powder on door and cupboard handles, door edges, taps and on the controls around all the appliances, which confirmed that Don Taylor had recently been there.

Angel made straight for the sink and peered into the water at the dirty pots and cutlery visible under areas of a soapy scum on the surface.

Flora Carter watched him.

Without disturbing them, he deduced that they represented a small meal for two people only. He then looked around for the waste bin and found it under the worktop. He opened the lid with his pen and inside, on top of other refuse, he saw an empty Coco Pops box with a used teabag lying on top of it. He closed the lid but left the bin out.

He turned to Flora Carter and said, 'Looks like the last meal served here was breakfast, and it was probably eaten by Wendy Green and her son Jamie, but I want Don to check on any prints on that Coco Pops box before he leaves . . . just to be sure.'

'Do you want me to tell him, sir,' she said.

He nodded and Flora Carter went out.

Angel had a quick look round the rest of the downstairs rooms, the summerhouse, the garage and the well-kept garden but could see nothing helpful to his investigation. As he returned to the house, he met Don Taylor in the hall. He had just come down the stairs.

'I've finished up there, sir.'

'Any new prints,' Angel said.

'Don't think so, but I need Mrs Green and her son's prints for elimination.'

'Yes. Yes,' Angel said rubbing his chin. 'Of course you do. I'll get Flora to organize it.'

'I've just to do that breakfast cereal box and then I've finished here.'

'Right, Don. You push off when you've done. I won't be far behind you. You didn't come across a woman's hairbrush or comb upstairs, did you?'

'Yes. I tested for a print on the handle of a long comb, but it was smudged. It was on the dressing-table in the big bedroom at the front.'

'Good. Have you got a small evidence bag?'

Taylor rummaged in a pocket, produced one and handed it to him.

'Ta,' Angel said, and he dashed up the stairs.

Flora Carter was at the top waiting for him. She had overheard the conversation. 'I'll see that Don gets Wendy Green and her son's prints for elimination, sir. And I've seen that comb. There's quite a lot of hair round it. Is it for a DNA test?'

'Yes,' he said and he handed her the little bag. 'Hurry up. I'll just have a quick scout round the rooms. I have another urgent call I must make today.'

'Why do you want her DNA, sir?'

He looked at her closely, took a deep breath and said, 'Because Flora, I regret to say that it is becoming abundantly clear that Wendy Green is the second victim of the wild cat or cougar or whatever it is!'

10

Angel urgently wanted the specimen from the comb and hair taken from the victim's body to be despatched to the police laboratory at Wetherby by special post that day for comparison to confirm (or otherwise) that the deceased was indeed the woman, Wendy Green. So, as soon as he had finished at the house, he drove the BMW back to the police station with Flora Carter and dropped her off so that she could attend to it. He urgently needed to see Ephemore Sharpe. He had wanted to interview her himself and had postponed the meeting several times because other important matters had cropped up. If she was in any way responsible for the deaths of Julius Hobbs and Wendy Green, he didn't want to give her any more time to prepare an alibi or cover up evidence.

He drove the BMW purposefully through the town to Wakefield Road, turned right up Ashfield Road and up to the end to Ashfield Lodge Farm, where he parked the car by the side of the road, behind a pickup truck with a commercial lawn mower, a wheelbarrow and long-handled hoes and rakes loaded on it.

He crossed the pavement and reached out to open the farm gate. Then he heard someone speaking loudly. It came from a man standing facing the front door of the farmhouse.

Angel assumed he was addressing Ephemore Sharpe, so he dodged back behind the wall.

'It's only sixty pounds, Miss Sharpe,' he heard the man say. 'This is the third time I've been back.'

Angel recognized him. It was Philip Pryce, the jobbing gardener he had met cutting the lawn at the back of the St Magdalene's Hospital on Rustle Spring Lane.

'I said I'd take a cheque but you said you'd run out of cheques,' the man said.

Angel strained to hear her reply. She sounded huffy. 'I hope to get to the bank tomorrow, Pryce,' she said. 'I'll post it on to you then.'

'No, I prefer to call for it, Miss, if you don't mind.'

'Well, if you must. Make it tomorrow afternoon,' she said.

'I'm working tomorrow afternoon, Miss,' he said. 'I'll call for it on Saturday morning. Thank you very much.'

The door closed with a bang.

A solemn looking Pryce turned away from the door and made his way across the yard.

Angel opened the farmyard gate and stood back to allow Pryce through.

When Pryce saw him, his face brightened. 'Thank you,' he said.

Angel nodded.

Then Pryce looked back and said, 'It's Inspector Angel isn't it?'

'It is.'

'Thought any more about your garden, sir?' he said. 'I said I'd give you a special rate.'

Angel smiled. 'No thanks,' he said, as he closed the gate. 'I'm managing at the moment.' He nodded towards the house. 'Having difficulty getting paid? Couldn't help but overhear.'

He shrugged but didn't smile. 'I do her garden for her. Cut the lawn, do the weeding, keep it right, and I feed the cats for her when she's not well or goes into hospital. But it's always the same with her.'

'Sorry to hear it.'

Pryce smiled. 'She's loaded, you know. Just doesn't like parting. She'll pay me. I *know* she will, but I've got to keep chasing her for it.'

Angel nodded understandingly.

'Cheers,' Pryce said and he crossed the pavement to his pickup truck.

Angel frowned. He was wondering if Miss Sharpe really was as financially well favoured as everybody seemed to think. In his job, over the years, Angel had known many 'customers' who had put on a big front to give the impression they were wealthy, when all the time they owed the pawn shop for the shirt on their backs.

He made his way across the yard up to the farmhouse door and knocked on it. He waited a minute and there was no answer. He knocked again. On that occasion, the door was opened only four inches. Through the gap, Angel could see a crimson eye, purple coloured nostrils with zigzag shaped septum, and half of a pair of thin blue lips.

'Good afternoon, Miss Sharpe,' he said.

'Oh, it's you,' she said. 'Go away. I haven't time for you today.'

She then pushed the door to. But Angel already had his shoe in the gap. She trapped it in a vice-like grip.

'I am sorry, Miss Sharpe, to have to resort to this, but this is important and urgent,' he said.

She eased the pressure on the door and said, 'Remove your foot *at once*.'

He was totally unyielding. 'The alternative to you seeing me now is for me to get a warrant and have you brought down to the station, forcibly, if needs be,' he said.

'You *can't* do that,' she said, applying more pressure against the door. 'I've done nothing wrong. I am a highly respectable, retired, senior history teacher. I do not break the law. Why do you keep hounding me like this? This town is full of criminals, why aren't you out there arresting them? Have you nothing better to do?'

'I only want to ask you questions, Miss Sharpe, questions about two persons that perhaps only you can answer. Either open this door and let me in, or become the subject of a warrant for your arrest, and a possible charge of obstruction.'

'This is outrageous,' she said.

Angel felt the pressure ease off his foot again. He looked up. Ephemore Sharpe had gone.

'Come in then, if you must,' he heard her call.

He pushed at the door. It opened easily. He looked inside and saw the back of her waddling awkwardly away from him down the hall.

'You have no cause to harass an old woman like this,' she called without looking round. 'Close the door. I will see you in my study. This way.'

Angel closed the front door and made his way along the hall. Six or seven framed circus posters in wooden frames adorned the walls. They were clearly old, and all of them featured women.

One of them was of a big blonde woman wearing thigh boots and a basque decorated with ribbons and bows. She was smiling and holding a whip in front of a row of tigers who were baring their teeth. The poster read: 'Cirque Americanos, 1907. Madam Muriel and her six Bengal Tigers!'

Next to it was a poster in German for Circus Barum in Berlin in 1910. It featured a woman named Margarete Kleiser with a huge male lion called Pascha. Next to that was a poster for the Barnum and Bailey Circus, September 1915, which depicted Rose Flanders Bascom in the dress uniform of a US bandsman brandishing a whip, with a line-up of ten lions and tigers. Another poster showed a tiny woman in the middle of a whole cluster of wild cats. Her name was Mabel Stark. It read: 'Ringling Brothers Circus, Madison Square Gardens, New York', and was dated 1902. There were more posters, some repeats of the same characters illustrated differently and for different locations and dates. But they were all women with wild cats.

Angel rubbed his chin. Wild animal trainer. Very unusual work for a woman, he thought.

The last poster showed a woman with hair between three and four metres long. She was on exceedingly high stilts that put her level with the ceiling of the circus big top. Splashed across the poster were the words: 'Amelia Longlegs — 60 feet tall — head in the clouds. The tallest woman in the world.' Ringling Brothers. Madison Square Gardens. New York. August 17th thru 30th 1899.

Angel wondered if the posters might represent something of her secret ambitions. He was thinking along those lines when he heard her call out from the doorway at the other end of the hall.

'Come along, young man. I haven't got all day.'

Her voice was like a fork scraping on a dry plate.

'Admiring your posters, Miss Sharpe,' he said. 'That's all.'

He moved quickly up the hall to her study.

It was a small room. The central piece of furniture was an important looking antique desk with a leather chair, where she chose to sit. Facing her were two wooden upright chairs.

She pointed at them and said, 'Sit there. But don't get too comfortable, you're not staying long.'

The chair seat was hard and the back as straight as a cell door.

Angel thought he wouldn't be at ease in that house wherever he sat. He looked round the room. The walls were covered with scores of framed photographs. There was hardly a space where one could see any wallpaper. Miss E. Sharpe, MA (Cantab Hons) in mortar board and gown was the prominent subject in all of them. Others in the photographs with her were mostly groups of various numbers of school children.

'Well, what is it you want?' she said, glaring at him like a vulture about to dart forward and snatch out an eye.

Angel turned back to her and said, 'Yes. Well er . . . I am still making inquiries about the very serious matter of the remains of a body we found by the stream in the field behind this house on Monday morning.'

'I told you I didn't hear or see anything. What about it?'

'We didn't know the identity of the body at the time,' he said. Then watching her carefully he said, 'It has since been identified as that of a thirty-year-old property developer in the town, Julius Hobbs.'

She didn't flinch. Her face was as rigid as the menu at Strangeways.

'Does the name mean anything at all to you?' he added.

She lowered the left eyebrow, raised the right and said, 'I believe I taught a boy of that name.'

'Do you recall anything about him?'

'Not much. I seem to remember that he was pasty, skinny and his hair was plastered down with lard.'

Angel was angry. He ran his hand through his hair. 'Was he a good pupil, Miss Sharpe? Was he well behaved? Was he lazy, or was he industrious? Was he an academic genius or plain stupid? Did he make a contribution to the class, or was he a disruptive nuisance?'

'Oh I really don't remember after all these years. I think he must have been satisfactory among thousands of generally ignorant, ill-mannered, smelly and badly brought up children, or I would have remembered.'

'Anything else?'

'No.'

'You know how he died, Miss Sharpe,' he said rubbing his chin. 'Erm . . . have you any knowledge of such an animal in the wild or in captivity that might have killed the poor man?'

She raised her head, stretching the scraggy neck up four inches and said, 'No. But there does seem to be a presence of large, wild cats roaming around. Indeed there was an actual case recently in Cheshire where a wild cat killed a man while he was fishing from a stream.'

'I heard,' he said.

She pouted and gave a slight shrug.

He rubbed his chin. She seemed unmoved by the mention of Hobbs being killed by a cat and torn apart by it. He wondered if she would acknowledge that he had recently approached her to buy her farm, and the field behind. He was determined to flush out the truth. Selecting his words carefully, he said, 'Do you remember anything else about Julius Hobbs?'

'No,' she said quickly, then after a moment, she added, 'Should I?'

'I thought you might,' he said.

He pursed his lips and rubbed his chin. 'Didn't he recently approach you with a proposition?' he said.

She half closed her left eye and peeped at him briefly with her right again. 'I don't think so,' she said slowly, then suddenly she added, 'If he had, what has it to do with you?'

'Didn't he want to buy this farm and the land behind it to build houses?'

Her eyebrows shot up. 'How do you know that?'

'Well, did he? Did Julius Hobbs offer you a colossal sum of money for the farm and the field?'

'It *wasn't* a colossal sum, but all right, yes, he did,' she said. 'But that has nothing to do with you.'

'And didn't you turn the offer down flat?'

'I did.'

'So you *did* remember something else about Julius Hobbs. You knew full well who I was referring to from the beginning. Nobody would ever forget being offered a big sum of money. Why did you say you didn't?'

'It wasn't a big sum of money, and I insist that it is no business of yours.'

'If it has anything to do with a man's death, it *is* my business.'

'What do you mean?'

'Didn't Hobbs say that if he couldn't do a deal with you, he would approach the council, whom he knew were extremely short of housing and were also desperately short of funds? And didn't he say that he could offer to build an estate of council houses for the good citizens of Bromersley at very low cost, no doubt because of the current lowly state of the building industry, provided that the council contributed the land, *your* land?'

'He might have done.'

'But he *did*.'

'You couldn't *know* that.'

'But I do know that, because it is in the notes he left together with the draft of a letter to the council in his files. And you know how the council would get hold of your farm and the field, don't you?'

She didn't reply.

'By issuing a Compulsory Purchase Order,' he said, 'which means what it says. And they would pay you as little as they can get away with. Very much less than the sum offered by Julius Hobbs. But you like living here, Miss Sharpe, don't you?'

'You ask too many questions.'

'You like living here. A view of the field and trees beyond, a garden, privacy, not too far from the shops, and plenty of outbuildings to provide accommodation for your cats. I could understand that you would not be eager to move.'

She said nothing.

'You have a number of cats, don't you?' he said.

'Indeed I do.'

'Feral cats . . . as well as pet cats . . . and you feed them every day?'

'Of course,' she said. 'I also treat them for their illnesses, neuter them, sometimes administer drugs to cure them, and, when it becomes necessary, put them out of their misery. And I have never received so much as a scratch from any one of them.'

'So Julius Hobbs was a threat to your peaceful existence here?'

'You *could* see it like that, I suppose.'

'There's no suppose about it. Then, after living here all your life, Hobbs came along and gave you an ultimatum. Either sell to him or sell to the council.'

'What are you getting at, young man?'

He decided not to take that line any further at that time. If she was in any way responsible for the death of Julius Hobbs, she would now know that he was on her trail.

'I'll come back to that,' he said. 'There's something else, Miss Sharpe. Last Tuesday morning another body was found. It was that of a young woman. She had also been attacked, killed and partly devoured by a wild cat. It was discovered on the side of the footpath of Fish Lane, that's between this farm and Salmon Cottages.'

'I *know* where it is.'

'You should. It's not two hundred yards away. I imagine you could see *that* from an upstairs window.'

She blinked. Her mouth dropped open.

'It happened Tuesday evening, sometime in the night or in the early hours of Wednesday morning. Did you see or hear anything strange around that time?'

'Of course not,' she said. 'It's a coincidence.'

'It's not a coincidence,' he said. 'Two people killed by a big cat less than two hundred yards away from here in two days. It's not a coincidence, it's an obvious pattern. Almost on your doorstep. Your house is the nearest building to where both bodies were found. Can you explain it?'

She shook her head.

'The dead woman was so very badly mauled that we are having difficulty in positively identifying her,' he continued. 'However, we are pretty certain that it is a Mrs Wendy Green, a divorcee. You may know her as Wendy Woods.' He looked at her for some reaction. There was none.

'Does that ring any bells?' he said.

She turned up her nose. 'It does. Not a nice girl. Not a nice girl at all.'

He waited then said, 'What do you mean?'

'You do ask a lot of questions.'

He breathed in and out heavily, then said, 'It's my *job*.'

She simply stared at him.

'Well, did you teach her?' he said. 'Was she in one of your classes?'

'Yes, she was, and quite unmemorable.'

'Is that all you have to say about her?'

'There is nothing else to say.'

The muscles in Angel's jaw tightened. He ran his hand through his hair. 'Please tell me anything and everything you can about her.'

She thought a moment, then said, 'I cannot remember anything at all about her school days. They were quite undistinguished. She must have been a satisfactory pupil or I would have remembered. However, a few years after she left school, indeed I had retired — it was in 1999, I recall — I needed some domestic help on a temporary basis. In a weak moment, I engaged her. Four mornings a week, I believe. I knew the job was beneath her. She was going to Cambridge University. The money I paid her was supposed to be going towards paying off her student grant. But she was useless. I should have dismissed her on the first day, but I knew she needed the money.'

'How long was she in your employ then?'

'Two weeks, I think, or something like that. She *had* to go.'

'You gave her the sack?'

'Domestically, she was useless. Also, she was a thief. She stole things.'

'Such as?'

'She stole a pot cat that I had had for years. A figure of a rather special lion, Pascha. I liked it quite a lot. It was something my father gave me as a girl. Don't know what else she might have taken. If she would take one thing, she might have taken a dozen other things.'

'What did she say when you faced her with it?'

'She denied it, of course.'

'It might not have been her, then?'

Ephemore Sharpe's grey face went scarlet. Her eyes shone like headlights on the chief constable's Mercedes. 'It certainly *was* her, young man. Who else could it have been? No one else came into the house. She was the only person it could have been. It was in the bottom drawer of the sideboard.'

She illustrated her indignation further by puffing and sniffing for a few seconds more then added, 'You need to be very careful what you say, young man. Very careful indeed.'

Angel remained resolutely deadpan. He had been threatened by suspects before. No bad-tempered harridan would disturb his equilibrium.

'Did you report it to the police?' he said.

She glared at him then said, 'Of *course* I didn't. What use would that have been?'

'Well, on the one hand you might have got it back and on the other, there would have been a record of the crime.'

Ephemore Sharpe suddenly stood up, her face as black as fingerprint ink. 'I've had enough of this,' she said. 'It's time for you to go.'

He shook his head, pursed his lips and said, 'Settle yourself down, Miss Sharpe. I'm not leaving here until I have finished my questions. And I must warn you, if I do not get answers, you could very well find yourself drinking your goodnight cocoa down at the station.'

She stood a few moments unsure what to do. After a moment, she slumped down into the leather chair.

'This is intolerable,' she said. 'How much longer do I have to put up with this?'

He ignored the question. His lips tightened again. He wanted to get back on track. 'What else did she steal?' he said.

Ephemore Sharpe swallowed once or twice then said, 'I don't know of anything else for certain, I just thought that if she would take one thing, she would probably take other things, that's all. She had the morals of an alley cat.'

'What do you mean by that?'

'She had a following of at least three young men at the same time. They used to call for her here. It was disgusting. I had to stop it.'

'Do you have their names?'

'Oh no. I had no interest in them.'

'Do you remember anything at all about any of them?'

'I think her favourite beau was a boy called Kevin. He had the noisiest motor bike I ever heard.'

'Did you and Wendy Woods, as she was known then, part company as friends?'

'Certainly not. I was the employer and she was the employee, and a pretty useless employee at that. I paid her the sum we agreed, and that was that. I was not kindly disposed to her, considering that I had chosen her for the job out of six others because I knew she needed the money. And I received no thanks for it at all.'

Angel nodded in acknowledgement of the answer, then rubbed his chin. In an inexplicable way, he felt cheated because he didn't feel that he was much further forward with his inquiries. He was pretty certain that he would not be able to extract any more information from Sharpe without more data, therefore the interview seemed to have arrived at a natural conclusion. Exactly how and why the two people were killed still remained a mystery, although he had opened at least one new thought about it.

'Perhaps you would be kind enough to show me round this house and your barns, Miss Sharpe.'

She glared at him. 'Certainly not. This isn't Chatsworth.'

Angel pursed his lips. He should have expected that. Anyway, he resolved to get a search warrant as soon as possible and have the house, the outbuildings and the barns searched. It was not beyond her to have a pet cougar hidden away in the back of one of the barns.

He stood up. 'Very well, Miss Sharpe,' he said. 'That's all for now.'

She was soon following him down the hall to the front door. There was no chit chat. She wanted him to leave and he couldn't get away fast enough. He opened the front door, then it happened. Right in the nose again. Pungent and sickly sweet. The smell of cheap scent.

His eyes flashed around feverishly seeking the source. If wickedness had a smell, that was it. He stepped outside and quickly turned back to face her.

'What is that sweet smell, Miss Sharpe?' he said. 'Are you wearing perfume?'

She held up her hands in horror. 'Certainly not, Inspector,' she said.

'What is the smell then?'

She leaned out through the door and inhaled through her gigantic nostrils. 'I can smell nothing but good, healthy Yorkshire air, straight from the moors,' she said then closed the door with a loud bang.

But that wasn't what Angel could smell. He stood on the step and looked down the yard at the three barns for a few moments. He turned, gave a last sniff round the area, but the saccharine aroma had disappeared into who-knows-where.

11

'You're late,' Mary said. 'Tea's ruined.'

'It's only six o'clock,' Angel said as he removed his coat. He took it through to the hall, returned, crossed quickly to the sink, turned on the tap and reached out for the soap.

Mary looked across from the oven, saw what he was doing and said, 'Why don't you wash your hands in the bathroom? This is *my* working area.'

'I always wash my hands here,' he said.

'Sit down. I don't know what it'll be like. It's ruined.'

'Go on. Slap it out on the plate. I'll eat it, whatever it's like.'

She glared at him and said, 'We don't *slap it out* in this house. We *serve* it.' She jostled up to him carrying a hot pan of cauliflower.

He reached out for a tea towel to dry his hands.

With her free hand, she snatched it off him and pushed a hand towel at him.

He turned away from the sink, drying his hands and said, 'Why don't you just serve up, and stop being annoying?'

'You're in my way,' she said. 'Go and sit down.'

He went to the kitchen table which was already set. He pulled out a chair and sat down. He checked the cutlery, side plates, salt and pepper, then looked across at Mary and watched her bend down to take something out of the oven. It was then that he noticed the high-heeled shoes, the tights, the dress and, as she moved to the sink, the make-up and the hair.

He frowned. 'What you all done up for?' he said. 'Are you going out?'

'I hope you're hungry,' she said, as she banged an extra spoonful of mashed potato on a plate.

He rubbed his chin. She was not in high-heeled shoes at 5.30 in an afternoon without good reason. Somebody must be coming. He hoped she had not invited another villain like last time. She needn't have got dressed up for him. Or, of course, she could be planning to go out. If that was her plan, he couldn't think where she might be going. He definitely had no intention of turning out. It was raining hard when he arrived home and there was a strong wind blowing up. This was a night for staying by the fire.

They ate in silence which was unusual.

When Angel had cleared his plate, he put his knife and fork down together and said, 'Thank you. If you'll excuse me I'll go and catch up with the news.' Then he pushed his chair away from the table.

Mary knew he was still tetchy because he always said something about the meal, usually complimentary.

He went through the hall into the sitting room and switched on the television.

Mary pushed two sprouts and a potato to the side of her plate, got up from the table, switched on the kettle, and made the coffee.

The television picture came up showing President Obama again speaking about the huge oil leak off the south coast of the US and again insisting that the entire cost of the clean-up and compensation claims be paid by the giant BP oil company.

Angel yawned, pressed the mute button on the TV remote and closed his eyes.

Mary came into the room with two cups of coffee and put them on the library table. She looked at Angel and wondered if he was asleep. She sat down in the easy chair at the other side of the library table, glanced across at him again, took a sip of coffee, hesitated a few moments then in a very soft voice, she leaned over towards him and said, 'Too tired to talk?'

'Just resting my eyes,' he said.

'There's something I want to say,' she said, 'and I don't want you jumping down my throat.'

He couldn't imagine what it was. But he wasn't in any mood for any argument. He'd had a heavy day and was whacked, and he wasn't pleased the way the case was going. Nothing made sense. With very little real evidence, he was working on the slender assumption that Ephemore Sharpe was in some way responsible for the deaths of Julius Hobbs and Wendy Green. He needed a positive lead to advance that theory, and he needed it quick.

Suddenly the front door chime sounded, *ding dong, ding dong*.

Angel's eyes clicked open. His nose turned up. 'Who the blazes is that?' he said.

Mary was on her feet. She rushed out into the hall.

He looked across at the clock. It was half past six.

The door chime sounded again.

He frowned. 'If it's somebody selling something,' he called, 'get rid of them.'

He heard the sound of the door opening followed by the gruff voice of a man. He couldn't identify the voice nor tell what was being said, but he detected that Mary was giving the caller a friendly reception. He heard the front door close, followed by footsteps along the hall.

'Please go through,' Mary said. 'First on the right. My husband is in there.'

Angel frowned as he looked toward the doorway.

The beaming face of an elderly man peered round the door jamb at him. 'Well, good evening,' the man said. 'Remember me?'

Angel recognized him instantly and he wasn't pleased. He sat upright and said, 'Geoffrey 'Gelly Roll' Rollings.'

'You have a good memory,' Rollings said.

Angel's lips tightened. 'How could I ever forget?' he said.

In 1990, Angel had been responsible for Rollings being imprisoned for blowing open a safe in a glassworks. Also, Rollings's son was currently serving time in Marshgate Prison, Doncaster, for a similar offence. The family were well-known crooks and had a reputation for being able to open the most unyielding safes.

'What are *you* doing here?' Angel said.

Mary gently pushed past the old man and said, 'I invited him to come, darling, to look at the safe. I have explained everything to him.'

She then rushed back into the hall, opened the door under the stairs, pointed inside and said, 'There it is, Mr Rollings.'

'Ah!' Rollings said. His eyes twinkled like fingerprint powder as he looked at the maker's brass plate on the safe door. He dropped a small bag of tools onto the hall carpet, reached into his top pocket for his spectacles and put them on, wrapping the old-fashioned curled wire ends carefully round his ears. He then took a small torch out of his pocket and shone it into the keyhole.

Angel stood behind him rubbing his chin. His forehead creased and his nose wrinkled upwards. He made a decision and said, 'I am sorry, Geoffrey, don't do anything to that safe. I will have to ask you to leave.'

Rollings's jaw dropped. He turned and said, 'Don't worry, Michael. I don't intend charging you. Your missus said that you wanted this tin box opening. Well, you know, I'd be happy to do it for you. It would be in the way of a thank you. It's fifteen years since I came out of Lincoln. It was no fun, but I retired then. You taught me a lesson. I've been as straight as neat whisky ever since. And I've no hard feelings towards you, honest.'

Angel said, 'What you say might be the gospel truth, Geoffrey, but I can't be seen to exploit my position to get a favour from a villain.'

'*Ex*-villain, Michael, if you please.'

Mary came forward and said, 'While you two are settling world peace, I wonder if Mr Rollings would like a drink?'

'Yes, please,' Rollings said.

'No, you wouldn't,' Angel said.

Mary looked at Rollings and said, 'Tea or coffee?'

'He doesn't want anything, thank you,' Angel said. 'He's leaving.'

'A small brandy would be most acceptable,' Rollings said.

Mary's eyes opened wide, she smiled and said, 'Coming up.'

She rushed off to the sitting room.

Angel glared down at Rollings. He smiled back.

Angel said, 'I want you to go.'

'I thought you wanted this thing opening?'

'I've told you. I can't ask you to do it, and I've told you why.'

'I can open this thing in three minutes, Michael, for nothing,' Rollings said. 'And to think, I used to get paid twenty-five per cent of what's inside! And I assure you, my dear Michael, I won't be telling anybody. Nobody would know.'

'That's not the point. *I* would know. So thank you for turning out, drink up your drink and then hop it.'

Mary appeared with a tumbler containing two fingers of brandy and handed it to a delighted Rollings.

Angel observed the glass, pulled a disapproving face and glared at Mary.

'Are you two getting along better now?' she said.

'No,' Angel said.

'Yes,' Rollings said as he took the glass. 'Of course we are.'

Rollings flashed a row of choppers as white and even as a line of urinals in Strangeways.

'When he's drunk that,' Angel said, 'He's leaving.'

Mary glared across at her husband. 'If Mr Rollings can open that safe in three minutes why not let him?'

Angel's eyebrows shot up. 'You've been earwigging,' he said.

'Of course I have,' Mary said.

'It will take a quarter of gelly,' Rollings said. 'And I bought a new battery this morning. I've got all I need except a pillow. An old blanket would do.'

Angel's eyes narrowed. 'You've got some gelignite? Where did you get it from?'

Mary's eyes flashed. 'Michael, *Michael*!' she said. 'Mr Rollings is a guest in this house. I invited him to come. You are not to behave towards him as if you were still on duty.'

Angel's lips tightened. 'All right, Mary,' he said, running his hand through his hair. 'All right, but we cannot ask a known felon to help us in this way, or in any other way. You should be able to understand that. You and he are jeopardizing our livelihood. He shouldn't even be in *my* house.'

'*Our* house,' she said.

'All right, *our* house,' he bawled. 'Now please, Mary, ask him to leave, before I throw him out!'

Rollings heard Angel's threat. He emptied the glass and handed it back to Mary. Then he quickly took off his spectacles and closed his bag. He looked up at Angel and said, 'All right, you miserable bleeder. I'll go. I would have liked to have helped you, but I understand *exactly* what you mean. It's called principle. And there aren't many people with any principles these days.'

Mary looked from one to the other with her mouth open.

Rollings turned and made his way down the hall. He stopped with his hand on the door handle and looked back. 'You know, Michael, you're too bloody good for this world. But I'll beat you yet.' He turned to Mary and winked. 'This old Phillips safe only needs the lock blowing. That's all. And I'm going to tell you what I *would* have done.'

'I'm not going to listen to you, Rollings,' Angel said. 'You are wasting your breath.'

'Don't care,' Rollings said. 'What have I to lose? This is for the benefit of your good lady.'

Angel stormed off into the sitting room and slammed the door.

Rollings looked at Mary, smiled and said, 'Now, Mrs Angel. I would have pushed a quarter of a stick of gelly through the keyhole into the lock of the safe, fed the two wires with bare ends into the jelly so that they are only about a sixteenth of an inch apart. I would then damp the jelly down with about a pound of Plasticene inside the keyhole and on the outside of the lock and then covered that with a cushion or a folded blanket stuck on with sticky tape to muffle the sound.'

The sitting-room door opened. Angel put his head through and said, 'Mary, come in here!'

Mary looked from Rollings to Angel and back. 'I'm just showing Mr Rollings out,' she said.

Angel slammed the sitting-room door.

Rollings grinned and continued, 'Then, taking cover round the back on your stairs, I would have put the other bare ends of the wires to my torch battery terminals. There would have been a bit of a pop, some smoke, and hey presto, when it cooled down, you would be able to turn the safe handle and pull open the door.'

He finished, looked at her, flashed the urinals at her and said, 'Have you got it, lady?'

She nodded uncertainly, looked towards the sitting-room door and said, 'I think so. Thanks very much. And thank you for coming. I am so sorry, but you'd better go.'

'Aye. All right,' he said, then he added with a giggle, 'He-he, thanks for the brandy.'

'Good night,' she said and he was gone.

12

It was Friday 29 October. Dark clouds filled the sky which matched Angel's mood as he tramped down the police station corridor to his office.

The unexpected arrival the previous evening followed by the abrupt departure of 'Gelly' Rollings from the Angels' house had resulted in the most almighty row in the Angel household.

Angel repeated the point he had made that policemen can't be seen to use crooks for their own ends, and that it could lead to all sorts of embarrassment and the possible watering down of police authority. In reply, Mary said that that was bunkum, that 'Gelly' Rollings was now an ex-crook, and that a new age of understanding, maturity and forgiveness was due, also that Angel's behaviour in sending 'Gelly' Rollings home abruptly without thanking him and apologizing to him for a wasted journey was rude, unforgivable and stupid. She said that Rollings would have opened the safe there and then at no cost, and without any obligation, and that would have been the end of it. As it was, the safe was still locked and they had no idea how they were going to open it.

Neither side was prepared to move in the argument; there was not even a willingness to agree to disagree, a formula that had settled the very few disagreements they had had in the past. Consequently both antagonists went to bed angry and, regrettably, the difficult atmosphere still persisted throughout breakfast the following morning.

Angel duly arrived at the office at 8.28 a.m., threw off his coat and rang for Ahmed.

'I want to see Don Taylor as soon as he comes in,' Angel said.

'Right, sir,' Ahmed said.

'And get a warrant started to search Ephemore Sharpe's house and outbuildings, find out the duty JP, and —'

There was a knock at the door. It was DS Carter.

'Come in,' Angel said. 'What is it, lass?'

'Can I see you briefly, sir?'

He nodded, pointed to a chair then turned to Ahmed and said, 'Right, crack on with all that and then come back.'

'Yes, sir,' Ahmed said and he went out.

Angel looked across at Flora. He couldn't help but notice how pretty she was. He watched her sit down and cross her legs. At that moment she looked a damned sight more attractive than Mary; of course, she was several years younger.

'I've completed my inquiries into Celia Hamilton, sir.'

'Oh yes, lass, and what's the score?'

'She was in St George's Hospital, Maidenhead, having her appendix removed on the day in question. It was an emergency job. A doctor was called to her home early Sunday morning, the day Julius Hobbs died. She was whisked into hospital, had the op at ten, and she's still there, possibly coming out today or tomorrow.'

'Sounds like a rock-solid alibi. Anybody corroborate it?'

'Half the world. It was all over Monday's papers.'

'I didn't see it.'

'But anyway, sir, I spoke on the phone to the actual surgeon. He confirms the time of the op and said it would not have been possible for her to have been anywhere else but in a bed all of Sunday. Her face is so well known, if she had been up here some news reporter would have spotted her. Do you want me to take it any further?'

'No, Flora, that sounds conclusive. I'll accept it for now. Don't spend anymore time on it. There are two more reports to go.'

'You really think the two were murdered by Ephemore Sharpe, sir, don't you?'

'It's very confusing, Flora.'

Her mouth dropped open slightly as she looked at him. 'Well, if they *are* murders, sir, have you been able to discover the motive?'

'Ephemore Sharpe might have had sufficient motive to want Julius Hobbs out of the way,' he said, 'and she certainly didn't care much for Wendy Green, but if we can't show and prove how she managed it, then we've no case against her.'

'She seemed to dislike the children she taught, sir.'

'I think she did.'

'She had the opportunity, sir?'

'Yes. She had.'

Flora nodded. 'But however it was managed, after the killing of each victim, there would have been the dangerous business of rounding up the wild cat and caging it.'

'Aye,' he said. 'Only someone who knows about wild animals could have done that, Flora. The MO of the killer, in respect of both victims, whether it involved a human or not, appears to be very similar, if not the same. Therefore the two victims must have *something* in common. It would be helpful if we knew what it was. Now, I want you to take that on, Flora. See what you can find out. See where their paths crossed.'

Her eyes darted thoughtfully from side to side. She was pleased to be given the job.

'Right, sir,' she said. She jumped up from the chair. 'I'll get right on it.'

She went out as DS Taylor came in.

'You wanted me, sir?'

'Yes, Don. Come in. Sit down.'

Angel snatched up the phone, tapped in a number and as it rang out, he turned back to Taylor and said, 'It's time we got this case moving. It's time we heard from Mac. He should have something useful to tell us by now. If I can get him, I will put the phone onto speaker so that you can hear what's going on.'

Taylor nodded and leaned over the desk towards it.

'Mortuary,' a voice said.

'Dr Mac, please.'

There was a short delay before the Glaswegian medic said, 'Mac speaking.'

'Michael Angel here, you old Scottish wizard,' he said, 'I haven't heard a word from you since you took Hobbs's body. What can you tell me?'

'Dammit, Michael. I'm not Superman, you know. I got straight onto, and I am still at it. And this corpse, I have to tell you, is in the worst state I have ever had the tragic privilege to examine.'

Angel looked sad briefly. 'I know. I know,' he said. 'But do you know the cause of death yet?'

'I am coming to that. There are so many abrasions.'

'The wild cat expert from NCOF Wakefield said that pawmarks found in the mud at the scene are those of a cougar, and that the usual method the cougar employs is to bite its prey — typically a deer, sheep or horse — at the neck, which kills it outright.'

'Aye, well, not in this case, Michael.'

'Does it look as if the victim fought back at all . . . are there any indications?'

'It doesn't seem that he did. The remaining hand is unmarked and there is nothing significant under the fingernails.'

Angel frowned. 'Does the body look as if it has been killed by a wild cat, left wherever it was for several hours, then dragged to the side of the stream under over-hanging trees and some of the flesh eaten there, where it was discovered?'

'The body seems certainly to have been devoured voraciously by a big cat of some sort, Michael. And hypostasis indicates that it had been left for some time, face down and then later moved and placed face up as it was found. Also there are scratch marks made by its claws down the victim's legs and his remaining arm. And I am not sure whether the body was eaten at the site by the stream, at some other place, or at both places. But whatever. That wouldn't in any case account for the contusions.'

Angel's eyebrows shot up. 'What contusions?'

'Well, there are two contusions to the head . . . they couldn't have been caused by an animal.'

'Contusions?' Angel said. 'Well they must have been caused by a human, Mac? What sort of a weapon was used?'

'I don't know,' he said. 'Something very unusual and blunt. It has left round marks between two and two and half inches in diameter on Hobbs's temple. The blows would have been delivered with a mighty swipe.'

That was the defining news that Angel had been expecting. It confirmed that Julius Hobbs had been murdered. His heart began to thump. He had suspected that a human agency had been involved in the murder from the very beginning.

'I'll email the report through to you later today or Monday,' Mac said.

'Thanks, Mac. That's great. Now, what can you tell me about the young woman?'

'Haven't got far with the lassie, Michael, but I *can* tell you that she also has the same contusions on her left temple, and that the other abrasions, cuts and bites are very, very similar. I should get to her in detail later today or tomorrow.'

'Can you give me any more information about the weapon used?'

'No, Michael. Something unusual, with a round end, delivered with a mighty swipe.'

'Thanks, Mac,' he said. 'Have you enough evidence to be able to say that both murders were committed by the same person?'

'No, Michael, but enough to say that they were committed in the same way with the same or a very similar weapon.'

'That's close enough. Thank you, Mac.'

Angel slowly replaced the phone and switched off the speaker.

He slowly turned to Taylor and said, 'So we do have a serial murder case on our hands, Don.'

'Yes sir,' Taylor said, 'and I have been thinking. How was the dead man carried and deposited tidily at the side of the stream where it was found, without leaving footprints? Nothing and nobody could have done that on wet mud without leaving a mark of some kind.'

'I don't know,' Angel said. 'If it had been dragged over grass, it would have been absolutely soaked, and if it had been dragged along the edge of the stream, it would be all muddied up. It was neither and there is no other route it could have been taken.'

Angel ran his hand through his hair several times. 'I don't know. I simply don't know.'

'Maybe the murderer was suspended in some way from the trees that overhang the stream, sir? And swung from branch to branch.'

Angel stared at him, shook his head and said, 'You mean like Tarzan . . . while carrying the body of Julius Hobbs under his arm?'

Taylor's face creased. He could see it wouldn't have been feasible.

'And it wouldn't have been practical to have employed a crane, a helicopter or the Red Arrows Display Team either,' Angel said.

'No, sir,' Taylor said with a grin. 'But why would the murderer want to make us think that a wild animal had been the killer?'

'I don't know, Don. I really don't know.'

'He's gone to a lot of bother, hasn't he?'

'Or *she* has,' Angel said.

Taylor blinked. 'Do you really think it's Ephemore Sharpe, sir?'

'Well, she's the most obvious candidate, Don,' he said, rubbing his chin. 'At the risk of repeating myself, I don't know. Now push off, Don. I've got a lot to do.'

'Right, sir,' he said. He got up and went out.

Angel leaned back on the swivel chair and looked up at the ceiling. It was a position he often adopted when he wanted to think. He lowered his eyelids and pursed his lips. As the situation had changed, he was thinking that his first priority was to search Ephemore Sharpe's farm and outbuildings. And that was under way. Ahmed was sorting out a warrant. Then Angel reckoned that he needed to report the change to Superintendent Harker so that hereafter he could treat the deaths as murders and not be constrained by the notion that the two victims had been accidentally killed. Also he needed to have the suspect, Ephemore Sharpe, under surveillance.

He leaned forward in the chair and reached out for the phone.

'How's that warrant coming along, Ahmed?' he said into the mouthpiece.

'Be in with it in a minute, sir.'

'Good lad. Then I want you to find DS Crisp, DS Carter and DC Scrivens, and send them to me ASAP.'

'Right, sir.'

He returned the phone to its stand, then stood up. He must see Superintendent Harker. It wasn't a pleasant thought, but it was necessary, before he did anything else.

He left his office and tramped up the corridor to Harker's suite. He knocked on the door and pushed it open.

The skinny man was at his desk writing.

The room was stuffy and hotter than Strangeways cookhouse. Angel frowned and looked around for the explanation. Sticking out from behind the desk, he could just see the edge of an ancient portable two-bar electric fire.

Harker peered through the piles of papers, files, the box of Movicol and the packet of paracetamol, and in a dreary, bored voice, said, 'What is it?'

'I have some important news from Dr Mac, sir . . . about the wild cat killings,' Angel said.

Harker looked up. 'You're not still wasting time on them, are you? They only needed the paperwork preparing for the cases for the coroner's court, you know. And, as a matter of fact, Angel, I haven't had a follow up report from you about the break-in and subsequent robbery from the hospital of the bomb making substances.'

'I am still working on that, sir,' Angel said. 'There is nothing new there. However Dr Mac has just told me that he now has evidence that a human — or more than one — is involved in the two killings formerly thought to be by a wild cat. This means that we have two murders on our hands.'

Harker put down his pen and eased back into his chair. 'I don't think you could have heard me, Angel,' he said. 'I am very worried about the possibility of a repeat performance of 7/7. That would be a national, nay international matter. If that were to happen, it would be horribly intolerable if any of the constituents of the explosive device were traced back to that burglary on my patch.'

Angel took several steps nearer to the superintendent's desk. 'Well, yes, sir, it would. And I will take another close look at the witnesses' statements and the forensic and see if we can find any more lines of inquiry, but, in the meantime, I cannot ignore the new evidence that shows that two people previously thought to be killed accidentally were actually brutally murdered, and I want —'

'That's *two* people, lad. You may have forgotten that fifty-six people were murdered and around seven hundred injured in that 2007 bombing.'

'No, sir, I haven't forgotten.'

'Well what are you blethering on about then?'

'I want to save time and cut off a corner, sir, by advising you in advance that Mac's written report will show that the two victims could not possibly have been killed entirely accidentally, and ask you for your authority to treat the victims as murders so that I can quickly pick up where I left off.'

Harker's mouth dropped open. 'I don't know what you're talking about.'

Angel's eyes flashed like a press photographer's camera. 'You stopped me investigating the deaths as murders,' he bawled.

'Why would I do that? I would never restrict inquiries so early in the investigation. It must have been clear that murder was a possibility.'

Angel's breathing became heavy and laboured. His knuckles tightened. Harker was always going back on an instruction that later showed him to be in error. 'You stopped me investigating the death of Hobbs as murder, sir,' Angel said.

'No. No. No. You must have misunderstood. Show me the memo that shows that I took such a narrow attitude.'

'I don't believe there was a memo.'

'No. There never was one.'

'It was just a verbal instruction.'

'Nonsense. I think you've lost the plot, lad.'

'No, sir. But we may have lost the case,' Angel said, then he stormed out of the room, banged the door and bustled down the corridor.

Ahmed was waiting for him at his office door. He was holding a sheet of A4 in his hand.

'Is that the warrant?' Angel said, snatching the A4 from him as he passed.

'Yes, sir,' Ahmed said. 'And the duty JP is a Mrs Stone. DS Carter and DC Scrivens are on their way, but I've not been able to find DS Crisp.'

'Right. Come in and wait. This'll only take a minute . . . never can find that lad . . . don't know what Crisp gets up to.'

Ahmed waited by the desk and looked out of the window. The sun was beginning to shine.

Angel filled in the box headed: 'Reason for warrant', then signed it stating the date and time.

Scrivens knocked on the door and went in. 'You wanted me, sir?'

'Yes, come in,' Angel said, then he turned back to Ahmed and shoved the warrant into his hand. 'Run up to the Operations Room, give the duty sergeant my compliments and ask him to find some transport to take you to Mrs Stone's house urgently. She's a big woman and might seem a bit daunting, but she's really very nice. Give this warrant to her, with my compliments. She'll know what to do. Then bring it straight back to me. All right?'

'Right, sir,' Ahmed said and dashed out.

Angel looked up at Scrivens. 'Now then, Ted. Go round to Inspector Asquith's office and ask him if he could see his way clear to letting me have a team to search Ephemore Sharpe's farmhouse and outbuildings . . . ready to leave in about fifteen minutes. About twenty officers should do it. The farmhouse isn't very big. But there are three barns and a big garden . . . and I don't want to be there all day.'

'Shall I tell him what you are looking for?'

'Yes,' he said. 'Tell him I'm looking for evidence that she is a murderer, Ted.'

'Right, sir.'

Then Angel said, 'No, Ted. Tell him I'm looking for a cougar.'

Scrivens frowned. 'A cougar, sir? You mean . . . a wild cat, sir. *That* sort of a cougar?'

'Yes. *That* sort of a cougar.'

Scrivens's forehead creased, then he looked at Angel and began to smile.

But Angel's face remained as straight as a truncheon.

Scrivens suddenly realized that his boss was deadly serious. He promptly stopped smiling and said, 'Yes. Erm . . . I'll tell him, sir. A cougar.'

He dashed out and closed the door.

13

It was 10.20 a.m. when Angel's BMW, two marked Range Rovers and two patrol cars travelled down Ashfield Road. At the end, they halted briefly while an officer jumped out of the leading vehicle, opened the gate to Ashfield Lodge Farm, stood by it to allow the procession of vehicles to pass into the farmyard and then closed it.

A squad of uniformed officers headed by Angel went up to the front door. He knocked on it. A PC carrying a battering-ram pushed passed him up to the door.

Angel tugged on his high-profile yellow waistcoat and said, 'Wait a minute, Constable. Give her a chance to answer.'

Several officers began to shout. 'Come on. Police! Police! Open up!'

A few moments later the door opened.

Ephemore Sharpe glared down at them all.

The look of her astonished them. They stopped shouting and eased back from the door.

'What's all this?' she said.

Angel showed her the letter in his hand. 'Miss Sharpe,' he said, 'I have a warrant to search your property.'

She put her hands up to her face. 'No! No!' she said. 'You can't do this.'

Angel stood to one side and eight uniformed policemen pushed past him and in front of her, into the house.

She lowered her hands. Her face was screwed up with hatred. She turned, followed the men down the hall, and Angel heard her shout repeatedly, 'You've no right in here. This is outrageous!'

He turned away from the farmhouse and accidentally walked into a measuring tape across the front of the house. Two officers had been nominated to measure the external and internal lengths and widths of all the buildings to check for any false walls that could have been concealing space. They lifted the tape over him and he rushed across the farmyard.

He joined the rest of the outdoor team who had already opened the first barn door. They found that there were twenty trestle tables set up against the walls with six or eight boxes, originally made for hens to lay their eggs in, located on each of them. There were two cats snoozing in separate boxes. As soon as the cats realized that the visitors were strangers, they scurried out of the boxes and off through gaps under the bottom of the barn wall.

There were textile materials in the bottom of the nest boxes to make them comfortable for the cats. Angel instructed the officers to examine the improvised mattresses. They found them to be discarded domestic textiles such as towels, curtains or blankets. They rolled them up and put them back. There was nothing illegal or untoward in there. Angel indicated that all was satisfactory and the barn doors were closed.

The second barn contained more trestle tables with fifteen or twenty bowls on top, containing cat meat, biscuits, milk and water. Angel thought that there was plenty of freshly dispensed food, enough perhaps to feed an army of small cats.

Both barns were tolerably clean and didn't smell at all unpleasant. He signalled that that barn was all right also, and the doors were closed.

The third barn was being used as a garage. It had a small 2006 registered Renault car nearest the doors. Behind it was crammed full of old farm machinery and tools.

Angel looked through the frame of an old combine harvester and saw a turnip wagon, odd wheels, tyres, scythes, pitchforks and garden tools. He rubbed his chin. He was disappointed and there was no concealing it.

The outside search team leader looked at Angel and said, 'What do you want us to do, sir? How far do you want us to go?'

'Tow out that car and that combine harvester,' he said. 'Then have a good look round. See if anything has been used or moved recently, and check the floor. Make sure it is solid and has not recently been disturbed. If you find anything, I'll be in the house.'

'Right, sir.'

The driver of one of the Range Rovers produced a short towing cable from out of his toolbox.

Angel crossed the farmyard and through a side gate to the back of the house where there were two constables with a heat-seeking detector which they were passing across the garden. They systematically held the screen area along the borders and the lawn scrutinizing them from side to side. It would detect dead bodies up to three metres below the surface.

'If you find anything, I'll be in the house,' he said.

'Righto, sir.'

The inside team were working in pairs and had systematically undertaken a room at a time. He went through the back door, through the kitchen into the living-room where Ephemore Sharpe was sitting in a rocking chair, rocking furiously, gripping the chair arms with her red, bony fingers and her face almost purple with rage. She glanced up at him then turned quickly away.

He crossed to the officer he had nominated as the inside team leader and raised his eyebrows quizzically.

The inside team leader shook his head slightly. It was clear enough.

Angel nodded and turned away. He went all round the house and spoke to the officers in the bedrooms, the bathroom, the loft, the drawing room, the kitchen, the pantry and the study. They all reported that they had not found anything illegal or anything to indicate that Ephemore Sharpe was in possession of a large cat.

Angel's lips tightened back against his teeth. His face muscles were as tight as the chief constable's budget. He ran his hand through his hair. He felt also that some of the younger constables were sniggering at the fact that he was expecting to find a dangerous wild cat hidden away in the old woman's house.

He wandered back into the study as that had now been satisfactorily cleared by the officers who had been searching there. It was a place where he could be on his own and perhaps think things out. It was the room where he had last interviewed Ephemore Sharpe, and he glanced at the myriad of photographs of her, mostly formal school photographs with pupils dating back to 1968. They all had handwritten captions with the date underneath. He looked along the rows and rows for more recent ones and then began to look at them carefully to see if he recognized anybody. He found one photograph that caught his attention. It looked like Julius Hobbs. It was similar to one of the photographs he had seen of him in his mother's flat at The Old Manse, Ripon Road. He was one of about twenty-eight boys and girls in school uniform, some standing on chairs, some seated and some kneeling on grass. It was captioned at the bottom. It read: 'Form 5A, July 1998'. He looked along at the other fresh-looking faces of youth to see if he could see any others he recognized.

He was interrupted by the sound of three knocks on wood followed by a cough.

He turned. It was the outside search team leader standing in the open doorway.

'Sorry to interrupt, sir. Just to say that we've finished, and we haven't found anything. There was only old farm junk and garden tools in there . . . didn't look as if it had been disturbed for years. We've put everything back as it was and closed all the doors.'

'Right, lad,' Angel said. 'Did you break or damage anything?'

He grinned. 'No, sir. Nothing of any value there to break.'

'Right, lad. Thank you very much. Pack up here then, return to the station and report back to Inspector Asquith.'

'Yes, sir,' he said. He saluted and went out.

As he left, the inside team leader arrived. His eyebrows were raised. 'We might have found something of interest, sir,' he said. 'I'm not sure.'

Angel looked up. His eyes brightened. Was this what he had been waiting for? 'What is it?' he said. 'I'll take a look. Lead the way.'

The man went out of the study, along the hall to the room at the back of the house next to the kitchen. Angel followed trying to contain his excitement.

'Well, sir, there's a sort of big scullery tacked onto the building at the back. You would have to go through it to come in by the back door.'

'Yes,' Angel said. 'I know. What about it?'

'In a cupboard in there, there are a lot of pills and medication and stuff. Amongst it, we've come across a big bottle of ethanol and a paper bag containing saltpetre. Now there was a burglary report in recently about those two items.'

'There *was*, lad.'

'The scullery has a big old table in the middle and working surfaces all round,' the officer said, as they made their way into the room. 'And under them are cupboards. Most of the cupboards contain old pans and cooking utensils, but one cupboard is full of what looks like surgical instruments, long needles to give injections, packs of cotton wool, lint and other similar things . . . the sort of kit they use in hospitals. Then there are also packets and bottles of various drugs and stuff I've never heard of.'

The scullery had big windows on three sides, which made it light and airy, and as Angel looked at the scrubbed down table in the middle of the room, it reminded him of pictures he had seen of hospital operating theatres of years ago.

On the table was a large, brown-glass bottle with the handwritten word 'Ethanol' on a plain white label stuck on it. Next to that was a paper bag similarly labelled but with the word 'Saltpetre'.

Angel didn't touch the items, but he looked at them closely. He noticed that the bottle was about half-full and that the paper bag had been opened and resealed with sticky tape.

He nodded then reached into his pocket and took out his mobile. He opened it and tapped in a number. It was to DS Taylor.

'Hello, Don. I'm at Ephemore Sharpe's farm at the end of Ashfield Road. Drop everything and bring yourself here.'

Taylor instantly sensed Angel's excitement. 'On my way, sir.'

He closed the phone, pushed it into his pocket and turned back to the officer. 'Now, lad, where did you find them?' he said.

'They were in there, sir,' the man said, pointing to a cupboard beneath a worktop area.

The doors were wide open and Angel squatted down and looked inside. He could see packets of drugs and bottles of medicines and chemicals, as well as kidney dishes, glass flasks, glass piping and rubber paraphernalia.

He stood up, turned to the man and said, 'Right, lad. Well done. Leave these two items here. Put everything else back as it was. Thank your team for me, then pack up and report back to Inspector Asquith.'

'Right, sir,' he said.

The constable threw up a salute, closed the cupboard doors and went out. 'Right, lads, pack up, let's go,' he called as he went out.

Angel looked out of the scullery windows across the garden to the field beyond and the stream near where the two dead bodies had been found. He rubbed his chin and wrinkled his nose. He wasn't pleased. The search may have exposed a thief but he was looking for something far more crucial. Where did Ephemore Sharpe keep the wild cat? The question went over and over in his mind.

Then he heard men's boots down the hall, the sound of voices, then the front door was opened and closed several times, then eventually, silence.

There were just the two constables in the garden with the heat-seeking detector. They had not yet reported to him. He went out of the house through the scullery door and down a path along the side of the house to the garden. The two policemen were not immediately visible. He looked round for them. They were among some bushes at the bottom of the garden. One of the men was raking over a patch of earth. The other was standing by with a spade. On the ground, to one side, he could see the silver-coloured handle of the detector. His immediate reaction was that they must have found something. He took in a lungful of air and felt his heart kick into top gear. He ran up the garden. When they heard him kicking through the dry, fallen leaves, they looked up.

'We were just about to call you, sir,' the older man said. He pointed to the area at his feet about two metres long. 'I've had a strong signal for this area here. I was coming in to report it.'

Angel felt his pulse banging away. 'All right, lads,' he said. 'Dig away.'

He intended staying with the dig until the search was completed, but he heard a motor vehicle arrive followed by a door slamming. He wondered if it was Taylor.

'I'll see who this is,' he said. 'Back in a minute.'

He went down the garden and followed the path to the front door. It was Don Taylor and he was carrying a big black bag. Angel was pleased to see him. He took him through to the scullery and showed him the ethanol and the saltpetre.

'I want a result on them sharpish,' Angel said.

‘I’ll do what I can, sir,’ Taylor said. ‘But it will depend on St Magdalene’s. I may need fingerprints from them for elimination.’

‘I know. I know. Do what you can. See yourself out. Must go.’

He went back up to the top of the garden. The two men had marked out the suspect area between the bushes, with pegs an area two metres long by about sixty centimetres wide, and had started carefully to remove a few centimetres of earth.

‘It’s easy to work, sir. The ground seems to have been freshly dug over.’

‘Crack on with it. I’m not going anywhere.’

Angel stood there, watching every move.

The men worked quickly, removing a minuscule amount of soil at a time until they were working at about a depth of twelve centimetres. Then they began to reveal something black and shiny.

Angel crouched down and leaned over the find. His heart was pounding as solid as a hammer on Dartmoor rock.

It was a plastic bag, the sort commonly used for household refuse. The men used purpose-made brushes with long, soft bristles to remove the soil from the top of it. Then next to it was revealed another black bag, the same. They cut big inspection flaps in the bags making long incisions with a Stanley knife. The openings released the most abominable smell, indescribably strong and foul. Peeling back the flaps showed that each bag contained the remains of a dead cat.

Angel peered over the trench and had a close look at the cats’ remains. His jaw muscles tightened. He stood up and turned away. He observed that the bodies seemed to be in good condition and had plainly not been buried long. They looked as if they were asleep except that they were both baring their teeth. He knew that there was nothing illegal about killing cats, or putting them down humanely, if that’s what had happened. He couldn’t see that the find had any bearing on the case he was pursuing.

'What do you want us to do, sir?' one of the men said.

Angel shrugged, shook his head then wrinkled his nose.

'There's nothing there I can use as evidence,' he said. 'You'd better close up the bags, cover them with earth and put the ground back to how it was.'

'Right, sir.'

Angel then turned and walked towards the house. He was not a happy bunny. He had expected to find evidence that would help him to make a case against Ephemore Sharpe, but she was too clever for him, or she was totally innocent of the murders.

Then he suddenly had a thought. He stopped, turned round and went back up to the site.

The two policemen looked across at him.

'Will you humour me, lads?' he said. 'Seal up the bags as best you can, put them to one side, then run the machine over the same area and see if anything has been buried underneath.'

The two men looked at each other and smiled wryly. They had heard what a shrewd old fox Angel was.

They fastened up the bags roughly with sticky tape and put them over to one side, then took hold of the detector, put on the headphones and ran the detector slowly over the area.

Angel watched the constable wearing the headphones. He knew that an unusual movement of his eyes would be the tell-tale sign that he had detected something.

The heat-seeking detector team passed the machine over the area and beyond very slowly three times and eventually — regretfully — declared the ground was absolutely clear.

'Right, lads, thank you,' Angel said, through gritted teeth. 'Put the ground back to how it was and make your own way back to the station.'

'Yes, sir,' they said.

Angel then turned away and walked slowly down through the garden. He had to consider what he was going to say to Ephemore Sharpe. He reached the house and made his way to the sitting room. The door was wide open. He stood looking into the room. Ephemore Sharpe was still in the rocking chair, no longer rocking wildly. On the table was a bottle of sherry. She was holding a glass tumbler and looking down into it. The glass was half-full. Two bright pink spots as big as the end of a truncheon glowed on her otherwise pasty white cheeks. She suddenly became aware that she was being observed. She turned and looked across at the doorway. When she saw it was Angel, her face changed. If she could have killed him with a look, he would have been dead.

'Miss Sharpe,' he said. 'We've finished our search.'

After a few seconds she took a deep breath then said, 'And did you find what you were looking for?'

'No,' he said. 'You've been very clever.'

She shrugged. 'I don't know what you mean.'

Angel's face changed. His eyelids lowered. The corners of his mouth were turned down. His voice dropped an octave. 'Where do you keep it?' he said.

'Keep what?'

'The cougar. The wild cat. Where do you keep it?'

She laughed. It was the forced laugh of a woman who never laughed and had had a little more to drink than she should have.

'Huh! I thought you were that brilliant detective I've read about,' she said. 'The wonderful Inspector Angel. Always in the papers. Always gets his man. Like in the Mounties. Except in this case. It's not a man. It's a woman. Ha!'

He thought she might be right. He also thought that this could be the case that shattered his record.

'You don't deny it then,' he said. 'You have a wild cat hidden away?'

'You stupid man,' she said. 'I have no wild cat hidden away anywhere. It would be a lovely idea, but impractical and expensive. And, by the way,' she added, 'do you realize that you are addressing a history teacher of over thirty-five years' experience, and a highly respected pillar of this community? I have lived in this town all my life and so have my father and his forbears. My family have a history of serving the townsfolk in one way or another for over two hundred years without at any time being in trouble with the police. That must count for something.'

Angel didn't believe it counted for anything. 'Some ethanol was found in the scullery cupboard,' he said. 'What do you use *that* for?'

'That's my business. It has nothing to do with you.'

'It could be used as an antiseptic, I suppose. Ethanol is pure alcohol. I suppose it could be taken for recreational purposes.'

She gasped for breath. Her red eyes stood out like those of a cartoon cat. 'Outrageous,' she said.

'There's also saltpetre. What do you use that for?'

It took her a few seconds to regain her equilibrium.

'They are both perfectly innocent substances,' she said. 'It is not illegal to own either of them, is it? Mind your own business.'

'I can only imagine that you use the saltpetre to keep fresh meat that you buy for the big cat.'

'There you go again with this ridiculous notion that I have a wild cat hidden away somewhere.'

'Do you have some other properties somewhere you haven't told me about?'

'Of course not.'

'Where did you get these two substances?'

'I don't remember. They've been there years. Now if there's nothing else, I have a lot to see to. You have held me up long enough. You must go.'

'A five-litre bottle of ethanol, and a twenty-kilo paper sack of saltpetre were stolen a few days ago.'

'This is ridiculous. I am not a thief. I don't know anything about it.'

'Where were you last Sunday night?'

'Oh really. What a remarkably stupid question. Where else would I be, but in my bed?'

'Can you prove it?'

'I don't have to prove it. Who do you think you're talking to?'

'You may *have* to prove it.

'I am a spinster, Inspector, and I live here on my own; of course I can't prove it.'

Angel was seething with anger. He searched his mind as he stood there. He wanted to ask her more questions, but there weren't any. He wanted to charge her with something and lock her up, but there wasn't any evidence. Up to now, it had been the waste of a morning.

'In the absence of satisfactory replies from you, Miss Sharpe,' he said, 'I am impounding a bottle labelled ethanol and a brown paper bag labelled saltpetre. If they prove to be part of a consignment stolen from St Magdalene's Hospital on the 24th/25th October last, you will be charged with breaking and entering, and burglary. Have you anything to say?'

'Yes,' she said. 'Go to hell.'

14

Angel was relieved to arrive back in the office. He picked up the phone, summoned Ahmed, then took off his coat, put it on the hook stuck onto the side of the stationery cupboard and sat down in the swivel chair.

Ahmed knocked on the door and came in. 'You wanted me, sir?' he said.

'I want you to find out what properties Miss Ephemore Sharpe owns or rents besides Ashfield Lodge Farm. You can find that out from the Town Hall, Community Charge office. If you don't get any joy there, check with the Inland Revenue and Customs. If she owns it, she'll be paying the community charge, and if she is renting a property from somebody she'll be paying them for it.'

'Right, sir,' Ahmed said and made for the door.

'There's something else, lad. This is also urgent. I want you to draw up a notice for the canteen notice board. It mustn't go up in reception or anywhere where the general public can see it. I want it to say that I would be grateful if any members of the force who attended Bromersley Grammar School and were taught by Miss E. Sharpe, particularly in the years 1993 to 2003, would contact me urgently in person to assist with inquiries. Word it nicely, lad, and be polite.'

'Right, sir,' Ahmed said and rushed out.

A few seconds later, there was a knock at the door. It was DS Crisp.

'Have you a minute, sir?'

Angel blinked. 'You've come without me sending for you. Yes, come in. Sit down. Have you finished your inquiries into Julius Hobbs's ex-wife?'

'I have, sir. She's a nice lady. Dorothea Webber. She still lives in Bromersley.'

'She's nice is she? You think all women are nice.'

Crisp grinned. 'Well, sir, she looks pretty. Nice figure and everything. She doesn't think much of her ex.'

'Well she wouldn't, would she? Anyway, get on with it. Has she got an alibi for Sunday p.m. and night?'

'She went with her father and mother to her brother's wedding which was on Saturday afternoon in a little village church between Peterhead and Aberdeen. On Sunday morning, they went to church and then, with her father and mother they travelled down to Edinburgh by car and stayed Sunday night at the MacStewart Hotel there. Then on Monday they arrived back in Bromersley.'

'Were you able to corroborate it?'

'Yes, sir. I spoke with the minister of the kirk and with the manager of the MacStewart Hotel where they stayed on the Sunday night. The hotel manager gave me a physical description of her over the phone. And it was a perfect fit. Do you want me to take it any further, sir?'

'No. That'll do for now, Trevor. That seems to rule her out.'

'Yes,' he said.

Angel rubbed his chin. There was a lot to think about.

'There's something else, sir,' Crisp said. 'I was in reception, and there was a little Irish nun from St Magdalene's Hospital —'

Angel frowned. 'Sister Mary Clare?'

'That's her, sir. She's just reported that a large bottle of iodine is missing, believed stolen, from the hospital pharmacy. She particularly asked for you, sir. I was told you were out.'

'Iodine? The brown antiseptic stuff you put on scratches and spots?'

'Yes, sir. A big dark glass bottle of the stuff, she said, worth forty pounds. Who would want to steal a shipload of iodine?'

Angel rubbed his chin. 'Leave it with me, lad. I'll see to it.'

Crisp looked pleased to offload the query.

'But there's something I want you to do as a matter of urgency and importance, lad. It might interfere with any weekend arrangements you may have with your young lady.'

Crisp hesitated a second then said, 'There *is* no young lady at the moment, sir.'

This surprised Angel as he knew that Crisp had a particular interest in the opposite sex. Indeed, he was known frequently to be dating at least two young ladies at the same time.

'I thought you were going strong with that pretty young civvy in accounts,' Angel said.

Crisp hesitated again. 'Yes, sir,' he said. 'I was.'

Angel expected more information.

Crisp, not eager to volunteer any, turned away.

Angel pursed his lips. He wasn't prepared to be put off. 'Well, what happened?' he said.

'She . . . she got married on Saturday.'

Angel's eyes flickered several times and his mouth dropped open. He wanted to smile but he didn't. 'Oh,' he said. 'Well, erm, anyway, I've just had a squad of men go through Ephemore Sharpe's place looking for that wild cat. There was not a trace. I can only conclude that she must be hiding it somewhere away from the farm. Now she would have to visit it every day or so, to feed it and clean it out, so I want you to get a team together and watch her day and night. She must lead us to it eventually. When she moves, I want you to ring me on my mobile. Doesn't matter what time it is. Three of you should be enough. It shouldn't take above two or three days. And the weekend is coming up. You'll get overtime, of course.'

Crisp smiled. The overtime would be welcome.

'Right,' Angel said. 'Crack on with it.'

'Yes, sir,' Crisp said, and he went out.

Angel sighed and ran his hand through his hair. It was difficult for him to accept that they hadn't found a single clue that would lead him to the hiding place of that elusive wild cat or evidence that Ephemore Sharpe had murdered Julius Hobbs and Wendy Green. Confidence was draining away from him like oil from a BP pipeline. He had that feeling that he would never solve this case.

The phone rang. He reached out for it. It was Dr Mac. He sounded quite animated.

'I've almost completed the PM on that female victim, Michael,' he said. 'And I have just discovered something you would want to know about urgently.'

Angel was all ears. 'Yes, well, what is it, Mac?'

'The woman had sexual intercourse shortly before she died.'

Angel's eyebrows went up. 'That's interesting,' he said. He wanted to say that it certainly wasn't a wild cat, but he didn't.

'Have you sorted out her ID yet?' Mac said.

'We believe that she was Wendy Green, a divorced woman, aged 30, who, by reputation, was no Mother Teresa. The donor wasn't likely to be her ex-husband and I don't know of any other suitor. Will you be able to retrieve a semen sample?'

'Already have done. I'll send it off to Wetherby today. It could be your lucky day.'

The find was potentially a big step forward. The semen sample could be checked against DNA records held in Wetherby and if the man was on file, he could be positively identified. Angel was buzzing with questions.

'How long before she died had she had intercourse?' he said.

'Could have been minutes. Possibly several hours.'

'Well, was she raped, Mac?'

'Hard to say. So many contusions. So many lacerations. Who knows? But I can say that she had been regularly sexually active lately.'

Angel nodded. 'Right, Mac. Thank you,' he said. 'Thank you very much indeed. Goodbye.'

He tapped the cancel button followed by Don Taylor's number.

'Yes, sir,' Taylor said.

Angel told him about the conversation he had just had with Dr Mac and then went on to say, 'Drop the ethanol and the saltpetre. Do that later. Go straight to Wendy Green's house and check for evidence of the recent presence of a man there . . . on the bed, in the bed, in the bathroom. Examine the towels and the bedding and check them. If a man's been there, there'll be something: a fleck of dead skin on the carpet, a hair on a towel, a stain on a sheet, perspiration on a pillow. Whatever there is, Don, don't miss it. I want it!'

'I'll do what I can, sir.'

Angel returned the phone to its dock, rubbed his chin, then reached in the desk drawer for his address book. He found a number and tapped it into his phone.

A voice said, 'St Magdalene's Hospital. Can I help you?'

'Sister Mary Clare, please. Detective Inspector Angel.'

'Thank you, Detective Inspector. Hold the line, please.'

The music 'Greensleeves' abruptly assailed Angel's ear. He patiently heard it played through three times and sighed. The music suddenly stopped and the voice returned.

'Sister is not in her office. I'll put a call out for her. Hold the line, please.'

'Greensleeves' is certainly pleasant enough the first time but becomes annoying on its sixth rendering. Angel began drumming a Sousa march on his desk until he suddenly heard the music stop and a man's voice with an American accent said, 'I say, Inspector Angel, how very pleased I am to speak to you again. It's Dr Edward G. Rubenstein. I'm afraid we cannot find dear Sister Mary Clare. Is it anything I can assist you with?'

'She reported the loss of a bottle of iodine to my sergeant, I understand.'

'Did she? I didn't know,' Rubenstein said. Then he added, 'I mean, I knew about the burglary, I didn't know that she had reported it. I wouldn't have bothered you with anything as trivial as a broken window and the loss of a fairly innocuous item like a bottle of iodine. I'm sure you have many more serious crimes to deal with.'

'Kind of you to consider our time, Doctor.'

'Not at all, Inspector. Not at all. So, I don't think there is any need to pursue this little matter any further.'

Angel frowned. His stubborn streak came to the fore. 'That's all right, Doctor. Whenever the law is broken and we've been notified, we can't ignore it.'

'Oh. Yes. Er . . . right,' Rubenstein said. 'By the way, Inspector, I'm hoping that you and your dear wife will come round to my house for dinner in the near future, you know.'

Angel remembered he had asked him about this before. Mary wouldn't want to go and he certainly wasn't keen. 'Well thank you, Doctor. Most kind. However I am overwhelmed with work at the moment —'

'It's those killings by that wild cat, isn't it?'

Angel never freely gave out information to anybody. It cost too much to acquire in the first place. 'I have several difficult cases at the moment,' he said.

'Well, I'll leave the invitation open.'

'Thank you. Goodbye, Doctor,' Angel said quickly. He smiled knowingly as he cancelled the call and replaced the phone.

Almost straight away, the phone bell rang out. He was still smiling as he snatched it up. He could hear coughing and laboured breathing. He knew it was Superintendent Harker. The smile vanished.

'Hello! Hello!' Harker said at length.

'It's Angel, sir.'

'*There* you are lad,' he said. He was breathless and angry. 'Been trying to get you for ages. Always giving the engaged signal. I want you up in my office, *now*!'

There was a loud click in the earpiece and the phone went dead.

Angel blew out a balloon's worth of breath. He wondered what Harker wanted him for. The meetings with him were never helpful, supportive or productive.

He stood up and charged out of the office. He knocked on the superintendent's door, determined to get it over with as soon as possible.

It was still hot and sticky inside the room.

Harker looked up from the cluttered desk, his wrinkled face as red as a judge's robe. He coughed several times and, at the same time, pointed to a chair the other side of the desk and clawed a tissue out of a box on the desk.

Angel sat down.

Eventually Harker said, 'I think you've excelled yourself this time, lad.'

Angel looked at him expressionless.

'There are not many highly reputable, professional, honest people who have a perfectly clean record, in this town. No, but you manage to find one . . . an elderly, retired schoolteacher who has served the community for over thirty-six years. You intimidate her, cross-question her, then take a squad of men in uniform and search her home and property for — of all things — a live wild cat, a cougar. After you make a thorough search, you find — amazingly — no wild animals, no cougar. Instead you find a part bottle of ethanol and a quantity of saltpetre. You impound them and tell her that she may be charged with burglary.'

Angel knew it would be a waste of time, but he decided he must make an effort to defend his actions.

'When I asked her where she got the ethanol and saltpetre from, sir,' Angel began, 'she said that she couldn't remember. I didn't think that that was a satisfactory answer. When I said that she might be charged with burglary and asked her if she had anything to say, she said, 'Go to hell'. I didn't think that an innocent, highly reputable, honest schoolteacher would make a reply of that kind in those circumstances. Anyway, SOCO are checking them out to try to determine whether or not they were the items stolen from the hospital.'

Harker sniffed, then reached forward and took a couple of sheets of paper stapled together off the top of one of the piles of documents on his desk. He glanced at them then said, 'Well Angel, I can save you and SOCO the trouble. Miss Sharpe's solicitor, Mr Cardinal, who left my office only five minutes ago, gave me these two invoices showing that the purchases were made from a wholesale chemist in Leeds in 2009.'

He passed them over the desk to him.

Angel took them. His jaw muscles tightened as he pored over them. 'She could have told me that at the time and saved herself a solicitor's bill,' he said.

'Could you seriously imagine that a woman of her standing, age and physical limitations would slap a treacle paper on the hospital window, in the middle of the night, break the glass, and climb inside to steal a few pounds' worth of chemicals?'

'Potentially dangerous chemicals, sir,' he said. 'It *has* been known.'

'Not by a schoolteacher of her age and standing, lad,' Harker said. 'Why, only last month the chief constable was consulted by the Home Office — and it was passed down to me — to advise on the suitability or otherwise of appointing Miss Sharpe to be a Justice of the Peace. And there was absolutely nothing known against her. I might tell you that her name was approved with flying colours. I tell you this in the strictest confidence, of course.'

Angel was tired of this offensive. It was unjustified. Ephemore Sharpe was a monster.

'Have you met the woman, sir?' he said.

'That is irrelevant,' he said.

Angel nodded knowingly.

'As a matter of fact,' Harker continued, with a sniff, 'my parents couldn't get me a place at Bromersley Grammar.'

'I thought you hadn't, sir,' Angel said. 'If you had *met* her you would have thought differently.'

'Well, that is your opinion and fortunately not that of everybody else,' Harker said. 'I know that you think you are something special on this earth, Angel, because you keep getting your photograph in the papers, articles written about you, and are frequently referred to as *the* Inspector Angel, who — like the Mounties — always gets his man. But you don't impress me any, and I am ordering you from now on to leave Miss Sharpe strictly alone. Her smart-arse solicitor has threatened a writ against the chief constable if she is pestered again. I want you to understand that I mean what I say. In the past, I have taken a lenient view when you have sneakily disobeyed my orders. You may have thought that I was stupid and that I didn't notice. Well, on this occasion, lad, for once in your life, you will do as you are told, or you will find yourself out on your ear. Do you understand?'

Angel sighed. Enough was enough. Sweet reasonableness had flown out of the window. He knew when he was beaten. He stood up. 'Anything else, sir?'

'No. Get out.'

Angel stormed down the corridor, while under his breath calling Harker every rude word and expletive he knew.

He reached his office door, put his hand on the knob then changed his mind. He wanted some fresh air. He turned and went back along the corridor towards the back door. He needed a change. He needed a holiday. And a new job. And £38,000 to pay off the balance of the mortgage, the community charge and the gas bill. And somebody who could open an old safe without a key. And he needed to solve the most difficult case he could ever remember. Most of all he needed Mary, but he didn't want any more argument. He simply wanted peace and quiet.

Outside was dry, cool and dull, but the air was fresh . . . came in direct from the Pennines. He stood there a few minutes, cool breeze on his cheeks and forehead, hands in pockets, looking out across the car park, the green fields and the Pennines beyond, undecided what to do. Eventually, he made for the BMW, and climbed into the driver's seat. He switched on the radio. Dreamy music with violins and a harp filled the car. It was something by Fauré. He started the engine and drove into the town centre . . . eventually he found himself turning into the Forest Hill estate on the outskirts of Bromersley and then to his own house on Park Street. When he realized where he was, he left the car on the drive and went into the house.

When his wife saw him, she knew something was wrong. She frowned, glanced at the kitchen clock, saw that it said twenty-five to five, which confirmed it. 'What's the matter? You're early. You're *never* early.'

His shift ended nominally at 5 p.m. but he rarely arrived home before 5.30 and many a time it was several hours after that.

He went up to her, kissed her gently on the lips.

Mary frowned. 'There *is* something wrong, Michael. What is it?'

He shook his head.

'Somebody died?' Mary said.

'Yes,' he growled, 'me.'

The row about 'Gelly' Rollings was instantly forgotten.

Angel was bursting to talk to her, as she was always a sympathetic listener. As always, she was willing to listen.

He told her about the heated conversation he had had with Harker and the instruction he had had to leave Ephemore Sharpe alone. He followed on with a detailed account of both murders and the case against the wild cat and the woman.

After some thought, Mary said, 'It seems to be a very complicated case, Michael, but you worry too much. You must take it easy. If you get —'

'I *can't* take it easy, Mary. If I wanted to take it easy, I'd write poetry, take up knitting or be a back-bench MP. I *have* to solve this case.'

'I know that it is important to you, but —'

He wasn't listening to her.

'The trouble is,' he said, 'there are no traces of the presence of a human anywhere near the corpse. There are plenty of signs of the cougar . . . its paw marks are all over the place . . . and yet, both victims died from hefty blows to the temple with a round, blunt instrument that must have been applied by hand, a human hand. I can't think of any other way they would have been delivered. A wild cat, such as a cougar could not possibly hold an instrument in its paws and deliver such hefty blows.'

'What makes you so certain that Ephemore Sharpe is involved in the case?'

'Both victims were found within two hundred yards of her farmhouse. She knows more about cats than just about anybody in Bromersley, with the possible exception of old man Fairclough, the vet. Her family — her grandfather in particular — has a history of the keeping and training of wild cats, and there is a poster in her house of Haydn Sharpe, her grandfather, with a group of tigers. And she appears to need to have power over people. As a schoolteacher, that was perfect for her. Now she is retired, that power over children has been taken from her. Power is important to her. This seems to be a trait in the Sharpe family. She has substituted animals for the children. Now if she could train a wild cat to go out and kill a human selected by her, that would surely pick her out as an exceptionally powerful woman. That's what I think she seeks.'

'Is there anything else?'

'Huh. She is obnoxious, obstructive, hates the police and me in particular.'

'That's not evidence.'

'*None* of it is evidence, love. What I have just rattled off to you are facts.'

Mary said: 'Well, maybe she is innocent?'

He wrinkled his nose. He didn't want to admit it. He shrugged. 'Maybe.'

His mobile phone rang out.

He frowned and dived into his pocket. He saw Trevor Crisp's name on the phone's LED. His jaw muscles tightened. He looked at Mary. 'Then again,' he said, 'maybe she isn't.'

'Sorry to bother you, sir,' Crisp said, 'but I know you wanted to know about any movement of Ephemore Sharpe. About twenty minutes ago, she left her house carrying something . . . it is too dark to be certain what it is . . . looks like a plastic shopping bag. Anyway, I am following her on foot. She's walking on Rustle Spring Lane towards St Magdalene's Hospital.'

Angel's heart jumped. 'Don't lose her, lad. I'll come down. Where is she now?'

'Just passing Mawdesley Cemetery on the left-hand side.'

'Be with you in five minutes.'

Mary stared at him. 'You're not going out now, are you? You haven't had anything to eat.'

'Ephemore Sharpe is on the move. I want to find out what she's up to. It would help my case if I could catch her breaking into St Magdalene's pharmacy again.'

'You won't be late, will you?'

'No, love,' he said.

She watched him rush out of the room. She thought for a moment then called after him, 'What would you like for your supper?'

The back door slammed and he was gone. It was too late.

It was a clear sky so the moon made it easy to follow somebody but not easy to hide from them.

Angel drove the car the mile or so round the houses so that he could travel along Rustle Spring Lane in the direction required to have Mawdesley Cemetery on his left. There was very little traffic about at that time . . . several private cars and a taxi . . . a man walking a dog . . . a courting couple stopping at every entry that provided minimal shelter for another quick kiss and a squeeze.

The streetlights were efficiently bright and unhelpful when you were trying not to be observed.

After he had passed the cemetery gates, he slowed the BMW down almost to walking speed and switched the car headlights onto long beam. It was only a couple of minutes later he spotted the back of a tall, dark-haired young man in a black overcoat. It was unmistakably Trevor Crisp.

Angel looked further ahead to see if he could see anything of Ephemore Sharpe, but she was not visible to him. He overtook Crisp by a short distance, parked the car at the side of the road leaving the sidelights on, got out, locked it and made for the pavement. A few moments later Crisp caught him up and they walked side by side.

'Have you still got her, lad?' Angel whispered.

'Oh yes, sir. She's there. Almost at the main gates to St Magdalene's Hospital.'

They walked together in silence. They had to walk quickly.

Angel thought it quite remarkable that Ephemore Sharpe could set such a pace, as she was sixty-nine years of age. Eventually his eyes became more used to the dark and he could see the tall, skinny, tilting stick of humanity, like a Lowry figure, in a light-coloured coat and no hat scurrying ahead, taking small, quick steps. She carried something that seemed to be about as big as two grapefruits in what looked like a white plastic bag swinging from her left hand. He watched her particularly carefully as she arrived at the hospital gates as he was anxious not to lose her, and was surprised when she didn't turn up the drive. She walked straight past. She didn't hesitate, she didn't even glance at the building.

'Where *is* she going?' Crisp whispered.

Angel began to wonder what would be of interest to her in the vicinity of Rustle Spring Lane. The top end of the lane met Park Road, which led to Jubilee Park and Creesforth Road. That was the classy part of Bromersley on the edge of the town.

Maybe she was going to lead them to a place in the country where she hides the cougar. Now that would be a revelation!

He began to wonder if she was aware that she was being followed.

'Has she looked back at all? Have you noticed?'

'No. I don't think so. Haven't seen her.'

The two policemen followed her for a further eight minutes, carefully keeping the regulation minimum of 200 metres behind her as recommended for those particular conditions, and eventually found themselves on Creesforth Road.

Wendy Green had lived at number 16, and Angel could see the silhouette of the house just ahead. He remembered that Don Taylor had not yet reported back to him about the possibility of finding evidence of the recent presence of a male visitor there.

Ephemore Sharpe was surely not returning to the home of one of her victims?

Indeed she was. She turned up the drive which was in darkness and strode out to the front of the late Wendy Green's house as Angel and Crisp crossed the road to be out of the moonlight and into the shadows. They peered at number 16 from behind a stone pillar at the entrance to the drive of number 13.

They saw her reach up to the door knocker with her right hand to give it a vigorous rat-a-tat. The left hand was still holding onto the white plastic bag. There was no reply. She turned round and looked up and down the road. It seemed deserted. Then she tried the door handle. The door was locked. She lowered her head, stamped her foot and her body shook with anger. She quickly turned, went across the front of the house and down the side of it out of the policemen's sight.

Crisp looked at Angel.

Angel said, 'We'll wait here . . . for a couple of minutes anyway. Looks as if she's trying to get into the place.'

'We might get her for house-breaking, sir,' Crisp said.

'I want her for more than that,' he said.

Five minutes passed. Angel began to get worried. Then she appeared from the other side of the house. She stood for several seconds at the front corner of the house looking round. Then she went purposely along a path towards the double garage door facing the drive. Angel noticed that she was still carrying the white bag.

A heavy wagon suddenly roared along Creesforth Road with its headlights blazing.

Her eyes flashed. She crouched down and stayed stiff.

The policemen pressed themselves back against the drive wall. They had no wish to be illuminated either.

When the heavy wagon had passed and quiet returned, Ephemore Sharpe stood up, crossed quickly to Wendy Green's garage and tried the door. It wasn't locked. She pulled at it several times and eventually managed to lift it upward and over, then she went out of view. It was too dark to see anything from across the road.

'Damn,' Angel said.

'I think she's gone inside, sir.'

'Mmm, yes,' Angel said, rubbing his hand across his face.

A minute later they saw her again. She had come out of the garage and was pulling down the door. Then she came straight down the drive, turned left at the bottom and began the quick walk back towards Park Road.

When she was safely out of earshot, Crisp whispered, 'Did you notice, sir, she wasn't carrying that plastic bag? Must have left it in there.'

Angel had noticed. He was thinking that whatever it was, it wasn't enough to feed a big cat, and he knew that Don Taylor had been through that garage as thoroughly as a prison doctor doing a bowel search for a condom of heroin. He clenched his fists then ran a hand through his hair.

'We'd better follow her. See if she calls anywhere else.'

They soon reached the hospital. Angel collected the BMW *en route* and the two men operated a leap-frog pattern surveillance in the car and on foot the rest of the uneventful way to the farm. Crisp was not far behind when Ephemore Sharpe unlatched the farmyard gate, closed it and made her way to her front door which she opened quickly, entered and closed. In the quiet of the night, he heard the bolts slide across and the click of the old lock when the key was turned.

Angel parked the BMW halfway down Ashfield Road in sight of her front door. Crisp walked back to the car and got inside.

'I don't think she'll be going anywhere else tonight, sir,' Crisp said.

Angel's mind was everywhere. He couldn't make sense of anything anymore.

'What did she want to go back to Wendy Green's house for?'

Crisp shrugged. 'We can go and find out, sir.'

They waited twenty minutes until Angel thought that she had completed her excursions for the night then drove the BMW back to 16 Creesforth Road. He parked up the drive right outside the garage, reached into the glove compartment of the BMW, took out a torch and then they made for the garage door. Inside Angel waved the torch around to see what there was. There was a low slung, expensive-looking car inside, an exercise bike covered in dust and an old chest of drawers covered in tins of engine oil, car polish and the like.

'Not much here,' Angel said. Then he handed the torch to Crisp and pulled open the drawers of the chest. The top two contained an electric drill, spanners, socket sets and domestic tools. The bottom drawer contained rusty spanners, tyre levers and similar. At the back of the drawer a piece of white plastic showed. He pulled the drawer out further.

'It's there!' Crisp said.

Angel snatched up the bag and opened it. 'Shine inside it, Trevor. I don't want to contaminate it with my prints.'

Angel peered inside the bag.

'What's inside, sir?'

Angel frowned. 'It's a pot, or plaster ornament of some kind,' he said. 'It's quite old . . . a few chips . . . knocked about a bit. It's the figure of a lion. It's got a name printed on a sort of chain round its neck. I think it's called Pascha, yes.'

Crisp's eyebrows went up. 'What sort of a name is that?'

Angel said, 'There was a German woman who trained and performed in a circus with a lion called Pascha. Saw it on a poster in Ephemore Sharpe's house.'

Angel thought a moment. He recalled what she had said to him and added, 'She said that the pot animal was a gift, and that Wendy Green had stolen it from her.'

'Well, she couldn't have done, sir, could she?' Crisp said.

Angel nodded. It was exactly what he had been thinking.

15

Angel arrived home that Friday night as the church clock bell struck eleven. He was tired and he was hungry. Mary had waited up for him. She quickly made some scrambled egg and toast, and he sat down at the kitchen table and ate appreciatively while telling her about the events of the evening.

'She lied to me,' Angel said. 'Ephemore Sharpe lied to me simply because she didn't like Wendy Green. And the poor girl isn't here to defend herself.'

Between bites of toast and egg, he prattled on about the pot tiger for quite a time until all aspects had been aired and some aspects had been repeated.

Eventually Mary pouring tea into a cup said, 'Can we talk about something else, Michael?'

'Of course. Of course,' he said quickly.

Mary had always been a patient listener and he was well aware of it. But it helped him to say out loud what he was thinking, and to air all the different facets of a piece of information. Mary's reactions and contributions had often assisted him in solving a case.

'What's the matter, love?' he said. 'Sorry to go on.'

'It's all right. I know how this case is bothering you, Michael. But it's twelve minutes to midnight, and then it will be Saturday. That's a day off work. A day of relaxation. A day for a change.'

He looked across the table at her. She was smiling. She was very beautiful, and she had a beautiful smile, but it made him suspicious. He frowned. 'You're not decorating again, are you?'

Her smile turned into a grin. 'No,' she said. 'But we can't do with that safe in the hall cupboard for ever. We have nowhere to put our coats and we can't even close the door properly.'

He was much relieved that he would not have to spend the weekend with a scraper, stripping wallpaper off a wall, and the house upset with clobber from the room that was being decorated. He hated that. Nevertheless Mary had raised a subject he would have rather forgotten about: finding a key to open Uncle Willy's safe.

'There might be your money in there, or even some beautiful silver. And it would be nice to catch up with our mortgage payments,' she said. 'And the gas people have sent us a reminder. They want us to set up a direct debit. Did you know we owe them two hundred pounds?'

He wrinkled his nose and said, 'Yes, love, well let's deal with that in the morning.'

* * *

The following morning, Mary was in the kitchen preparing some vegetables for a soup for lunch when she heard the clatter of the letterbox. She wiped her hands on her apron, went into the hall and pulled a newspaper out of the slot. It was the local rag. She opened it and glanced at it on her way back to the kitchen. Something she saw made her stop and call into the sitting room.

'You are mentioned on the front page of the *Chronicle*, Michael,' Mary said. 'With a photograph. It's an old one. You look about sixteen.'

'Thank you,' he said.

'You didn't tell me you'd been interviewed,' she said.

He frowned. 'What's it say?'

She smiled. 'The headline is, SUPER COP NEEDS YOU.'

He winced. He wasn't pleased. It meant he would have to put up with more insults and sarcasm from Harker when he returned to work on Monday.

'I'll read it to you,' she said.

'I can read it myself.'

'It's only short,' she said. 'It says, *Detective Inspector Michael Angel of the Bromersley force — the cop who, like the Mounties, always gets his man — needs your help in solving a mystery. He wants you to report the sighting of any large wild cats in the neighbourhood. Two local people, a man and a woman, have been viciously attacked and have subsequently died from wounds received from a large wild cat believed to be roaming free around the district at night. The identities of both victims are not confirmed at the time of going to press. If you see the cat, please note the size and colour of it, the time, date, where seen and send or bring the details — with a photograph (if at all possible) — to the* Chronicle *offices on York Street. Full details will be reported in next week's edition*. That's all,' she said, handing him the paper. 'You didn't tell me about this.'

He nodded. 'Didn't I?' he said. 'Well, I must have forgotten. It's been a very busy week.'

Then he put his nose into the paper and Mary returned to the kitchen.

A few moments later there was a knock at the front door.

'It'll be him here now,' Angel said. He stood up, threw the newspaper into the chair behind him, walked up the hall and opened the door.

On the step stood a tall, grey-haired man with a bright, cheery face. 'Hello there, Michael. How are you?'

'Come in, Sam. Thank you for turning out and coming all this way. On a Saturday, your day off.'

'I've only come from Castleford,' he said with a grin. 'Twenty minutes. And believe me, every day is my day off. This is a trip out for me.'

'Mary,' Angel called. 'This is ex Inspector Sam Holiday. Used to head up the CID unit, S19. It dealt with crimes involving bank security vaults, safes and things like that.'

Mary came into the hall, smiled sweetly, then returned to the kitchen.

Angel showed Holiday the safe and the two men sat in the sitting room drinking coffee.

'This safe is very old by today's standards, Michael. Must have been made about 1936. I'm sure you will have noticed that the copper keyhole is dusty and a patina has developed. A key has not been in that keyhole for some time. As a matter of interest, what's inside?'

'We don't know exactly.'

Mary called out from the kitchen. 'It might have some jewellery, or maybe some antique silver inside, Sam. Uncle Willy was in that line of business.'

Angel looked towards the room door then back at Holiday.

Holiday smiled. 'Well,' he said, 'it should be fairly easy to open by blowing the lock.'

Angel frowned. 'Yes, but where can you get dynamite?' he said.

Holloway shook his head. 'You can't. Not for breaking into a domestic safe. The best way, Michael, is to find the key.'

'The key was lost years ago. The owner has died and left the safe to me.'

Holiday scratched his head. 'There is a way. That is to drill a small hole just above the lock. However, that depends on the sort of metal the safe was made from. If the casting is made from cobalt-vanadium alloys with embedded tungsten-carbide chips, it would shatter the cutting tips of the drill bits, which are more than fifty pounds each. The process could cost more than a thousand pounds . . .'

'Can't you find out what metal it has been made from, Sam?'

'Can't be sure. You can only find out by actually drilling. Don't know how long that will take. Would take a few hours. Do you want me to have a go?'

Mary called out from the kitchen, 'Yes please.'

Holiday looked at Angel smiled and said, 'When do you want me to start.'

'Right now, Sam, would be fine!' she called.

Angel's eyebrows shot up.

* * *

Two hours later, after the second tungsten-carbide-tipped drill bit shattered before their eyes, Holiday switched off the drill, turned to Angel and said, 'It's no good, Michael.'

Mary came into the hall. 'What's happening?'

'Sam can't get through this casing,' Angel said. 'This is the sixth try. He's only drilled half an inch and the second drill bit has shattered.'

'There's something in the casting,' Holiday said. 'Might be a composite hard plate that is making it impossible to get through even with these special drill bits.'

'Can't you keep trying, Sam?' Mary said.

'It's not practical, Mary. I can't keep spending your money, like this. It would be like throwing it in the bin. Besides, if I got through to the lock there is still no absolute certainty that I would be able to open the safe.'

Mary's face dropped.

Angel rubbed his chin. 'What options are left to us now then Sam?' he said.

Mary said, 'I have heard something somewhere about thermal lances. Could we not get one of them?'

'The trouble with thermal lances and plasma cutters, apart from the cost,' Holiday said as he turned the key in the chuck to remove the damaged bit, 'is that they create such a high temperature that they might burn or melt whatever's in the safe. Your best bet — if you really can't get the key — is to use an oxyacetylene torch.'

'Could you do that then, for us, Sam?' she said.

'I've never used one,' Holiday said. 'I don't know much about them. We never used them in S19. If we had found ourselves in this position, we would have gone for blowing the lock. But Michael could soon learn to operate one, I daresay. You could then hire a torch and the bottles of gases . . . and you'd need a good pair of goggles.'

Angel frowned.

'I'm sure he could,' Mary said.

Angel turned round and looked at her, his mouth and eyes wide open.

Holiday showed him the place on the safe where he would need to direct the torch. Angel tried to look intelligent and interested and made the appropriate noises, but it wasn't for him.

Mary invited Holiday to stay for a meal and he and Angel talked over past cases, particularly where their paths had crossed. Angel paid him for the two shattered drill bits (which was £110) and gave him £10 for petrol. Holiday wouldn't take any more even though both Michael and Mary Angel thought he had earned it.

Holiday had thoroughly enjoyed his afternoon and was reluctant to leave, but he wanted to arrive home in Castleford before it became dark. It was twenty minutes to five when the Angels stood at the front door and saw Sam Holiday drive away.

Angel was not disappointed that it was too late in the day to pursue the business of hiring oxyacetylene equipment, because, as he pointed out to Mary, he had to change all the clocks in the house, including the central-heating clock. Tomorrow was the end of British Summer Time. Mary was not pleased, particularly as while he was upstairs putting the clocks back an hour, she phoned both local hire shops and discovered that they were both on the point of closing, that they would both be closed the following day, Sunday, and would not reopen until Monday morning at 9 a.m.

* * *

It was 8.28 on Monday, 1 November. It was raining, cloudy and cold.

Angel arrived at his office carrying a white plastic bag. Inside was the pot lion, Pascha. He placed it gently on the desk. He threw off his coat, sat down and fingered through the pile of letters and reports in front of him.

There was knock at the door. It was Ahmed.

'Come in.'

'Good morning, sir,' Ahmed said. 'You wanted me to check with the Community Charge Office in the Town Hall and the IRC to see if Miss Sharpe owned any properties or paid rent for any.'

Angel looked up, wide-eyed. He certainly did. That information was just what he needed, the place where she kept the big cat. 'Yes, lad?' he said. 'And what have you got?'

'Both inquiries came back negative, sir.'

Angel's face dropped.

Ahmed continued: 'The Community Charge Office said that they were certain that she didn't pay the corporation for any other property in the borough, and the revenue office could only say that there were no standing orders or regular payments being paid out of her bank accounts that could be regarded as rent.'

'Oh,' Angel said. He wrinkled his nose. There was another line of inquiry down the pan.

There was a knock at the door. It was Scrivens.

'What is it?'

Scrivens looked at Ahmed and then back at Angel. 'Can I have a word, sir?'

'I'm waiting for a report from you, aren't I, lad?' Angel said. 'About Hobbs's old girlfriend, Miranda somebody or other.'

'It's Imelda, sir, Imelda Cartwright. That's just what I want to see you about, sir. I could have done it more quickly, but you've had me on other jobs, you know.'

'All right, lad. All right,' Angel said. 'Don't get excited.'

He turned to Ahmed, picked up the plastic bag on his desk by its handles, passed it to him and said, 'Take that to Don Taylor and ask him to check it for fingerprints. It's a pot ornament so don't drop it.'

Ahmed's eyebrows went up.

Angel said, 'Tell him I'm looking for the dead girl's dabs. If they are *not* on it, ask him to phone me without delay.'

'Right, sir,' Ahmed said, then he went out and closed the door.

Angel turned back to Scrivens. 'Now tell me. Has this Imelda Cartwright got an alibi for Sunday night?'

'She was on the Zeebrugge to Hull ferry, sir,' he said, 'coming back from a holiday, touring with three other friends. She has the ticket, the tan, the car stickers and the friends to prove it.'

Angel groaned. 'And I suppose the three friends were enthusiastic in corroborating the alibi?'

'Absolutely, sir.'

'Thought they would be. That brings us back to exactly where we were — nowhere!'

'Sorry, sir,' Scrivens felt impelled to say.

Angel smiled weakly. 'It's all right, lad, it's not your fault. Sounds as if you've done a perfectly splendid job.'

He stood up and said, 'Tell Ahmed, if anything urgent crops up I'm going down to that hospital on Rustle Spring Lane.'

* * *

It was ten minutes past nine when Angel arrived at St Magdalene's Hospital. He went straight up to the reception desk and the beautiful Candy Costello, who looked more fragrant than ever. She fluttered her eyelashes, raised her eyebrows, smiled, looked at Angel as if she had known him all her life and said, 'Can I help you?'

He asked for Sister Clare. The receptionist put out a call for her, then right on cue, as before, out of his office came Dr Rubenstein. The doctor made straight for Angel, smiled and rushed across the lobby, hand outstretched to greet him.

'I am so glad to see you again, Inspector,' said, while shaking his hand. 'As a matter of fact, you're just the man I want to see.'

Angel smiled courteously, but he wasn't particularly pleased to see him. He hadn't time for any social chit chat. The double murder inquiry was his priority, and there was a lot to do that morning.

When he had retrieved his hand, he said, 'Pleased to see you, Doctor. But I have specifically called in to see about another breaking and entering case . . . iodine stolen this time, I understand.'

Rubenstein waved his hand in a casual way and said, 'Yes. Yes. *That's* not important. Please come into my office, Inspector. There's something cropped up that I need your advice about. Can you spare me five minutes?'

'Of course,' Angel said. What else could he say? He couldn't have said anything else. 'But I must see the sister before I leave,' he said.

'Of course. Of course. Come in.'

Angel followed him into the plush office.

Rubenstein closed the door and when they were both seated, Angel said, 'Now then, Doctor, how can I help you?'

The doctor seemed to have difficulty assembling his thoughts. He frowned and had his hands as if in prayer, the tips of the opposite fingers touching lightly, with fingers splayed. He separated his hands and brought them back together, several times. The corners of his mouth were turned downwards. He looked about as happy as a man with toothache waiting to be interviewed by Her Majesty's Inspector of Taxes.

Eventually Rubenstein said, 'Can I speak to you unofficially and in confidence?'

Angel looked back at him and slowly rubbed his chin. Sounded as if the doctor was about to make a confession.

If so, Angel wanted to hear it, but didn't want to walk into making a promise he couldn't keep.

'You can,' he said, 'except, of course, Doctor, if a crime has been committed and you told me about it, I may very well be obliged to follow it up.'

Rubenstein frowned again. He pursed his lips.

'It's my job,' Angel continued. 'And anyway, I can't help myself, Doctor. It's what I do. Tell me, is it you? Have *you* broken the law?'

'No. No,' Rubenstein said quickly. 'It's to do with a patient, a very unhappy person, who I think I can only completely heal by telling you about the crime and allowing the law to take its course. However, I am forbidden to do that.'

'Has *he* broken the law?'

'No, but —' He broke off. 'You understand, I have to abide by the special confidential relationship that exists between doctor and patient,' Rubenstein said.

'Of course. Of course,' Angel said.

He mustn't frighten Rubenstein off. Information was the lifeblood of all criminal investigations, but there were standards to maintain in the police force as well as in the medical profession.

'Supposing you approach the subject from a hypothetical point of view, Doctor,' he said. 'Would that work for you?'

Rubenstein pursed his lips. After a few moments, he began, choosing his words carefully. 'Well, supposing while hypnotized, a patient had told me that a murder had been committed and it was clear to me, in my professional capacity that it had significantly adversely affected that person's psychological and physical health and — it would be no exaggeration to say — quite severely ruined their life . . .'

'Yes?' Angel said.

'In such hypothetical circumstances, what could I do about it? I need to heal my patient.'

'I take it that he is unwilling or unable to tell the police about it?'

'That's correct. Both in fact.'

'Is that because he is to blame or partly to blame for the murder?'

'No. Not at all. Love and fear combined constitute the basis for the reluctance.'

Angel rubbed his chin. He reckoned it must be someone very close.

'In your opinion,' he said, 'is the patient ever going to be able to speak to the police about the crime?'

'No.'

'In your opinion, will your patient only recover when the guilty party is revealed, tried and punished?'

Rubenstein's face brightened. He was pleased that Angel seemed to understand the situation perfectly. 'I *am* of that opinion.'

'And yet the patient will not give a name or provide any information to help secure a conviction?'

'That's how it is, Inspector. That's exactly how it is.'

'Well,' Angel said after some thought, 'the problem seems insurmountable.'

The doctor sighed.

'Are the police already aware of the murder?' Angel said.

That seemed a difficult question for the doctor. He pondered a few moments before he answered. 'I won't answer that question, Inspector, if you don't mind.'

Angel smiled to himself. Rubenstein was no fool. If the force had already known of the unsolved murder, Angel could have produced a list of them and by process of elimination, perhaps, have been able to identify the case, and who knows what else. He wondered if it was a murder committed some time ago that was soon to be discovered. He was certainly intrigued, and he also had sympathy for the patient. He wished he could help the situation, if it was genuine.

He realized that what was required was that he should solve a murder that he wasn't allowed to know had happened.

A distant bell rang. He wondered what it was. He looked at his watch. It was ten o'clock.

This speculation was getting him nowhere. He stood up. 'I'm sorry, Doctor. I don't think I can help you with this one. If you can tell me anymore . . . ?'

Rubenstein got to his feet. 'Regrettably I can't, Inspector.'

Angel nodded. 'Well, if the circumstances change, you know where I am. Now I must see Sister Mary Clare.'

'I will take you down there, Inspector. It won't take us long.'

'Right. Thank you.'

The two men came out of the office and walked down the long corridor towards the pharmacy.

'I remember having iodine daubed on my knee when I grazed it as a boy,' Angel said, 'but does it have any other uses, Doctor?'

'Iodine is mainly used as a germicide and an antiseptic.'

'Really? All to do with treating wounds and keeping us clinically germ free.'

'Yes. And as a dye used in certain radiology applications.'

Angel frowned. It sounded very boring. He couldn't see why anybody would want to steal a large bottle of iodine.

They arrived at the pharmacy door. Rubenstein produced a big bunch of keys, unlocked it, opened it and switched on the light.

It was all tidy and clean. The window was boarded up.

'The bottle was kept up there,' Rubenstein said, pointing to a space between other bottles on a shelf shoulder-high. 'There is another bottle on order but it doesn't seem to have been delivered yet.'

Angel turned to look at the boarded-up window. 'And I suppose access was made through that same window again?'

'It was smashed, Inspector, the catch was unfastened and there was broken glass everywhere, just as last time. We were having it boarded up permanently, but the carpenter hadn't got round to it.'

Angel looked down at the floor. 'I don't see any glass around, Doctor.'

'Oh no. It's all been cleaned up. The staff couldn't have worked treading on broken glass. It was sharp and gooey and sticking to their shoes.'

Angel shook his head and pulled a face. He was wasting time. He couldn't solve crimes where the evidence had been swept away.

'I can't do anything here, Dr Rubenstein,' he said. 'If there had been any evidence, it has all been cleared away or contaminated by your staff. Please tell Sister Mary Clare that I called to see her. I'll find my way out. Good morning.'

16

Angel returned to his office, threw off his coat, reached out for the phone and tapped in a number. It was promptly answered by Trevor Crisp, who didn't seem very happy.

'Hello, yes,' he said.

'Anything happening, Sergeant?'

'Nope. She's been out to feed the cats in the barn,' he said, 'otherwise it's quieter than a mortuary.'

Angel took in a lungful of police station air and blew it out rapidly. 'What's the matter with you, lad?' he said. 'Have you forgotten who you are speaking to?'

'No, sir. Sorry, sir,' he said quickly.

'What's the attitude for?'

'Well, erm . . . I'm sat here in the car, sir . . . it's like watching paint dry.'

'Would you like a job with a pretty young lady, aged about twenty-six, with strawberry-blonde hair and legs so long that it's snowing at the top?'

Crisp hesitated then frowned. He had to be careful with Angel. 'I don't know, sir,' he said.

'Well, make your mind up, lad. I'm not hawking this job round the station. There are plenty of coppers who would snap it up. The other day you told me you didn't have a regular lady friend. Is that still the situation?'

He hesitated. 'Well, er, yes, sir. Are you serious?'

'Well, you can stay there for the rest of the week, if you prefer to.'

'Oh no, sir,' Crisp said. 'What's it all about? What do I have to do? And who's going to relieve me? Ted Scrivens is on the rota.'

'I'm cancelling the obbo. I can't spare any more time watching Sharpe. I simply haven't enough men. If she had been going to visit the animal I reckon she would have done it by now.'

'Maybe it's dead, sir.'

'I don't know. Anyway, make your way to my office smartish. We are wasting time.' Angel replaced the phone.

He managed to find ten minutes of uninterrupted time to begin to clear the two weeks of accumulated paperwork on his desk, when the phone rang. He put down his pen and reached out for it. It was Selwyn Plumm from the *Bromersley Chronicle*.

'I thought you would like to know, Michael,' he said. 'We only had three replies from my piece about the wild cat.'

Angel frowned. He had to direct his thoughts back to the news appeal Plumm had made on the front page of the *Bromersley Chronicle*.

'Oh good,' Angel said. 'Any photographs?'

'No. The trouble is that each reader described the cat they saw differently. You would think there were *three* cats. But all three readers said that the cat they saw was the biggest cat they had ever seen!'

'Where do they say they saw them? Any two in the same place?'

'No. Afraid not.'

'Does any of them say they saw a cat anywhere near the field at the back of Ashfield Lodge Farm?'

'Let me see . . . one in a garden in Tunistone . . . one coming out of an outhouse in Carlton . . . and one at the rear of St Magdalene's on Rustle Spring Lane. Huh, a woman has written in to say that her mother saw it from her hospital bed in the middle of the night. No, Michael, I'm afraid not. Is that where the victims were found?'

Angel rubbed his chin. 'I wonder if any of them saw anything resembling a cat.'

'Sorry, Michael.'

Angel was becoming used to lines of inquiry leading nowhere.

'See that they are courteously acknowledged, Selwyn. And perhaps this week you would thank your readers for being such good public citizens. Tell them the police appreciate it.'

'Of course I will, Michael,' Plumm said. 'Now then, have the two victims been identified yet?'

'Yes,' Angel said and proceeded to give him their names and ages. Plumm then followed that with a stream of other questions about the two killings. Angel only answered matters that could be confirmed (which was very little) and declined to say anything about his suspicions. Plumm said that he hoped that the wild cat, whatever it looked like, would soon be caught and returned to wherever it belonged. Angel thanked him and replaced the phone.

Angel's thoughts drifted back to Dr Rubenstein's patient and the predicament the doctor was in, when there was a knock at the door. It was Don Taylor.

'Wendy Green's house, sir,' Taylor said. 'We've been through it thoroughly and there are no recent signs of the presence of a man anywhere. I checked the bedroom, the bed and the bathroom and there were absolutely no fresh signs of anybody other than Wendy Green and her son Jamie. If she was playing around, she wasn't playing at home.'

Angel looked as miserable as Friday's fish on a Monday morning.

'Anything else?

'Yes, sir. I can confirm that the ethanol and saltpetre found at Ephemore Sharpe's place were *not* taken from St Magdalene's Hospital on the 24th/25th October. That copy invoice her solicitor produced dated 2009 must have been the genuine article.'

Angel looked as if he was ready to jump off Beachy Head. 'Anything else to cheer me up, lad?'

Taylor nodded. 'That pot lion, Pascha, sir. You'll be pleased to know that the only prints on it are Ephemore Sharpe's. Almost a complete set.'

Angel was pleased about that.

'That's good, lad. That's very good.'

Taylor said, 'But if Wendy Green *didn't* steal the pot lion from her what was the point of it all?'

'To make a liar out of Wendy Green,' Angel said.

Taylor looked puzzled.

'Look, Don,' Angel said, 'Sharpe told me how useless Wendy Green was. She also said she was a thief and that she stole a pot lion from her. She would have seen me write it all down. Afterwards she must have thought that we might check on it. Therefore it wouldn't do for the pot lion to be found in her house, would it? So she got hold of the ornament intending to dispose of it somehow, then thought what better place was there than to plant it in Wendy Green's house? After all, the woman's dead. She can't deny it. However, what Sharpe didn't know was that we were watching her and actually *caught her at it.*'

Taylor nodded. 'So she told a lie and was actually trying to prove it was the truth.'

Angel nodded. 'Exactly. She told a *whopping* lie, making a thief out of a woman who is probably as straight as a parson's pencil.'

'What a nasty, evil bitch she really is,' Taylor said.

There was a knock on the door.

'Come in,' Angel called.

It was Crisp. He looked very breezy and smart.

Taylor and Crisp exchanged nods then Taylor looked back at Angel and said, 'Was there anything else, sir?'

'Yes, Don,' Angel said. '*Ephemore Sharpe has to be stopped*, before we find another dead body. But there's nothing else for now, lad. That's all. Carry on.'

'Yes sir,' he said and went out.

Angel turned back to Crisp. 'Now then, Trevor, sit down. It's like this . . . a new inquiry has cropped up, and I urgently want the names and medical records of all the patients in St Magdalene's Hospital. If I ask for it openly, it would show my hand to the very person I need to hide it from, so I want you to get it for me — quickly, quietly and surreptitiously. I think the best bet, the easiest bet, would be via the pretty bird on reception. All right?'

Crisp blinked.

'That should be easy-peasy for you, lad,' Angel said.

He shook his head. 'I don't know, sir. Depends what she's like. You know how weird women can be.'

'Yes, I know, but this one's a real eye knocker, all right.'

'Well, then, she'll be in great demand, sir. She's probably already got a regular partner.'

'She might have. You can't tell. She might be fed up with him.'

'She might be very happy.'

Angel shook his head. 'None of these modern lasses are really happy,' he said. 'They don't know what happiness is. They don't know what they want, and when they've got it they don't want it.'

'I don't know, sir.'

'Besides, men often shy away from really good-looking girls. They think the competition might be too strong. She'd probably welcome a new face.'

'Yes, sir, but it might not be mine,' he said. He scratched his head. 'And she'd take a little time to get to know.'

'We've not got a lot of time.'

'Is she really a cracker?'

'She makes Cheryl Cole look like one of Ken Dodd's Diddymen. Believe me.'

Crisp smiled. He was warming to the idea.

'Mmmm. What about expenses, sir?' he said.

'Anything reasonable would be all right, but I am not talking about two months in the Maldives. I want you to crack this quickly — very quickly indeed.'

'And how would I get this info, sir?'

Angel opened his desk drawer, reached inside, took out a small paper bag and handed it to him.

Crisp took it and opened it. Inside was a bubble pack of a card and a memory stick for a PC.

'Do you know what that is?'

'Oh yes, sir.'

'Well, at the first opportunity stick that into a USB socket in the computer on her desk in reception, and the rest is easy. All right? It'll only take you a minute, if that.'

'When am I going to have the opportunity?'

'Don't worry. I am working on that.'

Crisp seemed a little more confident. 'Right, sir,' he said.

'Hop off, put on your best suit, get to that hospital and start the charm offensive. I'll contact you on your mobile.'

Crisp grinned and went out.

Angel watched the door close and smiled.

He resumed his wrestle with the endless paperwork and was thinning it out nicely when there was another knock on the door.

It was DS Carter.

'Have you a minute, sir?' Flora said. 'I've managed to find out a little bit about Julius Hobbs and Wendy Green or Woods, as she was known then.'

Angel pointed to the chair Crisp had not long vacated. Flora Carter sat down. She took out a small notebook from her bag.

'What have you got?'

'Well, sir, according to their respective mothers, they were not aware of any liaison of any kind between them, but both mothers were willing to agree that their kids didn't tell them everything about their friends and relationships, particularly at that age. I found a neighbour of Wendy Woods who was a similar age, and she said that when they were at school, they shared confidences particularly to do with boyfriends, but she never knew of any relationship between Julius and Wendy, so I have tended to rule that line of inquiry out. I did find out that they were both in the same class from being eleven years of age up to seventeen so they couldn't have avoided knowing each other. They were both born in 1980, so that's not surprising. Also her friend said that Wendy was almost always at the top of the class. Julius Hobbs's mother said that *he* was always top of the class, from when he first attended school also. They can't both be right. Anyway, they both left school at the end of the summer term in 1997. Julius Hobbs went to work in a travel agency in town and then as an estate agent selling houses, while Wendy Woods went straight to university. I couldn't find any indications that their paths ever crossed again. And that's all I've got, sir,' she said closing her notebook.

Angel had been listening carefully. 'Sounds as if there might have been a bit of competition between them to be top of the class?'

'Might have been. I don't think it was serious.'

Angel pursed his lips then said, 'Did either of the mothers mention Ephemore Sharpe?'

'No, sir. I asked each mother if their child had at any time mentioned any of their teachers by name. They both said they couldn't remember. They didn't think so. When I mentioned the name Ephemore Sharpe, both mothers said that they didn't know of her.'

'Did it seem genuine?'

'Oh yes, sir. It did.'

'And is that it?'

'That's all I could manage to dig up. Is it of any help?'

Angel shrugged. He tapped the tip of his forefinger quickly at his temple several times. 'It all goes in the pot, Flora,' he said. Then he ran a hand through his hair and said, 'If I could find where Ephemore Sharpe keeps hidden a big cat that kills to order, how she gets it to obey her and not harm anybody else, her motive for murdering two of her ex pupils, and sufficient evidence to secure a conviction, I'd be a very happy man. As it is, I seem to have a million facts milling around in there but not the right ones. In addition, there seems to be another murder case that I will have to solve involving a patient at St Magdalene's Hospital.'

Flora Carter lowered her eyebrows. 'I thought that was a breaking and entering and burglary job, sir?'

He pulled a face, moaned and said, 'No. But there's *that* as well, lass.'

The phone rang. He glared at it. He hesitated then reached out and snatched it up.'

It was Mary. 'Can you talk a minute, love?'

He wanted to say 'no,' but he didn't want another row. 'Yes,' he said, 'DS Carter is with me. She won't mind waiting one minute. What is it?'

'Give DS Carter my apologies and tell her I look forward to meeting her in the near future.'

'That's half a minute gone. What do you want?'

'Don't be mingy. That was only ten seconds, if that. There's a car breaker at Barnsley Common. Car breakers use acetylene torches all the time, don't they? Shall I ask him if he can collect the safe and cut it open for us?'

Angel blew out a truncheon's length of air. 'All right but get a quote from him first.'

'Right, love. Bye.' There was a click and she was gone.

His nose went up and the corners of his mouth went down. He slammed down the phone, blinked several times, turned to Flora Carter and said, 'Where was I?'

'I was thinking, sir, the two pupils who were in the same class may have witnessed something or were involved in something with Miss Sharpe which she now doesn't want to become public knowledge . . . something criminal.'

Angel nodded. 'It's possible, Flora. It's possible, but I think that the most significant thing you have found out is that both mothers said that *their* child was always top of the class.'

'A typical proud mother's boast, sir, don't you think?'

There was a knock at the door.

'Come in,' Angel called.

It was PC Sean Donohue, a car patrolman from Inspector Asquith's uniformed team at Bromersley.

'What is it, Sean?' Angel said.

Donohue looked at Flora Carter and then back at Angel. 'Oh. Er, I just wanted a word, sir,' he said. 'But if it's not convenient . . . ?'

'No. That's all right. Come in. You know DS Carter?'

Flora thought that Donohue wanted to speak to Angel on his own. She jumped up and said, 'If you gentlemen will excuse me? I'll get off.'

Angel nodded. Donohue smiled and she went out.

Angel looked at the patrolman, pointed to the chair and said, 'What is it, Sean?'

Donohue did seem more at ease when there was only the two of them. He sat down and put his flat hat on his lap. 'That notice in the canteen, sir. About Miss Sharpe, the history teacher at the grammar school.'

'Aye, what about her.'

'I was in her class from about twelve until I was sixteen, the same form as Julius Hobbs and Wendy Woods.'

'Oh yes? We were just talking about them, Sean. Which one was the cleverest?'

Donohue frowned. 'They were both pretty slick, sir. I guess Hobbs was the cleverest, but Wendy Woods came a very close second. They were the two smartest in the class. Is it important?'

'Probably not.'

'Huh. I know I came way below them both.'

'Tell me about Miss Sharpe.'

Donohue shook his head and looked down. 'She was a horrific monster, sir, if the truth be known. She was scary and all the class was terrified of her. She used to rant and rage and scream at us if we got a date or a name wrong. She was an absolute terror. There was never any nonsense in her lessons.

If she picked on you, you could expect a rough ride. There were some girls she reduced to tears. Her subject was history which she pumped into us hard. Her lessons were boring and uncomfortable.'

'And was there anything of a relationship . . . I realize that you were only in your teens, but was there anything of a relationship between Julius Hobbs and Wendy Woods?'

'I never noticed anything, sir. Relationships did exist but they were, in the main, kept secret, because if they got found out, they would get teased something rotten.'

'Anything else you can tell me about Julius Hobbs, or Wendy Woods?'

'I don't think so, sir. They were ordinary kids, just like we all were. It's just that they always seemed to know the answers and get the best marks, that's all.'

'Can you remember if they were good at history?'

'They were brilliant at everything, sir.'

Angel frowned, then he looked up and said, 'Thanks for coming in, Sean.'

Donohue went out and Angel sat there, rubbing his chin. He could not see a motive for the horrible Ephemore Sharpe to want to kill her two best pupils, unless it was deliberately to confuse him. Because confuse him it certainly did. He ran his hand through his already dishevelled hair. He had never hated a case as much as he hated that one at that moment.

The phone rang. He reached out for it. 'Angel.'

'It's Sergeant Clifton in the Control Room sir. I wouldn't bother you, but as you know the super's off sick and Inspector Asquith is up to his proverbials with this football match. The chief constable said I was to ask you to deal with it. He said, it needed your tact and diplomacy . . .'

Angel pulled a face like tripe on a plate. 'Yes, Sergeant. What is it? Don't wrap it up. Spit it out, lad.'

'Yes, sir. Well, there's been a call from Mrs Councillor Regan about sixty-one Huddersfield Road, near Fairclough's veterinary practice. She lives close by. It was a woman's fashion shop, but has been empty more than a year, I reckon.'

Angel's hand clenched the phone tightly. '*What about it?*' he said.

'Oh, she says that there is an unbearable sickly sweet smell coming from the building,' Clifton said.

Angel's eyes went up and then down. He knew about sickly sweet smells. His heart began to pound. He stood up and reached for his coat.

17

Six minutes later he was steering the BMW along Huddersfield Road towards the empty shop a few doors from Fairclough's veterinary practice where he had arranged to meet Flora Carter.

Angel understood from Sergeant Clifton that the shop was about six doors down from Fairclough's veterinary surgery. He saw the sign and slowed the car down.

Number 61 had been a smart shop with imitation marble frontage and two display windows now covered with sheets of white paper.

Angel stopped the car and got out.

His old friend, the sickly sweet smell began to pervade his nostrils.

He went up to the shop entrance. There was a big steel padlock locking the door. There was no indication that anybody was occupying the building, indeed it looked desolate. He banged loudly on the door and waited a few seconds. He gave the door another good thumping. There was still no response.

He stood back and looked up at the fascia of the two-storey stone building. He couldn't see any alarms, CCTV cameras or wiring.

He heard a car engine roar behind him. It was Flora Carter arriving in her Honda Civic. She stopped the car, got out, smiled then she also noticed the smell. She pulled a face and waved a hand in front of her nose.

Angel went up to her. 'I don't think there's anybody in there. I'm going to have to break in,' he said. He opened his car boot, took out a crowbar and used that to lever the hasp off the door jamb.

When he opened the door, the smell was stronger than ever. They looked round the shop but there was nothing there. It was completely empty. It was just one empty room with a door leading to stairs.

There was still no sign of the source of the overbearing odour.

They went up the stairs together. At the top was a door. He tried the handle. It was locked. He put his weight against it and burst it open at the second attempt. A cat zipped out of the room and down the stairs.

The smell in the room was more powerful, the fumes overwhelming.

He quickly pushed the door open all the way back. It banged on the wall behind.

'Protect your eyes, Flora,' he said, and he half closed his own eyes and shielded them with his hands. He needed to open a window. He could hardly see his way across the room the fumes were so strong, but he could see the daylight. He arrived at the window. It was the old-fashioned type. The fastener thankfully was broken off. He opened it and stuck his head outside for a second then looked round the tiny room.

The walls were lined with glass showcases. Flora put her hand to her mouth when she saw that one of them contained bones and skulls. In the other showcase was a collection of stuffed animals. There was an otter, a rat and a cat.

She pulled a face and said, 'What sort of a person is interested in stuffing dead animals?'

'Taxidermy, Flora,' he said. 'You'd be surprised. It's a hobby to some people.'

'Yes, sir. Taxidermy. Couldn't think of the word.'

'What an awful smell. I couldn't work in this all day. Yet all kinds of people are mad keen on this sort of thing . . . doctors, medical students, people interested in animal welfare, all sorts of people.'

'Do you know whose place this is, sir?'

He pursed his lips. 'I expect it's somebody we know.'

Flora shook her head, then said, 'Whoever it is, I expect that sickly perfume is used to cover the dreadful smell the animal's skins give off.'

There was a ten-gallon copper tank on the floor filled with a white crystalline powder. Angel leaned over it and discovered that it produced another ghastly smell. Next to it was a brown paper sack with the one-word label 'Saltpetre' stuck on it.

Angel's eyebrows went up then he nodded knowingly.

'We may have found our saltpetre thief, Flora.'

'And there's a big bottle of iodine up here, sir,' she said looking up at a high shelf with an array of bottles. 'It fits the description.'

At the back of his memory, Angel knew that iodine combined with salt (then called iodized salt) was used for curing skins and body parts in taxidermy. He learned that at school. He could have kicked himself.

Below the shelf, on the floor, were the remains of a smashed brown-glass bottle, but the area around it showed no stain or trace of the contents.

Flora pointed to the broken glass. 'What do you suppose was in that, sir?'

'That might have been the source of the stink. If it was alcohol based, it would have evaporated, wouldn't it?'

She nodded.

Angel noticed that there was an empty saucer and a half-bottle of milk on the floor next to the smashed bottle. He looked back up at the shelf and then said, 'I think that cat must have knocked that bottle down.'

He straightened up, took another quick look round the room and said, 'Look Flora, you finish off here. Find the person who is using this place. Ask him or her about the saltpetre and the iodine. You might find some traces of that bottle of ethanol also. It could have been used in that perfume concoction, I suppose. Get SOCO to see if they all or any came from St Magdalene's. And be very careful, do you hear? If the person whose place this is turns up, you might not be entirely welcome.'

She looked at him carefully.

'I have reasons to think we could be dealing with the murderer,' he said.

'Why do you say that, sir?'

'Do you remember when I said that I could smell a rich, sickly sweet smell at Wendy Green's house the day she was found murdered?'

'Yes, sir.'

'Well, I also came across the same smell at Ephemore Sharpe's house, and then again at St Magdalene's Hospital. These last few days, that smell has haunted me. I can't explain it yet but I believe that it is the smell of the murderer. Wherever the smell was, there was also some crime. Well, *that* smell was the same smell as this and it looks as if it was originated here.'

Flora straightened up and stared at him. She could feel her heart beating a tattoo. She knew she must keep on her toes.

'Right, sir,' she said.

'Leave it with you then, Flora. Keep in touch.'

Angel went out of the room, and out of the building, glad to be away from the stink of the place, and elated at the early possibility of being able to put his finger on the murderer. He climbed into the BMW as his mobile rang out. It was Crisp.

'Now, lad. What do you want?' he said.

'I've met Candy, sir.'

'Isn't she a picture?' Angel said beaming. 'I wasn't exaggerating, was I? What progress have you made?'

'I'm taking her out tonight.'

Angel's head went up. 'Tonight's no good, lad. I expect access to the computer will close when she leaves at the end of the day. Why not *now*?'

Crisp blinked. '*Now*? She never leaves the desk, sir.'

'What, *never*?'

'No. And I can't hang about her all the time. Visitors and patients look at me funny, and Dr Rubenstein pops out of his office now and again. He's already given me a strange look.'

Angel rubbed his chin. 'You haven't told her you're a copper, have you?'

'Of course not,' he replied indignantly.

'Good. What you need there is a diversion. Does she have a car?'

'She was saying that she'd just got a brand-new Volkswagen Polo.'

'Has she come to work in it?'

'I think so, sir. I don't know for certain.'

'We'll soon find out. Where are you speaking from?'

'I'm in my car in the car park.'

'Well stay in your car but park so that you can see the hospital entrance, because in about twenty minutes, Miss Candy Costello is going to come running out. And that's your cue to go running in. Access to that computer should be easy. You'll have about four minutes, which should be ample. I want the full list of patients in the hospital at the moment, plus their medical records. All right?'

'I'll do my best, sir.'

Angel cleared the line and then tapped in another number. It was DC Scrivens.

'Yes, sir?'

'Go to the armoury, Ted, see the duty sergeant and ask him for a six-minute white smoke bomb for me. Tell him I'll call in and sign for it later. Then bring it to St Magdalene's Hospital ASAP. I'll be waiting for you in the car park.'

'Right, sir.'

Angel closed the mobile, dropped it in his pocket and drove straight to St Magdalene's Hospital. He spotted Crisp in his car in the front row of the parked cars strategically placed facing the hospital doors.

Angel busied himself scouring the hospital car park for all the recently registered Volkswagen Polos. There were only two newish ones. He noted their registration numbers, phoned them through on the special police line to Swansea and eventually found which one was registered to Candy Costello. Then he waited by her car and looked round for Ted Scrivens who should be arriving with the smoke bomb any second.

Right on cue, his car came through the gates and Angel gave him a wave. Scrivens drove his car up to Angel and parked it.

'Everything all right, lad?' Angel said. 'Have you got the bomb?'

'Yes, sir,' Scrivens said handing him a small box. 'What's it for?'

'I'll tell you later. When I say 'when', I want you to rush through that door up to the reception desk where you will see the most beautiful girl in the world. Tell her that there's a car on fire on the car park. Tell her it's a new Volkswagen Polo and that you don't know what to do about it. Got it?'

'Yes, sir.'

'Then you can go back to the station.'

Scrivens frowned. 'You're not really going to set fire to it, are you, sir?'

Angel clenched his fists. '*No*! Now do you know what to say?'

'Yes, sir.'

'Make it sound urgent and desperate, lad. Imagine it was your own car. And make sure you say it to the pretty girl at the reception desk. Her name is Candy Costello. She's got a name badge on. Understood?'

'Yes, sir.'

'Right. Off you go and *run*. It will look good if you're puffed.'

Scrivens rushed off.

Angel took out his mobile and tapped in Crisp's number.

'Yes, sir?' he said.

'Stand by. Candy is going to come running out in less than a minute.'

'Right, sir.'

Angel closed the phone, moistened his little finger to see which way the wind was blowing, moved to the other side of the little car, looked round to make sure he was not being observed, and then he threw the smoke bomb hard onto the ground close to the car. It made a slight crashing sound as the glass capsule shattered.

Angel then walked slowly away whistling 'The Flower Duet' from *Lakmé*.

White smoke billowed out all round the little car.

Seconds later, Candy Costello came rushing out of the hospital, as Crisp, carefully avoiding her, discreetly entered.

Candy rushed over to her car, her hands up to her face.

Angel turned and approached her.

'What's the matter, Miss?'

'That's . . . that's my car!'

'What's happened to it?' he said.

'I don't know. It's new. I've only had it a month. What shall I do? Oh dear.'

'What have you done?' he said. 'Is it on fire or what?'

'It's on fire,' she said.

He pulled out his mobile and said, 'Do you want me to call the Fire Brigade?'

'Oh yes, *please*.'

A small crowd of people was gathering, watching the white smoke billowing round the car and then drifting away in the gentle breeze.

Angel tapped in 999, then pressed the 'cancel' button instead of the 'send', and spoke into the mouthpiece. 'Yes. Fire please . . . the car park at St Magdalene's Hospital, Rustle Spring Lane, Bromersley . . . car on fire . . . I'm phoning on behalf of a young lady, it's her car . . . yes, I'll tell her. Thank you.' He closed the phone, put it in his pocket, turned to Candy Costello and said, 'The Fire Brigade is on its way. The fire officer said it won't take five minutes to get here, and he said to ask you to stay near your vehicle until they arrive?'

'Thank you,' she said. 'You're very kind.' Then she gave him a wan smile that would even have melted the heart of Alan Sugar.

* * *

As Angel was walking down the station corridor to his office, he could hear his phone ringing. He dashed into the office and picked it up.

It was Dr Mac.

'I'm worried about this wild animal case of yours, Michael.'

Angel blinked several times. 'You and me both,' he said. 'Have you got some fresh information, Mac, or are you just ringing me up to make me more miserable than I am already?'

'It occurred to me last night. My wife and I were watching a ghastly film about eating habits and there were a few close-up and distasteful shots of wee kiddies, you know, chewing gum. And that got me to thinking about the way animals eat, and, do you know, Michael, in the case you are working on, at no point did I see any animal saliva on or near to either of the victims — not a drop. Now there should have been *some*. So I got in touch with my opposite numbers in both Glasgow and Edinburgh and they agree that an amount from a teaspoonful to a ladleful, in, on or near the victim, would be the norm. I would expect to have seen small or tiny pools, enough to have been able to recover sufficient to check the DNA, and that would have shown the breed of the animal and possibly more. But there was none.'

'Mac,' Angel said. 'What are you saying? Where are you going with this lack of saliva tale?'

'It isn't a tale, laddie: it's a fact. There are no physiological reasons why there wasn't any. Mammals cannot masticate without saliva, and wild cats produce much greater amounts than humans. There should have been an indication and there was none. And we have *two* crime scenes — two instances — where this phenomenon is illustrated. There must be an explanation.'

'I am utterly confused, Mac. Are you saying that the victims were definitely *not* killed by a wild cat?'

'Of course not. I am saying that . . . I suppose I'm saying that . . . that it's a possibility.'

Angel shook his head. '*A possibility?* But what about the claw marks, the teeth marks, the paw prints in the mud? How were the bodies moved, because you said that they were both killed elsewhere and moved six or twelve hours later? And remember there were no human footprints in the mud anywhere near the bodies.'

'I don't know, Michael. I'm just a doctor. I tell you what I know are facts. It's up to you to interpret them. I know it's a difficult case, I know that the facts seem ridiculous, but that's — that's science.'

'Well, I have a partial theory about some of it, Mac. Ephemore Sharpe comes from a circus family. She could possibly walk on stilts, and stilts would not leave a permanent indent of the floor of the stream. The movement of the water would soon level off any depression that might be made, wouldn't it?'

'Brilliant!' Mac said. 'Sounds great, Michael. I see you haven't lost any of your unique skill as the master detective.'

Angel beamed but was immediately suspicious. Mac was a good friend, but he never ever handed out compliments. There was a catch somewhere.

'Tell me,' Mac said. 'This suspect of yours, Ephemore Sharpe, is she strong enough, while balancing on stilts to walk up the stream carrying the first victim, Julius Hobbs? He was a big man, you know. Twelve stone, ten pounds. She must be young and very strong.'

Angel pulled a face. There it was. Mac had set a trap and he had walked right into it.

'All right, Mac,' he said. 'You win. Ephemore Sharpe is in her seventies and I suppose she couldn't possibly have lifted him.'

He could almost hear Mac grinning.

'But I'm not finished yet,' Angel said. 'I'll find out how she did it before I have done. You know, Mac, this is one of the most annoying and mystifying cases I have ever worked on.'

'Aye. But I'm sure you'll solve it in the end, Michael.'

'Thank you, Mac,' he said. 'You've more faith in me than I have. Goodbye.'

He put the phone back and turned to the endless pile of letters and reports on his desk in front of him. But he couldn't concentrate on anything. His mind was in turmoil.

After an hour or so, there was a knock at the door.

It was Trevor Crisp. He was waving a sheet of printed A4. There was a glint in his eye as he passed it over to Angel and said, 'I think this must be the case you were looking for, sir. So I have printed it off.'

Angel's face brightened. 'Sit down, lad,' Angel said taking the sheet of paper from him. He glanced at the heading, then passed it back to him. 'Read the bits that matter.'

'Well sir,' Crisp began, 'It refers to a Maisie Evans, a widow of 11 Royston Mews, Bromersley, date of birth 23.4.1954. There is a lot of medical stuff and mumbo jumbo then — I think this is the important bit, sir — it says,

Transcript of consultation on 27 October 2010 under hypnosis.

Dr Rubenstein: Now, Maisie. You wanted to tell me about the time you got your broken ribs.

Maisie Evans: Oh yes, Doctor . . .

(Pause of ten seconds)

Dr Rubenstein: Well, Maisie?

Maisie Evans: Oh yes, Doctor . . . My husband, Charles and me was very happy on our own but he didn't get on with Philip. He's my son. I was married before, you

see. They was always bickering. It started when he started at Bromersley Comprehensive. You see he wasn't very good at school work. He said he couldn't do certain things like algebra and trigonometry and geography and things like that. My husband said that he must work harder, and that it looked like he took no notice of the teachers and didn't pay attention in class. Philip said that he wasn't made out for things like that. He was better with animals. He wanted a little dog, but Charles wouldn't let him have one. Well, I wouldn't have minded, but Charles said that he *would have finished up looking after it. Anyway, they was* always *rowing. It didn't improve with the years. It got so bad that when Philip left school, he straightaway got a job labouring for the council at Jubilee Park and he left home. He took a little flat over a pub near the park. Then on 19 October 2007, it was a Friday, he visited me one afternoon, Philip, when he should have been at work. He was in his overalls. I was surprised to see him. He said that he'd heard that his dad had been having it off with that girl from the fish shop. That his dad had finished early from work that day and called in at the Fisherman's Rest and then gone on to the Market Hotel. Well, I didn't believe it. But he'd been with her before and I thought it was all over. She was a real tart. Well, that made me furious, and when he came home I faced him with it. He stank of beer. And I could tell by his face that it was true. Well, we had a right set to. The worst we ever had. Anyway, in the middle of all this, Philip came back. When his dad saw him, he blamed him for everything and flew at him and began to belt him in the face with his closed fist. It was terrible. I pleaded with him to stop and I got two cracked ribs for my trouble. Then Philip pulled out a dibber from a long pocket down his overall leg and began trying to defend himself with it. They was in the kitchen at the top of the cellar steps. I was crying and holding my chest. It was hurting and I couldn't stop coughing. And every time I coughed it hurt all the more. And in between I was . . . I was shouting at them to stop it, but, of course, they didn't* take any notice. They were still going at it hammer and tongs. Philip waved that dibber around and caught Charles a right crack at the side of the head. Charles staggered backwards at the top of the cellar steps. Next thing I know, I heard a shout from Charles and a lot of noise. It was Charles falling down the cellar steps. Then it was quiet. Too quiet. We waited a bit then Philip went down.

Maisie Evans cries for 1 min 20 secs.

Dr Rubenstein: Do you want any more tissues, Maisie?

Maisie Evans: Mmmm . . .

Dr Rubenstein: You were saying that it was quiet down the cellar and that Philip went down to investigate.

Maisie Evans: Yes. I wondered what had happened. I shouted down to him. He didn't say anything. I went down to have a look for myself like. Charles had his head on the bottom step and his body on the cellar floor and he wasn't moving at all. It was awful.

(Pause of ten seconds)

Dr Rubenstein: What happened then, Maisie?

Maisie Evans: I sent Philip off. There was no point in involving him. I didn't want to lose him as well as Charles. He didn't want to go, but I persuaded him. Then I straightened the place up and dialled 999 for an ambulance. The ambulance man looked at Charles and said he was dead and sent for the police. Two men came. One of them took a statement from me. I said that he came in drunk, we had a row, he punched me in the chest, then went to the cellar top looking for a half-bottle of whisky he said he had put there. Then he staggered, lost his footing and fell the full length all the way down. They wrote it all down then sent for a van from the mortuary and took him away. It was dreadful. Then they took me to hospital. They later sent me a report — I have it somewhere at home — where the coroner's conclusions are that he died accidentally while under the influence of alcohol. I knew that wasn't right, but I couldn't let poor Philip be charged with murder, could I, Doctor?

Suddenly Angel said, 'Trevor, stop there.' He had been listening intently. He was looking down towards the floor and he didn't look up. He was deeply disturbed.

'There isn't much more, sir,' Crisp said.

'No, lad. That's quite enough.'

Angel reached out for the phone and dialled the mortuary at Bromersley General Hospital. 'Hello, Mac, this is Michael Angel. Would you kindly look up the PM report on a Charles Evans of 11 Royston Mews, who died on 19 October 2007?'

'Now what are you up to?' Dr Mac said.

'Will you have a read and let me know if you find anything interesting?'

'All right, but I can't do it just now, Michael. I'll ring you back in an hour or so. But even if I was the one who did the PM, it's three years ago, I doubt if I will remember anything about it.'

'Thanks, Mac,' he said and replaced the phone. He turned back to Crisp, leaned forward, lifted out of his hands the paper with Maisie Evans's statement on it, pushed his chair back and fed it into the shredder suspended over the wastepaper basket in the knee hole of the desk.

Crisp stared at him open mouthed.

Before he had chance to say anything, Angel said, 'Clear that memory stick, lad, then re-format it. I don't want any record of this interview keeping, and I want you to forget all that you know about it.'

Crisp frowned. 'All right, sir, but why?' he said.

'It was confidential information between patient and doctor.'

'But *you've* heard it, sir.'

'Yes. Well, like you, I hope, I am now going to forget it. I have made a big mistake.'

'Oh,' he said, 'It's not *that* much of a mistake, sir.'

'Oh, it is, lad. You'll see.'

18

Angel drove the car into the garage and was locking it up when he heard the church clock strike six.

'Hello, love,' Mary called, as he came into the house and closed the back door. 'Everything all right?'

It wasn't. Far from it. But he said, 'Yes,' and gave her a kiss on the cheek.

He took off his coat and took it into the hall. Then he noticed the door to the area under the stairs was ajar and that the safe had gone. Then he remembered, Mary had phoned him . . . something about a car breaker at Barnsley Common who could open it with an acetylene torch. 'The safe's gone then?' he said.

Mary's eyes twinkled and she had a smile from ear to ear. 'Isn't it exciting?' she said. 'I phoned them up and spoke to a really nice man, Mr Jordan, and told him of our predicament.'

'We haven't got a predicament.'

'Well, you know what I mean.'

'Is he the owner of the business?'

'I don't know. I suppose so. Let me tell you.'

'Can he open it and what will it cost?'

'Mr Jordan said that he would send his team round straightaway and collect it, and they were here in twenty minutes. His team was his three sons. They're lovely —'

'What will it cost?'

'Well, he . . . he didn't know.'

Angel's jaw muscles tightened. 'He didn't *know*?' he said. 'I said get a quote.'

'Yes, er . . . He said that he usually had twenty-five per cent of the value of the contents.'

Angel's face went red. 'Those are crook's rates!' he said. 'That's the language of villains. You've got us mixed up with a gang of crooks!'

'I said no,' Mary said. 'I said ten per cent and he agreed.'

'Ten per cent?'

Her face hardened. So did her voice. 'Look, Michael,' she said, 'I thought that if I didn't do something, we'd never get that safe out from under the stairs and opened up. You're too busy with your work. Now I know you've got a difficult case on . . .'

His face was like thunder. 'We don't know what's in there, Mary. Could be worth thousands.'

'He says he'll start cutting tomorrow morning. It could take all day, or a day and a half, and I can go up there and stay with him until he's actually inside it, if I want to. You could get off work for an hour and join me, couldn't you? It's very important that you should be there, Michael. And if there is a really big diamond, I want it made into a nice ring for me.'

'If there's a really big diamond in there, we'll have to sell it to pay for transporting that safe up and down the country. What is he charging us for taking it to his place?'

'Nothing. That comes out of his ten per cent,' Mary said nonchalantly. Then she turned away and headed for the kitchen.

Angel shook his head in incredulity. Then he sighed. He'd had enough. There's only so much he could take in a day.

Mary opened the oven door. 'Tea's about ready,' she called.

Angel shrugged and went into the sitting room to look for the *Radio Times*.

* * *

After Angel had finished his coffee, he went out into the hall and came back into the sitting room in his overcoat and hat.

'I'm going out for a walk,' he said.

Mary looked up at him in amazement. 'Where to?' she said.

'Nowhere. Just a walk. Blow some cobwebs off.'

'Where are you going to?'

'Nowhere in particular. I just want to think something out.'

'Is it the safe? You are not worrying about the safe, are you?'

'No. No, it's not that. Anyway you seem to have taken that out of my hands. I'm leaving it up to you.'

'What is it then?'

He hesitated, touched his chin and then said, 'I know how those two murders were committed. But I have to work something out. I can do it best where it's quiet and I'm on own.'

Her face brightened. She knew what it meant to him.

'Oh, that's fabulous, darling. But you don't have to go out, Michael. You can go in the bedroom or . . . or the kitchen or . . .'

'No. No. The phone might go. Or you'll suddenly want to ask me an urgent question.'

She looked up at him and frowned. 'What sort of an urgent question would I want to ask you?' she said.

'Well, I don't know . . . whether I want peas or beans with the chops tomorrow, or something like that.'

She lifted her head and stuck out her chest. '*That's* not an urgent question,' she said.

'Well, you might have thought it was, love,' he said. 'Anyway, don't worry about it. I'm off. You'll be all right, won't you? Don't wait up.'

Her mouth dropped open. '*Don't wait up*?' she said. 'Why? How long are you going to be?'

The back door slammed.

* * *

It was 8.28 a.m. on Tuesday, 2 November, when Angel arrived at his office. He wasn't likely to forget that day: it was the day he arrested one of the cleverest murderers that he had had the misfortune to meet.

He threw off his coat, picked up the phone and tapped in a number.

'Yes, sir,' Ahmed said.

'Nip down to Don Taylor's office, lad. He's got a pot lion figure that belongs to Ephemore Sharpe. Ask him to give it to you and bring it up to my office. And *don't drop it*,' he said, and replaced the phone.

He stood up and went over to the window. He twisted the plastic control knob to angle the blinds to 90 degrees and then pushed up one of the slats and looked through. All he could see was a section of the grey stone wall of the building next door, which he knew was the offices of the local branch of the Weavers, Menders and Shoddy Workers Trades Union, the WMSWTU. He wrinkled his nose, withdrew his hand and turned away. It wasn't much of an outlook: it wasn't much of an office. He sat down in the swivel chair and tried to relax.

Ahmed arrived. He was carrying a plastic shopping bag.

'There you are, sir,' he said, carefully placing the bag on the desk. 'One pot lion. And I didn't drop it once.'

'Thank you. Now at four o'clock this afternoon, I am going out to Ashfield Lodge Farm, with DC Scrivens and some uniformed. Later on, we'll be bringing in Miss Ephemore Sharpe.'

Ahmed's eyes glowed like headlamps. 'You've solved the wild cat murders, sir? You've got the evidence? That's terrific news, sir.'

'Have you still got that blue and white teapot, and four-cup set that was nicked by the chief constable's secretary?'

'Oh yes, sir. It's on a tray in the CID cupboard.'

'Well get it out, lad. I'll be asking you to make us some tea in it when we get back.'

'Right, sir,' Ahmed said. 'I'll get it out now.'

He made for the door.

'Just a minute, lad. I've got another little job for you.'

Ahmed turned back. 'Yes, sir?'

Angel pulled out a small wad of notes, peeled off a dirty orange tenner and held it out for him. 'You know that little fishing shop on William's Walk,' he said.

Ahmed's mouth dropped open. 'Yes, sir,' he said, taking the note.

'Go there and get me a small, lightweight, collapsible fishing stool. They're only about eight pounds.'

Ahmed frowned. 'What's it for?'

'It's for fishing.'

The phone rang.

'Get off and fetch it now,' Angel said as he reached out to the handset. 'I won't need you until later on.'

Ahmed went out.

It was Flora Carter on her mobile.

'I'm still on Huddersfield Road at the taxidermist's place, sir,' she said. 'Don Taylor can confirm that the saltpetre, the ethanol and the iodine are all from St Magdalene's Hospital.'

'Good,' Angel said.

'Yes, sir. But I have still not been able to find out whose place this is.'

Angel had already worked out who the amateur taxidermist must be, but it was necessary to have documented evidence for the court.

'None of the other shopkeepers on the block has ever seen anybody arrive or leave,' she said. 'The Council Tax office thought the premises were unoccupied. Up to now, I seem to have drawn a blank.'

'Well, keep at it, Flora.'

'SOCO's fingerprint man is here lifting prints from those glass bottles, glass tanks and so on. There is plenty to go at. We might get a useful print that we can identify.'

'When you get the ID, seal that place up and come back here.'

'Right, sir.'

He cancelled the call and replaced the phone. He rubbed his chin, then reached out for the phone again. He tapped in his home number.

'I am glad you rang, darling,' Mary said. 'I was about to ring you. I've just had a phone call from Mr Jordan.'

Angel winced like a bald judge with a scratchy wig on a hot day. Very slowly he said, 'And who is Mr Jordan?'

At the same tempo Mary said, '*The man who is going to open the safe*. I told you all about him yesterday.'

'Oh yes. What about him?'

'He's run out of oxygen or something, so he won't be able to start cutting until he gets a delivery tomorrow. So there's no need to leave work early.'

Angel's eyebrows shot up. 'Well, that's what I'm ringing *you* about. I won't be in for tea, anyway. I'll be late home. Much later. Could be eleven o'clock or so.'

Mary wasn't pleased. 'Why?' she said. 'What's happening?'

'Just extra work with all this case.'

'Whatever is it that you can't leave until tomorrow?'

'Just things. Work. All to do with this case.'

'I'll just have to put a casserole on. I was going to leave that until Thursday . . . if I can thaw the steak out all right . . .'

'Whatever you like, love. Goodbye.'

He replaced the phone.

He sighed, then pulled the pile of post, papers, reports and the two most recent issues of *Police Reviews* towards him.

* * *

The sky began to get dark. Angel switched on the desk lamp. He was still at his desk.

The church clock began to chime.

There was a knock at the door.

'Come in,' Angel called.

It was DC Ted Scrivens. 'It's four o'clock, sir. The patrol car escort is ready waiting at the front. Are we going in your car?'

'Yes, lad,' he said and reached out for his coat.

* * *

It was 5.20 p.m. exactly when a sullen Ephemore Sharpe, in a grey tartan shawl and a long black skirt, escorted by Angel and DC Scrivens, one each side, followed by Patrolmen Donohue and Elders, trundled down the corridor of Bromersley station into interview room no 1.

Ahmed, and about twenty other police personnel peered from office doorways in shocked horror as the glowering woman passed them.

As the interview room door closed, Ahmed rushed off to make the tea.

After a couple of minutes, Angel came back out, went two doors down the corridor to his own office, sat down at his desk, picked up the phone and, referring to a handwritten number on a piece of card, carefully tapped out a mobile number on the keypad.

It was soon answered. 'Hello. Philip Pryce, who is that?'

'Ah yes, good evening, Mr Pryce. This is Michael Angel, I'm an inspector with Bromersley Police. We *have* met. You might remember me. I am sorry to bother you, but I am phoning on behalf of Miss Ephemore Sharpe.'

'Of course I remember you, Inspector,' he said. 'Good evening to you, sir. And what's the matter with Miss Sharpe? Why can't she phone herself?'

Angel rubbed his chin. 'She says she wants you to feed the cats. She says you know what they have and where the food is and so on.'

Pryce hesitated. 'Does she mean just today, or what?' he said.

'Oh, she means for the time being, until she can make more permanent arrangements.'

'Well yes, I suppose so, but why couldn't she have asked me herself? Have you arrested her or something?'

Angel never normally spoke about internal police matters particularly before they had actually been carried out. 'Miss Sharpe is here with me at Bromersley Police Station now,' he said. 'She has been arrested and will be formally charged later.'

'Oh dear. Goodness me. What on earth has she done?'

Angel had to think quickly. 'It's to do with some people being attacked and killed by an animal,' he said.

He thought that he had given him sufficient information. Then he added quickly, 'She said to tell you that she'll see that you are paid, of course. Can I tell her that you will see to it for her?'

'Yes, of course, Inspector,' Pryce said.

'Right. Thank you. Goodbye.'

He replaced the phone. He trapped his bottom lip lightly between his teeth and made small chewing movements as he thought about what still had to be done that day. Firstly, he must return to the interview room to settle all the arrangements for the immediate care and security of Ephemore Sharpe, then prepare himself for the other matter that urgently needed his attention.

He stood up.

19

The sky was as black as fingerprint ink.

It was eight o'clock that Tuesday night when Angel left his office and ventured out into the cold air. He jumped into the BMW and drove it through the town, then halfway down Beechfield Road, where he stopped and parked. He picked up a torch from the dash and opened the car boot, took out a flat plastic shopping bag, closed the boot and walked quietly through a ginnel to the street parallel to it, which was Ashfield Road, where he turned left.

He was approaching Ephemore Sharpe's farm.

A courting couple, with their arms round each other's waists, twisted, turned and giggled as they advanced taking a zigzag course towards him and then passed him by. A man walking a small white dog at the other side of the street suddenly took a turn to his left and disappeared down a pitch-black ginnel.

The street was deserted when Angel reached the farm gate. He opened it silently and went into the cobbled yard. Several cats running across the yard in different directions stopped dead, looked at him briefly, then ran off even faster.

He made for the garden which was at the rear of the house and opened the wicket gate in the wall. The hinges squealed louder than a cat on heat, which made Angel's heart leap. He froze, looked round, waited a few seconds to be certain he had not disturbed anybody then continued through it. It made the same noise in reverse on closing but there was nothing he could do about it. He carried on along the path adjacent to the side of the house, and past the tool shed onto the lawn and up to the uncultivated part of the garden where there were trees and bushes. He opened the plastic bag and took out a fishing stool, opened it up, pushed his way into the foliage, selected a spot where he thought he could observe without being seen, placed the stool safely and squarely on the grass, and took up his position.

He could see the back door of the house and most of the garden. He was out of the cool breeze, but there was no warmth in conifer branches. He hoped that he would not have to wait very long. He dug his hands deeply into his overcoat pockets. His hand felt the torch and a glove beyond. He pulled up the collar of his overcoat, put on his gloves and waited. And waited. And waited.

It was two hours later at about ten o'clock when Angel suddenly heard the squeal of the wicket gate being opened. He listened to hear it close, which it did. There was somebody else in the garden with him!

He sucked in a lungful of ice-cold air. His heart banged like the big drum at a Salvation Army Christmas service.

He became aware of a figure walking along the path to the tool shed.

Angel held his breath.

He could just see him in silhouette. It looked like a man. He was carrying a bag of some sort. He dropped the bag on the lawn. It made a rattling sound. He opened the shed, then flashed a torch and came out with a wheelbarrow and a spade. He switched off the torch and proceeded to shovel the top surface of a long section of the soil of the border nearest the window into the wheelbarrow. After several minutes, he stabbed the spade in the ground and began to open the bag.

Angel had seen enough. He stood up, aimed the torch at the man and switched it on.

The man visibly shook with surprise and fear.

'Frigging hell! Who is it?'

'It's Michael Angel, Philip,' he said walking down the garden towards him. 'What are you doing?'

Pryce gasped then quietly said, 'Erm . . . Just a bit of weeding. I might as well keep up with my work.'

'Funny time to be weeding. How can you tell what's a weed and what's a plant?'

'I can tell.'

'What's in the bag?'

'What bag? I haven't a bag.'

Angel pointed down to the bag on the lawn. 'That one.'

'Oh, that? I don't know. It's nothing to do with me.'

Angel sighed. 'You can't get away from it, Philip. I saw you arrive with it, and it will have your fingerprints on it. What's inside?'

Pryce stayed his ground, pulled a long-handled dibber out of a pocket down his boiler-suit leg and raised it above his head.

Angel said, 'Are you going to tell me, or do I have to look for myself?'

'Stay where you are, Angel. If you take one step nearer, I'll bray you with this. I have told you that bag has nothing to do with me.'

'It's no good, Philip. The game's up. I know you murdered your stepfather — with that dibber you are holding in your hand.'

Even in the dark, Angel could see the whites of Pryce's eyes. It made him look like some figure from a Hammer Horror film.

'He fell down the cellar steps,' Pryce said.

'After you hit him with that thing in your hand.'

'Who told you?'

'It wasn't difficult to work out.'

'Has my mother been talking to you?'

'No. It was in your stepfather's post-mortem.'

'But the coroner said that his death was the result of injuries caused by him hitting his head on the cellar steps.'

'That was one interpretation. And then you murdered your old school chums in the identical same way.'

'It's a lie.'

'And I think I know why. I have had a long talk with Miss Sharpe.'

'What! That old frigging bitch. You won't get the truth out of that old cow. She's never told the truth in her life. And she wouldn't say anything good about me. Besides it was her that murdered them, not me. It's just like her, trying to blame somebody else . . .'

'Why? Why would she do that?'

'She's batty, that's why. She needs her frigging head seeing to. She was my form mistress you know. She said that I had no brains. She said I was stupid. She was rotten to me. It didn't matter how hard I tried, how long I spent on my homework, she always gave me a low mark. So that at the end of term, Julian Hobbs, Wendy Woods, Scrap Scolding and that crowd would be at the top of the form and I would be at the bottom. It wasn't frigging fair. Not sometimes either, but *always*. Every term, every year. It was her plan, you see. She didn't like me and *she* was the senior mistress. She made my school life an absolute misery, and I couldn't do anything about it. I left as soon as I could. *They* went on to university. *They* got letters behind their names. If I had taken my GCE I wouldn't even have passed it. According to her I wouldn't amount to anything, but she was wrong, you see. I run my own business. I am self-employed. I am a qualified gardener. I have twelve regular customers, and I have a contract with the council. I earn thousands of pounds . . . more money than she ever earned being a bloody teacher.'

'Well, you'd need a fortune to pay to keep your sick mother in that expensive hospital, wouldn't you?'

'Who's been opening their mouths? I'll shut them for good if I find out who they are.'

'There aren't *that* many people called Maisie Evans in the world, Philip, whose next of kin is Philip Pryce. It wasn't that difficult to work out. What's in the bag?'

'You keep on about that bag. I found it. It's true that I was going to bury the stuff here, because it's hers, Miss Sharpe's.'

'And you were going to bury it here. Why here? There's fields and woods where you could have buried it. You could even have thrown it in the canal.'

'It's as good a place as any.'

'And you were going to bury it so badly, that when we searched the place again, which you thought we would now be certain to do because you thought that we had arrested her and charged her, that we would find it and think the contents were hers.'

'They *are* hers. I found them in her barn earlier this evening, when I was feeding her cats. And she is the murderer. I thought that's why you arrested her. That's why I'm feeding her bloody cats, isn't it?'

'No, Philip. I had Miss Sharpe brought to the station and made sure that you thought we had charged her with the murders expressly to flush you out.'

'Rubbish. That's friggin' rubbish.'

'It's no good, Philip. You can't make it stick,' Angel said.

Then he decided to take a gamble. The laboratory at Wetherby had the DNA from the semen found on her, but at the time, Angel knew that a match had not yet been found.

He said, 'We have forensic evidence that proves you had intercourse with Wendy Green, around the time she died. Did you rape her?'

'Huh,' Pryce said, then he sniggered. 'Nobody had to rape Wendy Woods. So what? Even if I did have sex with her, it doesn't mean to say that I had anything to do with her murder.'

'Yes, it does. And that, coupled with the contents of that bag you now have no use for, will send you to Wakefield for life.'

'Oh no, it won't, Angel,' Pryce said, and he lifted the dibber high above his head, and brought it down intending to hit Angel with the handle end on his head. Angel dodged away but the blow caught him on the arm. There were more attempts to hit him with the tool.

Pryce was intent on murdering him. He had nothing to lose and everything to gain.

Angel stood facing him, feet astride, hands at the ready, as Pryce rained down further blows. Angel managed to dodge each subsequent one, and eventually managed to grab the handle of the dibber with both hands and with successive pulling and pushing movements eventually pushed the surprised Pryce backwards over the wheelbarrow.

Pryce had to release his grip on the dibber in an effort to save himself. Angel snatched it away and pitched it over the garden wall onto the cobblestones where it landed with a clatter. Then he leaped on Pryce and brought him down on the lawn. Pryce reached up to Angel's throat and squeezed and tightened his grip thus cutting off his breath. The gardener had a grip of iron. He rolled over putting Angel on his back. Angel struggled to breathe and reached up to Pryce's hands in an attempt to pull them away. But it was useless. Angel's memory of elementary anatomy came to mind. He knew the approximate position of the jugular vein in the neck, and the vagus nerve just behind it. A hard enough blow on the right spot would incapacitate Pryce if not kill him. This was a desperate time. He was running out of air. He kept thumping and thumping at it. At the tenth blow, Pryce suddenly relaxed his grip and slumped over him. Angel stayed there a while, exhausted, his lungs pumping vigorously. After a few seconds, he wriggled from under him, got to his feet, rubbed his throat and looked down at the man.

Pryce was motionless.

Angel leaned down, put his fingertips to his neck, found a pulse, sighed with relief, pulled Pryce's arms out and up his back and handcuffed him. Then he stepped back, brushed his hair out of his eyes and reached into his pocket for his mobile.

* * *

Philip Pryce was duly arrested at 22.30, Ephemore Sharpe was taken home by police car at 22.35, and Angel was in bed by 2 o'clock the following morning.

It was a short night. He awoke at the usual time, made some phone calls to the office at 8.30 that morning, and actually arrived at the station at 10.30.

Everybody Angel passed on his way up the corridor smiled, those he knew well congratulated him.

He was followed in by Don Taylor carrying the bag Pryce was so secretive about. He quickly made for the SOCO office.

Ahmed came in with a tray of tea using the blue and white china tea set. 'Congratulations, sir. I knew we could do it.'

Angel smiled. 'Thank you, lad.'

About an hour later, there was a knock at the door.

Angel looked up from his desk. 'Come in,' he said.

It was Don Taylor. He wasn't smiling. 'I've had a look at the stuff in Pryce's bag, sir,' he said. 'His prints are all over them.'

'That's good,' Angel said and pointed to a chair.

Taylor sat down.

'There are three items,' he said. 'Most ingenious and horrific: pair of rubber moulds of a cougar's paws glued on to strong elastic garters that fitted over his shoes so that wherever he trod, particularly on mud, the only marks he made were from the moulds. That explains why there were never any human prints for us to find.'

'I knew it had to be something like that.'

'There is a contraption comprising four pieces of horn, shaped and sharpened to the exact shape and size of a cougar's claws, and set in a rubber mould. He used that to reproduce claw marks.'

Angel nodded.

'And there's a thing made entirely of steel that represents the full set of teeth of a fully grown cougar. The upper set and lower set were hinged at the back and fitted with handles like pliers so that the jaws could be opened, set round the flesh, the handle squeezed to replicate the bite, and then pulled.'

Angel said. 'They'll lock Pryce up as a nutcase.'

'You must come and look, sir.'

'I will. Later.'

'Where did he get all this information from, sir? The size of the jaw, the position of the incisors, the spread of the claws in the paw . . . everything so precise.'

'He'd pick all that up through his interest in taxidermy.'

'Oh. He was the man who had that place on Huddersfield Road then?'

Angel nodded and said, 'His prints will prove it.'

'So there was no wild cat, sir,' Taylor said. 'No cougar.'

'That's right. But Pryce knew Ephemore Sharpe's family's interest in them from the posters in her house and so on. He tried every trick in the book to pass the blame for the murders of Julius Hobbs and Wendy Green on to her.'

'He was most ingenious,' Taylor said.

'Before you go, Don, did you come across any scent spray or similar among his belongings?'

'I was coming to that, sir. In a pocket of his boiler suit, he had a small aerosol contrived from an air freshener can, filled with cheap commercial scent usually used diluted to sweeten the air in cinemas and theatres. The taxidermy business is a very smelly business. I suppose if ever he thought he or his clothes ponged a bit, he might surreptitiously pull out the little can and press the button.'

Angel nodded. He pursed his lips. That was exactly what happened, several times.

'Thank you, Don,' he said.

Taylor went out.

Ahmed came in. 'Finished with the tea, sir?' he said.

'Almost,' Angel said, picking up the cup.

'DS Crisp has just come in . . . I think he wants to see you, sir, privately.'

'Ask him to come in. He doesn't have to stand on ceremony.'

Ahmed picked up the tray, opened the door and called out, 'Come on in, Sarge, I'm just going.'

He went out and Trevor Crisp came in and closed the door.

'Ah,' Crisp said. 'Good morning, sir. You're on your own at last. I understand that Philip Pryce, the gardener, is the murderer, that he's in the cells, and that you have a watertight case that will put him away for life.'

'That's about right.'

'And that you fooled him into giving himself away.'

Angel nodded.

'That's great, sir. Fantastic. You always manage it in the end. I've seen you do it a hundred times, one way or another, but . . . well, sir . . .' Crisp ran out of words. He just sat there shaking his head and smiling.

'What is it, Trevor?'

'Is it true — I can hardly believe it — that you kept Ephemore Sharpe quietly sitting in the interview room drinking tea with two patrolmen for nigh on six hours?'

Angel nodded again. 'Yes.'

Crisp shook his head bewildered. 'For goodness' sake, how on earth did you manage to do that?'

Angel smiled. 'Wasn't that difficult,' he said. 'Yesterday afternoon I spoke to her on her own. And I said that I knew she had lied about Wendy Green stealing the pot lion, Pascha. I told her that you and I had followed her and seen her plant the ornament in the dead girl's garage. In fact, I took the ornament with me and showed it to her. Then I offered her a deal. I told her that I wanted her to come back with us in a police car and stay in the station for several hours while we flushed out Philip Pryce. Furthermore, I said that if she didn't do as I asked, I would tell Selwyn Plumm, the senior reporter on the *Chronicle* about the lie she had told about the dead woman, and the devious way she had attempted to prove it. I said that Plumm would publish the facts on the front page. Well, I got a torrent of abuse, a spiel about her family's good name, about the Sharpes giving public service to the town for over a hundred years, and so on, but when she simmered down, she agreed to it. And afterwards, I gave her back the pot lion. That's all there was to it.'

Crisp was agog with surprise and admiration. 'Where did the actual murders take place?'

'In a shed at the back of Pryce's house. I met Don Taylor there first thing this morning. We found the remains of Hobbs's coat there. Pryce had torn it up and was using pieces as cleaning cloths. And there was Wendy Green's purse with her credit cards and other stuff. It was pretty gruesome in there. He used his truck and his wheelbarrow to transport the bodies. It all checked out.'

A mobile phone rang. It was Angel's. He reached into his pocket for it.

It was Mary. 'Hello, darling,' she said.

'Just a minute, Mary, I've got Trevor Crisp with me. I think we've finished. Just want to see if he has anything else for me.'

Crisp said, 'No, sir. That's fine. I'm off . . . Give my compliments to Mrs Angel.'

'Now then, love?' he said. 'Anything wrong?'

'No, on the contrary. I'm at Jordan's Car Breakers, Barnsley Common. He's cutting open the safe. He should have it open in about half an hour. Can you come over?'

Angel winced. 'I don't know, Mary,' he said.

'Listen, Michael, Mr Jordan turned it over about an hour ago and something inside it made a noise. I heard it. Like a metallic clink. Come on. You can spare me an hour, can't you?'

Angel hesitated.

'Aren't you curious to find out what's inside,' she said.

He glanced down at the papers on the desk nearest to him, looked at his watch and said, 'Of course. Why not? I'm on my way,' he said. He stood up, closed the phone and put it in his pocket as he reached out for his coat.

The phone on his desk rang. He snatched it up. 'Angel.'

There was the usual heavy breathing, then the superintendent said, 'I see that you've got a suspect for those breaking and entering and stealing of chemicals from St Magdalene's Hospital.'

'Yes, sir. We have recovered the stolen items and they have the thief's prints on them, so it should go straight through.'

'It was the same man who murdered Julius Hobbs and Wendy Green?'

'Yes, sir. Philip Pryce.'

'And there never was an animal wild or otherwise involved.'

'That's right, sir.'

'That's what I said at the beginning. You could have saved a lot of time there, Angel. And another thing: the chief constable is not very pleased about your lad, DC Ahaz, stealing that pretty blue and white antique tea set from his secretary's office. No doubt he was following instructions from you. That tea set was given to this station in return for services rendered and it is only right that the chief constable should have first option on any such perks. What do you think the executive offices have CCTV for? If that lad ever wants promotion, he'd better return it smartish.'

* * *

Angel arrived at Jordan's Car Breakers. He drove through the open doors into a big enclosed field bursting with 5,000 old, battered cars, some piled five high. He drove down an alley through more wrecks to a gathering of four men and one woman huddled under a corrugated roofed shelter. The older man in the middle wearing goggles was sitting on an oil drum concentrating on holding an acetylene torch flame steady on the safe casing. The other four were standing around, shielding their eyes and watching the point of the flame.

They heard Angel's car arrive and all except the man with the torch looked round.

Mary Angel said, 'It's my husband.'

They glanced at him then returned their gaze to the safe.

She crossed to the car as Angel got out. 'You're just in time. Mr Jordan said he'll have it open in a couple of minutes.'

Jordan stood up. 'We're through,' he said.

He turned off the flow from both bottles to extinguish the flame, put the cutter down and reached out for a long crowbar which he pushed into the line of the cut on the top of the safe. He gave it a quick jerk and the entire front of the safe fell with a thud onto the ground.

Mary crouched down and looked inside. The only item there was an OXO tin. She took it out. It had something small but heavy inside. She put it on the top of the safe.

All eyes were on the tin.

She looked up at Angel who had moved up close next to her. He nodded. She opened the tin and inside it was a sealed envelope. There was something heavy inside it. It was addressed simply to Michael Angel's father, 'Ernest'.

'You'd better open it, love,' she said, passing it to Angel.

He took it and quickly tore it open. A key dropped out with a handwritten swing label fastened to it. He read the label. 'Spare key to safe.'

'Is that all?' Mary said.

Angel felt inside the envelope. 'There's something else.'

He poked it out. It was a folded sheet of paper. He unfolded it, read it and frowned.

'What's it say?' Mary said.

'It says "IOU £100". And it's signed, "Uncle Willy".'

THE END

OTHER BOOKS BY ROGER SILVERWOOD

YORKSHIRE MURDER MYSTERIES

Book 1: THE MISSING NURSE
Book 2: THE MISSING WIFE
Book 3: THE MAN IN THE PINK SUIT
Book 4: THE MORALS OF A MURDERER
Book 5: THE AUCTION MURDERS
Book 6: THE MISSING KILLER
Book 7: THE UMBRELLA MURDERS
Book 8: THE MISSING MILLIONAIRE
Book 9: THE MISSING THIEF
Book 10: FIND THE LADY
Book 11: THE MISSING MODEL
Book 12: MURDER IN BARE FEET
Book 13: THE MISSING HUSBAND
Book 14: THE CUCKOO CLOCK MURDERS
Book 15: SHRINE TO MURDER
Book 16: THE SNUFFBOX MURDERS
Book 17: THE DOG COLLAR MURDERS
Book 18: THE CHESHIRE CAT MURDERS

FREE KINDLE BOOKS AND OFFERS

Please join our mailing list for free Kindle crime thriller, detective, mystery, and romance books and new releases, as well as news on Roger's next book!
www.joffebooks.com/contact

Thank you for reading this book. If you enjoyed it please leave feedback on Amazon, and if there is anything we missed or you have a question about then please get in touch. The author and publishing team appreciate your feedback and time reading this book.

Our email is office@joffebooks.com

www.joffebooks.com

Follow us on Facebook, Twitter and Instagram
@joffebooks

We hate typos too but sometimes they slip through.
Please send any errors you find to
corrections@joffebooks.com
We'll get them fixed ASAP. We're very grateful to eagle-eyed readers who take the time to contact us.

Printed in Great Britain
by Amazon

71180236R00132